DARK DAYS FOR THE TOBACCO GIRLS

THE TOBACCO GIRLS BOOK TWO

LIZZIE LANE

Boldwood

First published in Great Britain in 2021 by Boldwood Books Ltd.

Copyright © Lizzie Lane, 2021

Cover Design by The Brewster Project

Cover Photography: Colin Thomas

A CIP catalogue record for this book is available from the British Library.

Paperback ISBN 978-1-80048-499-3

Large Print ISBN 978-1-80048-500-6

Hardback ISBN 978-1-80162-967-6

Ebook ISBN 978-1-80048-498-6

Kindle ISBN 978-1-80048-501-3

Audio CD ISBN 978-1-80048-492-4

MP3 CD ISBN 978-1-80048-493-1

Digital audio download ISBN 978-1-80048-495-5

Boldwood Books Ltd
23 Bowerdean Street
London SW6 3TN
www.boldwoodbooks.com

Dedicated to Cordelia and Rita at the Royal United Hospital, Bath, who kept me laughing when they stuck needles into my arm, gave me ice lollies as well as information about Zimbabwean tobacco!

1

BRIDGET MILLIGAN

The news from the British Expeditionary Force in France was bad and spread like wildfire, flashing from town to town, house to house and family to family. A whole army had been plucked from the beaches and the safety taken for granted had melted away. Britain was in danger of being invaded.

Feeling sick inside, Bridget Milligan gripped the newspaper with trembling hands, thankful that no member of her family was serving in the army. Being of a caring nature, she felt great empathy for those who did.

Her clear blue eyes exchanged a worried look with her father as she passed the newspaper back to him.

'It doesn't look good.'

He shook his head solemnly.

Studied on a map, the battleground and the retreat from Dunkirk in Northern France seemed a long way off from the city of Bristol, yet still they felt its effects. Bridget saw those effects on the strained faces of some of her workmates at W. D. &. H. O. Wills, the tobacco factory where she'd worked since she left school. She heard it in their voices, concern for their menfolk, not knowing whether they were injured, lost or listed amongst casualty lists that were as yet incomplete.

That night whilst brushing the hair of her sisters, she thought about her friend Phyllis. They'd worked together and been best friends for a long time, but she'd hardly seen her since she'd married Robert Harvey. Robert had joined up shortly after the wedding and Phyllis had moved in with her in-laws, a situation Bridget didn't envy. Had Phyllis heard from Robert? She was tempted to go round there and ask, but Mrs Harvey didn't welcome visitors, especially girls who worked in the tobacco factory.

Molly, one of her sisters, interrupted her thoughts. 'Will my hair be as long as yours one day?'

Bridget smiled down at her little sister who hadn't long turned six years of age, a fact Molly was inordinately fond of, as though six meant babyhood was left behind.

She patted Molly's head. 'Well, it's the same colour as mine and just as shiny.'

Molly's hair was indeed of the same brandy brown as Bridget's and just as glossy.

'I'm next,' said Mary, nipping under Bridget's arms to make sure that she was.

A year older than Molly, she had the same colour hair as all the girls except for Ruby, who, at eleven, was the eldest of Bridget's sisters and had just gone up into the big school. Her hair was dark blonde and, according to Bridget's mother, was inherited from her father's side of the family. Between Ruby and Mary in age was Katy, who had not been able to stay awake for her turn but fallen asleep, her hair a glossy sundial arrangement round her head.

The boys, Sean now thirteen, and Michael aged ten, were still downstairs in the bathroom.

'Now let me see if you've done behind your ears,' she heard her mother say, and smiled. Washing wasn't top of her brothers' agenda, though Sean was changing his attitude now his voice was breaking and girls didn't disgust him quite as much as they used to.

'The boys are growing up,' Bridget remarked once everyone, with the exception of Sean, was safely tucked up in bed.

She was standing with her mother, drying the dishes whilst her mother washed them in a mixture of flakes of Sunlight soap and a handful of soda.

'So are you,' murmured her mother with a sidelong look. 'They're not the only ones to have had birthdays.'

This year had been Bridget's twentieth birthday, but she was wise enough to know there was more to her mother's remark than it being another year gone by. There was no young man walking out with her, none she'd invited home and none she'd ever mentioned – none that were local anyway. There were only the letters – infrequently nowadays – from Lyndon O'Neill, an American, the wealthy owner of a Virginian tobacco plantation.

She'd formed a bond with Lyndon from the very first time they'd met, but the war had intervened in their relationship and he'd gone back to the United States with his parents, wealthy people with great ambitions for their son which did not include a factory girl.

Bridget knew very well where her mother's words were leading. 'I'm not an old maid yet.'

Her mother raised her hands from the suds and watched as her fingers dripped hot water, a slight frown worrying her brow. 'Don't aim too high, Bridie,' she said gently, using the familiar name Bridget was always called at home.

'I'm not aiming anywhere.' Bridget couldn't help the sudden sharpness in her voice. Lyndon had swept her off her feet, but she still harboured fears about falling in love with anyone. She'd watched her mother give birth and also miscarry, saw the pain and vowed she would never go through childbirth if she could possibly help it.

* * *

The terrible events on the beach at Dunkirk took the preparations for war up a gear. Fear and justifiable alarm spread. It felt as though a black cloud lay heavy on the land. France had fallen, and according to Mr Churchill, the new prime minister who'd taken over from Mr Chamberlain, England was next.

As a consequence, it was only a few weeks later that Bridget's father persuaded her mother that the children should be evacuated. Her mother cried at the thought of being separated from her youngest children, but responded to her husband, Patrick's common-sense statement.

On the allotted day of evacuation, Bridget took the day off work to help with getting the kids ready to be evacuated to a place where there were no docks, no important railway links and no aircraft factories. Bristol was such an obvious target.

Temple Meads Station heaved as though every child in Bristol had flocked there, gas masks in cardboard cases hanging from strings around their necks, bags or cases clutched in tight little hands. The noise was deafening, people shouting, children crying, chattering, laughing, and all against the tooting and steaming of great locomotives like the Bristol Castle and the Truro Castle, named after places built to fend off enemies.

Women with plummy accents seemed to be the ones in charge. Some wore uniforms and almost all of them held a pen in one hand and a clipboard in the other.

Patrick Milligan ushered his family forward, his wife Mary at his side, her face white, her brow furrowed with worry.

Bridget held tightly to the small hands of her youngest sisters as they shuffled forward in a queue that stretched far behind them, over the old flagstones of the concourse and down the hill towards the Bath Road.

The woman in the green uniform was short and dumpy, her hair grey and tightly curled. Discerning eyes swept over them, nostrils flaring as though she had the physique of a spirited horse rather than that of a short-legged donkey.

Patrick handed her a list of his children's names, gender and ages.

Thanks to the press of the crowd, Mary Milligan and the younger children were squashed between her husband and Bridget.

The woman briskly checked off the names. 'Yes. Your children are all destined for South Molton.'

Mary smiled down at her children, especially the youngest ones. 'There. You'll be going to a pretty little village in the countryside.'

'It's a town, not a village,' said the woman brusquely. 'A market town in fact.'

Despite her lack of stature, the woman had a high-handed attitude, as though working-class women had no knowledge whatsoever of anywhere outside Bristol.

Disliking her attitude, Bridget bristled. 'It's in North Devon,' she declared, looking down at the woman from her superior height, her blue eyes cold as ice. 'Not that far from Tavistock. Farming country, though not quite so lush as South Devon.'

Surprised by her knowledge, the woman looked momentarily as though she'd dislocated her jaw. 'You sound as though you know it well,' the woman managed to say at last.

'I'm very well read on that particular part of the Devonshire coastline, though I prefer Exmoor, just north of there. Lorna Doone country. As in the book written by R. D. Blackmore.' She said it in an aloof manner. If this woman thought she was going to make her feel small, she was sadly mistaken.

Having accepted she'd been put in her place, the woman dropped her gaze to her clipboard, cleared her throat and pronounced that the train would be leaving from Platform 12 in twenty minutes.

'I would suggest you get your family aboard as quickly as you can,' she said, turning swiftly away as though keen to get onto the next batch of evacuees and people she could more easily intimidate.

Patrick Milligan thanked her as courteously as the situation allowed, then shouted to make himself heard above the heaving, noisy throng.

'All keep together, children. All together now!'

Battling through the crowd was something of an ordeal. Bridget and her mother picked up the youngest two. Her father managed to lift Katy into his arms whilst the older three, Ruby, Sean and Michael, followed on behind, the two boys using their overladen carrier bags to bulldoze their way through the packed throng.

Their excitement was obvious. As far as they were concerned, they were going on a holiday, the only one they've ever had except for day trips to Clevedon or Weston-super-Mare.

Another woman with a clipboard supervised the boarding of children into the carriages. She checked their names off for a second time. Once it was done, she turned to their father. 'If you can't get them all into one compartment, some of them will have to go into another one.'

A whistle sounded and steam squealed in a white cloud from the engine.

'I wouldn't want them to be separated,' shouted Mary Milligan above the shrill noise. 'I want them to stay together.'

The surging crowd pressed all around.

The woman clasped her clipboard tight against her chest. 'Get them aboard. They can at least travel together. What happens at their destination is another matter entirely and it's very likely that they will be split up. But still, anything is better than living under a hail of bombs.'

Mary Milligan stiffened at the woman's words and Patrick frowned, worried at his wife's likely response.

The excited chatter of other children already on the train was infectious.

'Look at all of them kids,' shouted Sean.

Michael looked and, being one to always look on the bright side, added. 'I 'ope they all play football.'

The girls began to take an interest. Molly waved her rag doll; Mary followed suit and waved a one-eared teddy bear that went everywhere with her.

Pleased at their response and smiling hesitantly, Bridget's father patted his wife's shoulder. 'They'll be fine, Mary.'

'No!' The rest of what Mary Milligan said was drowned out with the sound of steam squealing from the engine. 'I don't want them separated,' she shouted.

People surged in a sudden rush between them and the carriage doors and they were pushed backwards.

'Patrick! I've changed my mind. I don't want them to go.'

Bridget hung onto her mother. 'Mum, you can't change your mind now.'

'Well I have.'

But it was too late. All six of her children had scrambled up into the carriage and hurled themselves into the seats. The youngest two, looking slightly confused, were the only ones to glance back. It had indeed turned into an outing, an adventure they'd never gone on before.

'Patrick!' Mary Milligan turned to her husband in alarm.

Fearing she'd get too close to the train, Bridget held onto her mother.

Bridget's father shrugged his shoulders as best he could in the tight crush of people. 'It's done, Mary. It's done.'

Out of sympathy for her mother, Bridget did her best to push through, but a railway guard intervened and slammed the door shut.

'My mother's changed her mind,' she shouted.

'Sorry, Miss. Too late. We're ready to go.' His manner was polite but officious. Without more ado, he waved his green flag and blew his whistle.

The station was a place of turmoil, noise, crowds and steam, the gritty smell of burnt coal hanging in the air and swallowed with every breath.

As the train began to slide along the platform, the crowd thinned and Bridget's mother lunged forward. 'I can't let them go,' she screamed.

Bridget and her father held her back, both using soft words of reassurance.

'Mary, me darling, the train is going now.'

Crowds of children waved excitedly from behind carriage windows, faces rosy with excitement. Here and there was a paler face without smiles, dumbfounded that the world of all that was familiar was slipping away with the increased speed of the train.

'My babies!'

Bridget held on to her mother.

Patrick Milligan draped a strong arm round his wife's shoulders. 'They'll be safer in the country. Come on, me darling. Let's be going home.'

Mary Milligan looked up into her husband's face as though he had not understood what was happening so she stated it slowly. 'Didn't you hear what she said? They won't necessarily be together.'

Patrick hugged his wife of twenty-two years tightly against his body, felt the heaving of her sobs, and buried his face in her neck. 'We have to let them go,' he murmured, his breath warm against her neck. 'They'll be safer in the country. Just you see. They'll be safer, me darling.'

Gradually there remained only a cloud of steam and gritty smoke where the train had been. The children were gone.

Gathering on the platform and the concourse behind them, another throng of children and adults replaced those already on their way to safety as another train pulled in.

Shoulders slumped, Bridget and her parents headed out of the station, leaving the noise and bustle behind them. Her mother was no longer crying, but there was an ominous silence between her parents. It was her father's habit to run a hand across his wife's back as they walked, even in front of the children. He did this now, an act of reassurance that on this occasion was instantly shrugged off.

2

MAISIE MILES

Since the very first time they'd met, when Bridget and Phyllis, who were three years older than her, had labelled themselves, the Three Ms, Maisie had regarded Bridget as a voice of calm in the midst of a storm, the sensible one when everyone else was running round like headless chickens.

Not so this week when Bridget had been very down in the dumps; even offers to go out and paint the town had met with disinterest, which was a great shame.

Maisie eyed Bridget and thought back to the days when she'd started work at the factory. She'd been glad of the money but more so of the friendship. Phyllis and Bridget had taken her under their wing, her a scruffy kid from the Dings. She owed both of them her support in any way she could..

It seemed an age since she'd lived in York Street. Her mother was dead now, but Frank Miles, her stepfather was still around. Rather than stay in the old house, she'd taken Aggie Hill up on her invitation to move into the Llandoger Trow, a spooky old place next to the water.

Aggie's husband, Curly, who was actually as bald as a new laid egg, ran the pub whilst Aggie continued to work at the tobacco factory; she reckoned the pair of them would kill each other if they had to spend twenty-four hours a day together.

There was plenty of life in the Llandoger as it was more commonly called, a black and white timbered pub on the Welsh Back, an ancient quayside where wood for shipbuilding used to be unloaded from barges called 'trows' which came down the Rivers Severn and Wye from the Forest of Dean.

Maisie had been over the moon when her stepfather, Frank Miles, had gone inside for thieving just before the last Christmas. For a time she'd thought she could stay in the house at York Street. Unfortunately, it wasn't for long enough. In order to gain his freedom, Frank had shopped Eddie Bridgeman, a nasty criminal who was into a lot of nasty things to the police for receiving. A terrified Maisie had fled and Aggie had offered her a room.

Even if Frank didn't go back to the old house, there was Eddie Bridgeman to think about. An arch criminal with his fingers in many pies, exploitation, nightclubs, protection and prostitution, He had the money to get out of difficult situations. Eddie might be inside, but his thugs were still out and about. He could also afford good lawyers so his term in prison wasn't likely to last for too long, and when he got out? He'd be out to get Frank, who would run like a rabbit and dive into the deepest hole he could find. That's where the problem was. No matter that she hated her stepfather, Eddie Bridgeman would assume she would know where he was. Fleeing York Street had made sense. Hopefully neither of them would track her down.

Whilst these thoughts whirled around her head, Maisie kept working, concentrating on stripping the tobacco leaves; she was making good progress.

She glanced at the leaves piled in front of Bridget. Her mild-mannered friend was usually way ahead of her, but today, and most of this week, her movements seemed lethargic. A little nudge was in order. She was sure she wouldn't mind her being concerned she would get her pay docked. The Milligans were a big family and although she'd never mentioned as such, her wages were vital. As gently as possible, Maisie informed her that she was falling behind.

At first, there was a round-eyed stare, as though she'd been caught out doing something quite outrageous. Then the legs of her stool screeched across the floor, making Maisie's teeth set on edge, and she was gone.

Maisie put up her hand to get Aggie's attention, letting her know she was off to the cloakroom.

When she got there, Bridget was leaning against the sink, the light from the frosted windows touching her face with porcelain clarity, a handkerchief held to her nose.

Maisie snuggled up close to her, folded her arms and gave her a dig in the ribs. 'Come on, old mate. A problem shared an' all that.'

Bridget chewed her lips and looked down at the floor. 'Everything seems so strange. The house is so quiet and my mother doesn't stop crying. My dad tries to raise her spirits. She's all right for a time, and then she's downhill again.'

'I'm not surprised. Poor woman's got nothing to do without them kids around.' Maisie was her usual outspoken self.

Although used to Maisie's frankness, Bridget didn't let it wash over her as she often did. 'What do you know about my mother? Or the rest of my family? I'll thank you not to make comment about something you don't know.'

The sharpness of her response was surprising, but Maisie kept her head. Her words were ice cold. 'I know nothing about your family or 'avin' a mother like yours. I ain't got one.'

Bridget's comment had smarted and, although Maisie wanted

with all her heart to support her friend, there was no point offering sympathy where none was likely to be taken, so she turned away.

'No.' Bridget grabbed her arm. 'I'm sorry, Maisie. I didn't mean to say that.'

There was genuine affection in Bridget's eyes. Maisie saw it there, and although her intention had been to march off in a huff, that look rooted her to the spot. 'No,' Maisie said softly. 'I know you didn't. Time to get it off yer chest.'

'It isn't easy. I know Mum would have them back in a trice if Dad would let her.'

'That would be daft,' said Maisie, shaking her head. 'There's a lot of parents in Europe who wished their children had been evacuated before the bombing began.'

She detected an instant change in Bridget's manner, as though such an observation had not occurred to her before. A faint smile that promised to spread flickered at her lips.

'You're right, Maisie Miles, but then you usually are.'

* * *

Back in the stripping room, their workmates sang and hummed along to the songs on the wireless.

Maisie exchanged a barely perceptible nod with Aggie, who had also been aware of Bridget's low mood.

'*Here is the news...*'

All hands stilled in their work. All conversation ceased.

The news main topic was the evacuation from France. There were mothers, wives and sisters who knew for certain that their men had survived the evacuation of Dunkirk. To date, 300,000 men had been rescued. A few still awaited news and Maisie's heart went out to them. She herself had no relatives involved but understood their feelings.

Each item of news was abrupt and delivered without a trace of emotion: France, Norway and attacks on Atlantic convoys bringing much-needed supplies; a switch to North Africa and ships lost in the Mediterranean; raids on Gibraltar and some little island few had heard of called Malta.

The silence lingered for some minutes after the broadcast had ended. Maisie fancied she could hear the beating of their hearts, all of them beating as one.

The music resumed.

Maisie sang out, determined to concentrate minds on love rather than war.

'*It had to be you. Wonderful you...*'

'*Pack up your troubles in your old kit bag and smile, smile, smile...*'

They were her workmates and perhaps a bit more; her family in the absence of any real one. Her mother was dead, her brother gone away to sea and she had found out that her natural father had died not long after she was born, beaten to death, according to her grandmother, by her stepfather, Frank Miles.

There were sounds of sniffling once the singing had stopped and was replaced by instrumentals.

A slow murmuring of conversation resumed, talk of those not yet home interspersed with tales of ordinary family life. All Maisie had was Alf, her brother, a small contribution to talk of family. Whilst growing up, Alf had been the most stable influence in Maisie's life and she missed him.

'I heard my brother's been to South America. Had a card from him,' she said.

'South America is a big place. Did he say which country he was in?'

'He couldn't say exactly but the place name was Spanish for *I see a mountain.*'

'Ah,' said Bridget. 'Montevideo. He's in Uruguay.'

'Is that what it means,' said a delighted Maisie. 'That's a pretty name.'

Bridget smiled. 'Yes, I suppose it is.'

Maisie had been purposely innocent in her response, but noted a sudden tension around that soft smile. 'I can read the papers. I do know what happened there, Bridget. But that was back in December. There's no pocket battleship waiting there now. I ain't that daft, you know. I 'ave 'eard of the battle of the River Plate. It's still dangerous, I know that, but Alf made 'is choice. It's the life 'e wanted.'

'Ah!' said Bridget.

Maisie smiled to herself. Well-read and interested in most things, she'd surprised her friend in being able to name the battle.

Before Bridget could fall into another thoughtful silence, Maisie patted her hand. 'Those kids will be fine. All them fields to run around in and all that food. There's more food in the countryside. Everybody knows that.'

Bridget was forced to agree with her. 'I know. They're probably having the time of their lives. I suppose we have to get used to it. For the duration.'

'Yep. For the duration!' Maisie said brightly. 'Heard anything from your American sweetheart?'

'He isn't my sweetheart.' Bridget's response was curt.

Maisie chewed her bottom lip as she considered what she could say next. 'Fancy the pictures tonight? I think it's something called *The Four Feathers*. Don't know what it's about though.'

Her question was met with a heavy sigh, then a thoughtful tilting of Bridget's head as though she were considering it. 'India.

The British in India and a man who's accused of cowardice. I read the book.'

'Oh,' returned Maisie, slightly deflated.

'Thing is...' Bridget began. 'I hate leaving my parents alone at night. I'm all they've got left...'

Maisie sighed. She fancied going to the pictures, though she had a vibrant social life at the pub where the customers liked her outspokenness and youthful personality.

'You're a cheeky minx and that's for sure.'

She smiled at the thought of the rough seamen who frequented the old pub on which Robert Louis Stevenson had based Long John Silver's quayside inn, the Spyglass. Some of the customers regarded her as they might a daughter. Others entertained more risqué thoughts, though didn't dare upset landlady Aggie Hill, who watched her young charge with an eagle eye and ready fists.

Maisie thought a bit more as she hummed along with the radio to a song called 'Stardust'. Once it had finished, she suggested they chance a bit of shopping in Castle Street on the coming Saturday.

'We're working Saturday afternoon,' Bridget pointed out.

'We can go after work. The shops are open until ten. Got any money?'

Bridget frowned. 'Yes. Why?'

Maisie beamed. 'You could buy some small presents for the kids and send them to that place they're staying... whatever it's called...'

'South Molton. I suppose I could,' she said thoughtfully.

Maisie breathed an inner sigh of relief. 'Well, that's settled then. Tell you what, instead of you goin' 'ome and us meetin' up, 'ow about you coming back with me and Aggie to the Llandoger? It's only for a couple of hours. You won't be leavin' yer mum and dad alone for too long,' she said quickly on seeing the sudden doubt on Bridget's face. 'Anyway, they might appreciate 'avin' a bit of free time together. What do you reckon?'

She waited with bated breath to see if her crafty ploy had worked and was relieved when Bridget agreed to it.

Bursting with self-satisfaction, Maisie slapped her hands down on the table. 'That's settled then. I'll tell Aggie you're coming back with us on Saturday and you tell yer mum and dad that you'll be a bit late 'ome after work.'

* * *

When Saturday came, Aggie, queen of the stripping room and landlady of the Llandoger, fed them liver and onions swimming in thick gravy. 'Spotted dick for afters,' she added. 'We don't do afters during the week, but we do on a weekend. A little bit of luxury we all deserve in these troubled times.'

As expected from somebody of Aggie's size, the portions were big.

'I'm not sure I can make it to Castle Street,' Bridget pronounced once the meal was finished. 'Does she always dish up such big portions?'

Maisie laughed and patted her stomach, which was far rounder than it used to be. 'How do you think I got this?'

Even though goods were scarce and shop windows were unlit, the shopping area in and around Castle Street was busy. Crowds of people, some in uniform, were taking advantage of a fine evening in May before darkness descended and everything was pitch black.

Some deep-seated instinct told Maisie that all this jollity was a brittle veneer and that beneath the surface these people were afraid. The news from France had affected everyone and the distance between England and France was very small indeed – just twenty-two miles of the English Channel. Rumours were rife that an invasion was imminent.

Maisie wasn't the only one aware of the electric atmosphere.

'It's as though everyone is out to enjoy themselves while they can,' Bridget suddenly pronounced.

'At least your youngsters are out of the way if they do start bombing. How about going into this shop?'

They had stopped in front of a plate-glass window. Though unlit thanks to the blackout regulations, it displayed small items and even a placard saying:

Small Enough to Send Overseas

The idea was that as little room as possible would be taken up on any form of transport heading to forces stationed overseas, military supplies having priority.

Maisie pointed. 'How about these? Not that you're sendin' 'em overseas.'

The small items, pencil sets, handkerchiefs, notebooks, drawing books and ribbons, caught Bridget's attention. 'Katy would love that colour,' she said, pointing at a silky blue ribbon.

Maisie pointed out that a queue was forming. 'I think other people got the same idea,' she remarked and before Bridget had chance to change her mind, she dragged her into the queue.

Once inside the shop with the items in front of her, Bridget became absorbed in choosing gifts for her siblings. For the boys it was pencil sets and notebooks. For the girls, ribbons, sketchbooks and packets of crayons.

'Do you need them wrapped?' asked the assistant.

Bridget opted for them to be wrapped, first in newspaper and then brown paper and string ready for posting.

'We can post it for you,' the assistant added helpfully.

Bridget didn't hesitate. 'Yes please. I only wish I could see their faces when it arrives. I've got the address of the local post office in South Molton. They collect regularly from there.'

Maisie sensed it was a different Bridget who exited the shop than the one who had gone in. It was obvious from the excitement in her eyes that this was a kind of link between her and her brothers and sisters. They were far away but sending the parcel somehow brought them closer.

They both stopped and took another look in the window.

'They've got some nice things in here. Hopefully they'll still have things at Christmas – unless the war's over by then of course.'

Maisie leaned forward beside Bridget and scrutinised the display. 'They'll still be here and Christmas will happen as it always does, no matter what.'

They stood for a few minutes admiring the display. Other people were also looking, their faces mirrored in the plate glass just as theirs were.

And they're all smiling, thought Maisie, glancing from one face to another. She too smiled until suddenly she spotted a face she'd wished never to see again.

'I quite fancy going for a drink before going home. How about you?'

Maisie jerked away from the window and faced Bridget, a cold shiver running down her back. 'What?'

It was obvious from her expression that Bridget noticed the sudden pallor of Maisie's face. 'What's wrong?'

'Nothing. I was miles away. What was it you said?'

'I suggested we go for a drink at the Bear. What do you think?'

Maisie recovered quickly. 'Yes,' she said with more enthusiasm than she actually felt. 'Yes. Why not?'

Her eyes scanned the crowds as they moved away from the shop window. The face she'd seen was no more. *Perhaps I was imagining it*, she thought to herself.

For reassurance, she slipped her arm into that of Bridget's. Not once did she look over her shoulder for fear she hadn't been imagining things, for fear that she really had seen Frank Miles, the man she hated most in all the world.

3

PHYLLIS HARVEY

Phyllis woke up and immediately clamped her eyes shut again. The sight of the dull green curtains hanging at the bedroom window made her feel sick, a stark reminder that she was living with her in-laws in Bedminster Road.

She'd been dreaming she was somewhere else where the curtains were rose-coloured and the room far prettier than this one. Perhaps it might have been more bearable if Robert had not gone away to fight, leaving her to fend off both boredom and the ongoing whining and barely concealed dislike of Robert's mother.

In her head, she was her old bubbly self, her titian hair gleaming, her greyish green eyes shining, her lipstick, powder and clothes exactly the right colour to suit her porcelain complexion. In the dream, she could hear her mates, Bridget and Maisie, laughing and singing as they walked along the prom at Weston-super-Mare last September. It had been the firm's outing and, to her mind, her last really happy time before marrying Robert Harvey – because she had to.

It was shortly after the trip that she'd begun typing lessons in a bid to better herself, only she'd got much more than that. 'A bun in the oven,' as the likes of young Maisie said. Only it hadn't been her fiancée Robert's 'bun'. It had been her typing teacher, Alan Stalybridge. Luckily for her, pregnancy had coincided with Robert insisting they get married. Robert had always made the decisions in their relationship rather than ask her opinion, and in this instance, she welcomed it. To do otherwise, she would have been ruined.

Now, here she was, married to a man she didn't love, heavily pregnant and living with his parents. His father, Tom Harvey, she could stand. His mother was an entirely different matter, a dried-up stick of a woman who found fault with everything she did.

Phyllis sighed and turned over in bed. Oh how she wished she was still working. Although most women gave up work when they got married, others continued and even when expecting continued to work for the allowed time of up to six months. Robert had insisted that no wife of his was going to work. So that was it.

Would things be better if Robert was here? Phyllis frowned and tried to remember how it had been with him. Nothing very eventful came to mind except that she recalled no softness, no real signs of affection. She'd turned to Alan for that, a one night stand that she'd wanted to be much more. He'd shot off even before she'd found out she was pregnant; just a fleeting moment that she'd wished had been so much more. Robert had assumed the child was his, conceived on their honeymoon, so at least her reputation had been saved. It was accepted that a girl wanted to save her reputation, but she wasn't so sure about that now. She'd been unhappy ever since tying the knot.

She squeezed her eyes more tightly shut, as if that alone might blot out the grinding whirr of the alarm clock when it struck seven thirty. Robert's mother insisted everyone was out of bed by seven thirty, though stretched it on Sunday to eight o'clock. Breakfast was only available within that sacrosanct first hour.

'If you can't be bothered to get up, there's no breakfast. I've no time to wait on people.'

Hilda Harvey's voice jangled the nerves – just like the alarm clock. Suddenly, there it was, rattling and jangling, vibrating across the bedside table as though it had suddenly sprung legs.

Phyllis slammed it into silence with the palm of her hand so hard that it hurt. She sighed, tucked her hands behind her head and stared up at the ceiling, visualising what her life might have been if she hadn't got hitched so hastily, but then, it was a case of needs must. Robert had insisted on it before he went to war.

When she'd announced her pregnancy only six weeks or so after their honeymoon, Robert had preened, accepting that the child was his. From the very first, suspicion lurked in Hilda Harvey's eyes.

One winter night when she was too cold to sleep, Phyllis had got up intending to go downstairs and make a hot drink, when she overheard her mother-in-law's acid voice express her doubts.

'Honeymoon baby indeed!'

'So what if they went to bed together before they tied the knot?'

Her father-in-law was yet again sticking up for her in that calm voice of his and she had blessed him for it. She had gone no further down the stairs but stayed to listen.

'Wash your mouth out, Tom Harvey! I know my son! He's God-fearing and upright. He would never commit such a wicked sin as that!'

Even from this distance, she had heard poor Tom Harvey's heavy sigh.

'Then it can only be a honeymoon baby, surely.'

Heart in her mouth, she had waited for the answer. It wasn't long coming.

'He's married beneath himself. I told him so, but he'd made his mind up. She's of the lower orders, just a common factory girl. What can you expect?'

Phyllis had slunk back against the wall, feeling her way back to the bedroom door with a sick feeling in her stomach.

As the weeks had gone by, Hilda's comments had become more pointed and a lot more worrying. Most were regarding what the baby would look like when it was born.

It was such a trivial respite from monotony, but each month Phyllis received a visit from the district nurse who would take her blood pressure and monitor her progress. Even then Hilda hovered, venting her spleen in waspish undertones.

'Robert was a very handsome baby. Very fair, almost white. I myself wouldn't want it any other shade.'

Her pompous comment was accompanied with a contemptuous glance at Phyllis's flame-coloured hair.

The district nurse had responded that all babies were beautiful, no matter what their hair colour. 'Or skin colour come to that,' she'd added. She had not seen the stony look on Hilda's face but kept her attention and care fixed on Phyllis. 'Just you look after yourself, Mrs Harvey,' she'd pronounced. 'Make sure you get your extra milk allowance and the free orange juice and cod liver oil. There are free vitamins too if you want them. You've only to ask. And plenty of fresh air. You and baby need it.'

Feeling bloated, Phyllis now swung her legs out of bed. For a moment she looked at a pair of podgy feet poking out from beneath the full-length nightdress her mother-in-law had thought a good present for a bride going away on honeymoon. The neckline was high, the hem reached to her ankles. It was made of winceyette, a welcome fabric in winter, but too warm for

May. Her ankles were puffy and her pregnant stomach obscured the upper half of her thighs.

In her dream, she'd been slim again and off for a night out with her mates at W. D. &. H. O. Wills. My, what wouldn't she give to be back working in the stripping room, the music on the wireless competing with the booming voice of Aggie Hill? Aggie was statuesque, broad in the beam and had arms the size of hams. Like a mother hen, though of far larger proportion, she took care of her girls, her 'chicks' as she called them.

The dream had been no more than that and left Phyllis longing for the old times when she could see her feet and dance all round the stripping room, out of the door and along East Street with her best friends.

They'd called themselves the Three Ms, Maisie Miles, Bridget Milligan and herself when she'd been Phyllis Mason. She was now Mrs Robert Harvey, a fact she was constantly reminded of by a mother-in-law who seemed to regard her as her son's personal possession.

Robert had been posted abroad, presumably to France, though he'd been reticent to tell them the exact details. In his absence, his mother had taken on the role of chaperone and surrogate nurse, as though the unborn child was some kind of valuable for which she was sole custodian and Phyllis a lockable safe.

At least when the baby was finally born, she would have someone to love, someone to love her and then it might all be worthwhile.

Sunshine streamed into the room when Phyllis pulled the curtains back and the sky was a crystal blue. She had to get out, escape this oppressing atmosphere for as long as possible.

She'd had her twenty-four-week check-up at the clinic and the next wasn't due until the twenty-eighth week, two weeks' time. However, the district nurse had told her she could pop in at any time if she had any worries.

Excited at the prospect of an unscheduled day out, she hummed as she washed, dressed and brushed her hair, even chancing a little face powder. Her mother-in-law didn't approve of face powder. Neither did her mother for that matter, but today Phyllis felt almost inebriated. Come hell or high water, she was going out.

Robert's father wished her good morning when she appeared in the doorway, the breakfast table set out before her. His smile was kind but there was a weary look in his eyes that had little to do with lack of sleep, more to do with his wife.

'It's going to be a nice day,' he said, his smile wavering on receipt of a withering frown from his wife. He cleared his throat and turned his attention back to his newspaper.

Tom Harvey worked for the local authority. He didn't talk much about what he did, except that it entailed piles of paperwork. The main thing he did talk about, which Hilda seemed keen to hear, was the new council building on College Green. Eventually a gold unicorn would stand at each end of the roof, just like the ones on the city's shield which also displayed a ship and a castle, above the Latin inscription, *'Virtue et Industria'*. It was the one piece of history that Hilda Harvey seemed to have swallowed whole and couldn't help regurgitating when the chance arose.

'Virtuous and industrious. That totally describes those who made this city great,' she snorted and made it sound as though she'd put in a lot of effort herself.

Tom Harvey looked the part of a council official, his tie and shirt collar tight round his throat so that his Adam's apple bobbed against it when he spoke as though trying to escape the breath-squeezing confinement. His black hair was plastered to his head with a copious amount of Brylcreem and his moustache looked as though it had been painted on.

'Don't take too much notice of my wife,' he'd said one day when Hilda's venom had really got to Phyllis. 'Her brain isn't always in tune with her tongue.' He'd patted her hand, and although Phyllis didn't quite understand what he meant, for the sake of his kind disposition, she had smiled readily and said that she did.

Hilda Harvey winced when he gave her a goodbye peck on the cheek, barely glancing up from the task of slicing bread that was at least two days old.

'It's fine toasted,' she said as she sawed through the hard outer crust and through the equally hard inner core. 'We can't waste anything. My Robert's life might depend on it.'

Once it was toasted, Phyllis applied a scraping of butter, aware her mother-in-law was keeping an eye on how much she dared use; ditto marmalade, a pale-coloured watery substance that slid off her knife. Hilda added water when it reached the halfway stage so it would go further. If any more was added, it would be easier to drink it, Phyllis thought.

She took a deep breath. 'I need to go to the clinic. I'm out of orange juice.'

Hilda's eyes narrowed, her pupils like chips of gravel in her narrow face. 'Do you now.'

'I could get some bread whilst I'm out.' It wasn't that far to the clinic where she collected the things an expectant mother was entitled to; she wanted to go further. She wanted a whole morning out.

Phyllis pretended not to notice Hilda's flinty expression. She thought on her feet, her words carefully chosen. If there was one thing Hilda could not tolerate it was somebody getting the better of her; what was hers was hers and belonged to nobody else. 'I've heard of bread being left on the shelf 'cause people ain't been in to claim what's rightfully theirs. Seems daft to me. Might as well claim our share whilst we can, don't you think? Before bread gets rationed too.'

So far bread was not rationed, a fact that many were grateful for, but it didn't mean that it wouldn't be.

Hilda was aghast. 'I suppose you'd better,' she muttered, her thin lips purple with disdain.

What joy, an hour or so at the clinic, plus another hour or so queuing for bread! A whole half day away from the depressing atmosphere of the Harvey household. 'Would you like me to get a pot of marmalade as well?' On the outside, Phyllis was innocent amiability, on the inside she was desperate, like a canary wanting to fly from its cage.

'Marmalade!' Hilda looked scandalised. It was as though Phyllis had suggested dancing nude down the street. 'We have enough to be going on with.'

Phyllis helped carry the dishes to the draining board. 'It'll be nice to get out.'

It was her one mistake. The moment the words were out, she knew Hilda would adopt a wounded expression. It turned out she was right.

'Well, I'm sorry my company and my house make you feel that way. I'm sure I've only done my best to make you feel at home.'

'I didn't mean anything by it.' She hadn't, but Hilda never flinched from the opportunity to make Phyllis feel of little value, that she knew nothing and was nothing without Robert.

Hilda tossed her head. 'I'll say nothing except that Audrey, who Robert once courted, wouldn't speak to me like you do. She was a respectable girl. Went to church and wasn't fast – not like some I could mention.'

Phyllis flinched but swallowed the insult. She apologised for a second time.

'As it happens, I've got a meeting at the church hall this morning for the association campaigning against women joining up, so I won't have time to buy bread so you might as well do it.'

Phyllis felt five pounds lighter. She would have her half day out. 'Your meeting sounds interesting.' The truth was she wasn't in the least bit interested, but Hilda did respond to flattery, her begrudging air hiding her inbuilt smugness.

'I'm starting a campaign to keep women out of uniform. Men go to war. Women look after the home front.' She puffed up with self-importance. 'Our aim is to persuade women not to put on a uniform. Not to join the services alongside men. It's not seemly.'

Phyllis knew it was useless saying that the government were in charge, not her mother-in-law and that if it was what a girl wanted to do, she would do it. 'It sounds a very good idea,' Phyllis offered instead and wished Hilda the best of luck with her meeting.

'No luck is needed,' came the sharp retort. 'God is with us. He knows as well as we do that women were never destined to wear a uniform. Wives and mothers. That's what he meant women to be.'

'There to look after the family,' said Phyllis as though she agreed with everything said. 'Feed, clothe and keep house.'

'Just a loaf,' snapped Hilda fixing Phyllis with a warning look sour enough to make milk curdle. 'Take the key from behind the mantel clock.'

Despite her girth, Phyllis felt like skipping round the room. It wasn't often she got her hands on a key to the front door.

'Make sure you put it back afterwards,' warned her mother-in-law.

'Without fail,' returned Phyllis, and felt a stab of pain that fast faded to nothing.

* * *

Phyllis gulped the fresh air in deep draughts. It felt so good to be out and away from Hilda's dark shadow. Sometimes she wondered whether her mother-in-law was just a little mad. Hilda Harvey was always complaining about her nerves and her sweet husband, Tom, tolerated behaviour that was becoming odder and odder. There were occasions when Phyllis caught a worried expression on his passive countenance as though he knew very well that there was more to her spiteful behaviour than nerves.

Sometimes when Hilda was at her church meeting, he'd relate to Phyllis how she'd once been and she detected true love shining in his eyes.

'She was quite a dish back then,' he said, his eyes sparkling in a way she'd never seen them sparkle before.

He seemed to like talking to her, but ultimately was defensive of his wife, excusing her manner as being due to the change. There was always an excuse, she thought.

At the clinic, Phyllis had collected her free bottle of orange juice and declined the cod liver oil.

'Everything all right,' the duty nurse had asked brightly.

'Fine,' Phyllis had responded with an equally bright expression.

Now Phyllis looked in the window of a shop selling baby clothes and smiled. Most of the baby clothes were for older than new born; it was taken for granted that people knitted matinee jackets, bootees, caps and bonnets. Although she already had some, Phyllis went in and bought two tiny flannelette night-dresses for which a ration book was not needed.

Feeling pleased with her purchases, she left the shop but stood in the doorway a while watching the world go by, the ordinary wonderfulness of a tram rattling past, the sky smudged with smoke from factory chimneys.

There were people everywhere, mostly women of course, all intent on getting what they could with their ration books.

The queues were long and the comments critical from the women queuing.

'It can only get better,' said one in a strong Bristolian accent, an unlit cigarette hanging precariously from the corner of a toothless mouth.

'Well, it can't get any bleedin' worse,' returned her companion, a trio of metal curlers jangling over her forehead. 'All this queuing for a pound of onions!'

Children cried, women nattered, and men shouted as they loaded or unloaded vans, lorries and carts. A pair of shire horses pulling a Georges' Brewery dray stamped their hairy hooves outside the green tiled walls of the Barley Mow.

Phyllis's steps slowed then halted when she was directly opposite the warm red brickwork of the tobacco factory and the entrance she knew so well.

The arched windows of the first floor held her attention and suddenly she thought how attractive they were. This was no ordinary factory thrown up cheaply so production could commence as quickly as possible. Skilled craftsmen, who would have been just at home building a castle as a factory, had made the East Street factory exactly that, a Gothic palace, a handsome edifice of which the owners, the builders and those who worked within could be proud.

Up until this moment she hadn't realised just how handsome it was. She'd been more familiar with the interior than the exterior, a sweet memory that brought a tear to her eye. If only, she thought, as she imagined her workmates inside, the air buzzing with gossip and laughter. Working there seemed a lifetime ago but was only a matter of months. She missed it desperately. If only she hadn't decided to learn to type. If only the typing teacher had been a woman and not Alan Stalybridge. It was a hard lesson to learn.

'You all right, luv?'

She started from her thoughts. The question was put by a woman pushing a pram. Two other children clung onto the handlebar.

Taken by surprise, Phyllis responded that she was: 'Just taking a breather.'

The woman laughed. 'Make the most of it, luv. There's barely time to breathe once they get to this age. Seven years ago, I was twenty-one and looking forward to 'avin' the first one. Seems a lifetime ago.'

Phyllis was horrified. Gaps in the woman's teeth showed when she laughed. Yet she couldn't be much more than twenty-eight, Phyllis thought. Expectant mothers were prone to losing their teeth and nobody could afford the price of a dentist. It was bad enough finding the price of a doctor or midwife.

Phyllis brushed at her eyes and turned away from the place where she'd felt at home, where she'd been one of the girls. At the same time, the baby seemed to lurch in her stomach making her gasp. She reassured herself that it was nothing to worry about. Getting ready to be born, she thought. Her mother had said something to that effect, how they twist and turn to get themselves in the right position to enter the world.

'Round about seven or eight months,' her mother had told her. She was almost seven.

A tram rattled past. A newspaper seller shouted the latest news and it wasn't good. Despite the evacuation from Dunkirk, there was still some action going on and men were missing in France and Belgium. So far there'd been no word from Robert, but it had been reported that communications were chaotic. Her mother-in-law was adamant that he'd be home soon.

'He'll be back. He knows he's got a good home awaiting and a mother who loves him.'

Her father-in-law had been more circumspect and had gone so far as to make excuses for his wife's abrasive manner. 'Don't blame her too much for trying to keep you and the baby safe, stopping you going out and suchlike. She's doing it for Robert.' His expression had turned awkward, almost embarrassed. 'Robert is all she cares about.'

Phyllis's heart had gone out to him and she accepted it was true. Robert was the centre of Hilda Harvey's world. Nobody else mattered, and that included her husband, Tom Harvey.

'You 'eard what I've 'eard,' said a woman in the queue outside the greengrocers. 'Them soldiers that's come back from France are being billeted in Victoria Park. There's tents everywhere, a rough roof over their 'eads, but better than nothin', I suppose.'

'Why ain't they goin' 'ome?'

The other woman shrugged. 'P'raps they've come back without all their marbles. A lot who came back from fourteen to eighteen went a bit like that. A bit doolally.'

Frightened by the women's comments, Phyllis quickened her steps, hurrying towards Bedminster Bridge and Redcliffe Hill, suddenly oblivious to the jangling of the trams, the shouts of horse drawn vehicles and the blowing of horns as she crossed the road without looking. What about Robert? Would he be a bit doolally? Was that why they'd heard nothing from him?

Ahead of her, the spire of St Mary Redcliffe church showed above the bank of trees at the top of the hill. The steamy smell of the faggot and pea shop lured her ever onwards. In the past she'd never been able to pass it without stopping, pressing her nose against the ancient bay window and drooling at the sight of the faggots – oversized traditional meatballs – simmering in thick gravy.

The bakery, just along from the faggot and pea shop, was the last stop. There were only a dozen people in front of her. Her stomach heaved. She felt a sudden heaviness between her thighs.

Take deep breaths, she told herself. *You've walked a long way. It'll do you good.*

A woman wearing a man's trench coat that reached her ankles gave her belly a sympathetic look and said the words Phyllis had hoped to hear. 'Go on in front, love. Wouldn't want you to drop it 'ere now, would we?'

Another woman wearing an old-fashioned black hat that seemed mostly to consist of ostrich feathers looked her up and down before making space for her. 'Your first is it?'

Phyllis said that it was.

The feathers fluttered when the woman laughed. 'I 'ad seven meself. The first is the worst, but you'll get over it.' A different look came to the woman's face. 'You look a bit pale, love.'

Phyllis did indeed feel a bit strange. The nagging ache she'd felt earlier intensified. As her head began to spin, she grabbed the counter. She gasped as a sharp pain shot across from one hip to the other.

'Feeling all right?' asked the woman in the trench coat.

Phyllis nodded and said that she was. 'I just walked too far. That's all.'

The pain retreated, but her heart was pounding.

Six people were still ahead of her, then five, then four, then three, then two. All that remained was a woman with two children, clinging to her coat, both demanding the crust from the end of the still warm loaf.

'Leave it alone, you little brat! You too!'

The sound of a slap across one face was followed by another. Both children burst into tears, one deciding to have a tantrum, throwing himself down on the floor, rolling around and kicking his legs in the air, screaming that he wanted a piece of bread.

Phyllis sucked in her breath and felt the blood drain from her face. Another pain shot across her ribcage. Her head began to swim, her vision became blurred. Those in front of her were no longer people but blobs of colour and movement. The lovely smell of freshly baked bread became noxious, too sweet for her taste buds and too strong for her head. Even the smallest sounds seemed to pierce her eardrums, as the mixed smells of bread, human sweat, tired clothes all added to a feeling of excessive nausea.

'Get 'er a chair,' somebody shouted.

The pain stabbed again and again, along with the feeling that her innards were too heavy for her body to hold inside. A great weight pushed down, her heart raced, thudding like a drumbeat against her ribcage. The blurring exploded, then became a fog of nothing as her legs crumpled, her head hit the floor and there was only darkness and pain.

4

BRIDGET AND MAISIE

It was some days later when Bridget and Maisie found out about Phyllis losing the baby. The mother of one of their workmates, Sally Grey, had been standing in the queue when she'd been taken ill.

'Lost it. Bound to 'ave,' pronounced Sally with a sad shaking of her head.

Maisie and Bridget exchanged worried looks.

The first person they told was Aggie. 'I'll do a collection. We can buy the poor chick something nice to take her mind off things. Chocolates or some nice fruit if we can get hold of it.'

They thanked Aggie before she marched off, ready to have her collection bag full of money before the bell went for lunch.

'Poor Phyllis,' whispered Bridget. 'I wonder how she is?'

'Still in hospital, I should think,' said Sally. 'You going to visit?'

'You bet we are,' Maisie said firmly. 'We'll phone at lunchtime.'

Bridget agreed and was given the job of phoning the hospital and finding out how Phyllis was getting on.

'Why me?'

'You've got the posh voice,' pronounced Maisie. 'And I've got plenty of coppers in my purse we can use. Anyway, I get confused with that pressing button A, then button B. I tried it with Sid.'

Sid was a mate of Bert, a workmate who had been sweet on Bridget, with whom Maisie was exchanging correspondence – when she felt like it. Their friendship had been fleeting – a couple of dates and the annual trip to the seaside, but when he'd been called up, she'd seen him off at the station and promised to write to him. She'd really meant to keep to her promise, but the truth was he wrote to her more often than she wrote to him. The last she'd heard; he'd been posted abroad. She resolved to write a letter.

'Give you something else to think about,' said Maisie.

Bridget pulled a face but didn't argue. She was still feeling a bit down since her siblings had been evacuated to South Molton in Devon. Sean had sent a postcard saying they were all fine and that he and Michael were billeted on a farm at the edge of the village. The two eldest girls, Katy and Ruby, had been taken in by the vicar and his wife. Molly and Mary, the youngest were with spinster sisters.

Longer letters had come from the four girls shortly afterwards. The letter from the two eldest were in their own handwriting and own words. The letter from the two youngest seemed to have been written for them and it was difficult to read between the lines, to get a feel for how they were really getting on.

In response to her mother's anxiety, her father had provided the voice of reason. 'Leave it for a month or so and then pay them a visit. There's bound to be a pub there with rooms. We'll do that, shall we?'

'If there's no bombing by then, I'm bringing them home,' Mary Milligan had declared in one of her most down moments.

Recognising he'd done no good, Patrick had retreated behind his newspaper.

Bridget hated the emptiness of the house without her younger brothers and sisters around, but at least their letters or postcards plopped regularly through the letterbox.

Letters from Lyndon O'Neill, the son of the plantation owner she'd met at the beginning of the war, were less frequent. She blamed the war. Everyone blamed the war for everything, but the lack of correspondence from Lyndon paled into insignificance on hearing that Phyllis had lost her baby.

They'd attempted to visit Phyllis during the last few months, but had been unsuccessful. The tobacco girls weren't welcome, Mrs Harvey telling them she was out or lying down.

'In other words, we ain't good enough for 'er,' Maisie had stated.

Bridget had agreed. 'But that doesn't mean we're abandoning Phyllis.'

'She's got 'er mum.'

'She needs her friends,' Bridget declared. 'She needs to see that we're there for her.'

Eating in the canteen, the only place where a really good main course and pudding was guaranteed, had to be pushed back until they'd phoned the hospital. Once the factory hooter sounded for lunch, they ran all the way, hoping and praying that the phone box was unoccupied. Of late it had become busier, thanks to girls phoning their beaus and mothers trying to get in touch with somebody – anybody – who might know whether their sons, husbands or brothers had survived the slaughter on the French beaches. Even being taken as a prisoner of war was preferable to being slain and gone forever.

Breathless and thankful, they arrived at the empty telephone box, heaved open the metal door and fell inside. Maisie fingered pennies from her purse and placed them on the black metal shelf. Bridget took four or five, picked up the phone and dialled. It rang and she pressed the requisite button. The pennies clanged into the metal container and finally the call was answered.

'Hello. I'm enquiring about Mrs Phyllis Harvey,' Bridget said nervously. 'She lost her baby and I was wondering how she was.'

Even when they squeezed tightly together, receiver pressed between them, it was hard for Maisie to hear what was being said. Frowning at Bridget, she shook her head and mouthed, 'What?'

Bridget shrugged helplessly. She didn't like phones either.

'We would like to visit her. Can you tell me visiting times please?' she asked.

Her face dropped when she heard the answer.

'It's relatives only,' she hissed to an impatient Maisie.

'Say we're her sisters,' urged Maisie.

Bridget shook her head at Maisie and put down the phone.

'Relatives only.'

'You mean like Robert's mother?' Maisie pulled a face. 'Phyllis needs friendly faces not that sour old puss. Can't you ask them again?'

'No.' Bridget pushed open the door and waited until Maisie had poured her coppers back into her purse. 'Come on. People are waiting.'

In the short time they'd been in the telephone box, a small queue had formed. Few people had their own phone at home and in this war the public telephone box was in great demand.

Maisie was thoughtful and uncharacteristically silent as they hurried back to the factory canteen, keen not to miss the best meal of the day.

As usual, Maisie was full of what Bridget considered, hare-brained schemes. First she suggested pretending they were close cousins.

Bridget shook her head. 'I'm not sure we'll get away with it. There are nurses and there's a matron who is always a bit of a dragon. We'd be lucky to get past reception, let alone get to the ward.'

Maisie frowned at Bridget. 'How do you know that?'

Bridget gave a lofty toss of her head. 'Because I read about it in a book. The matron is always a dragon.'

When they got back to the stripping room, there was a hubbub of noise and a fug of cigarette smoke.

Aggie informed them that she'd collected over two pounds but was intent on making it three. 'Five, if I twist a few arms,' she laughed.

Maisie was still thinking deeply as she threw the last of the leaves from the pile into the first basket. She'd become very quick at stripping leaves and had filled three that morning. Miss Cayford, the woman who had taken her on, came by and complimented her on the deftness of her fingers, then smiled at Bridget. 'She'll be as good as you before long, Miss Milligan.'

As she began to fill the fourth basket, Maisie thought to herself that Bridget had read more books than anyone she knew, but she'd been reading a few herself of late. George, Aggie's husband, kept some old tomes that had once belonged to his mother on a dusty old bookshelf. Old Mrs Hills, George's mother, seemed to have had a preference for mysteries, crime and adventure. Maisie had read one where two young women had disguised themselves as sailors in order to get aboard a vessel they suspected of smuggling brandy. Nobody had suspected their true identities and the thrill of the story had stayed with her.

'I've got an idea,' she said brightly as a plan formed in her mind.

Bridget eyed her warily. 'I'm not sure I want to hear it.'

'Of course you do. We're Phyllis's best friends!'

Bridget groaned. 'Nothing too hare-brained.'

Unperturbed, Maisie carried on.

'If we can't get in as relatives, we could dress up as nurses. We'd look good as nurses. Nobody would suspect.'

Bridget's eyebrows rose almost to her hairline. 'Are you serious?'

'Course I am!' She giggled and an impish look came to her dark brown eyes. 'Are you scared?'

'You bet I am. Mainly of what you'll come up with next!'

'Go on,' said Maisie and dug her elbow in Bridget's ribs. 'I'm game if you are.'

'Oh, Maisie,' murmured Bridget, shaking her head. 'You are crazy sometimes and that's for sure.'

'All we need are two nurses' outfits. That shouldn't be difficult, should it? We're surrounded by uniforms. Everyone in the city is wearing uniforms. Nobody will take notice.' She cocked her head and grinned mischievously. 'How about asking your nurse friends upstairs in the medical unit?'

Maisie knew the whole story of Bridget showing Lyndon O'Neill round the city and how it had all started with her lying on an examination couch in the medical unit when he'd come in with a group of VIPs. Cordelia and Rita, the two nurses present at the time, though Bridget didn't know their names until afterwards, were very friendly and approachable. Even so...

'I can't believe you're suggesting such a thing,' said Bridget. 'No. It's impossible.' She shook her head in utter consternation. Maisie and her crazy ideas!

Maisie winked. 'Come on, Bridget. Where's your spirit of adventure? Go on up and see 'em now? Ask 'em if they can 'elp.'

Bridget glanced tellingly at the wall mounted clock ticking away the seconds, minutes and hours of the day. 'It's gone four.'

'So what? You aint' got no need to rush 'ome, ave ya? Not with all the nippers evacuated.'

It was a home truth that hit Bridget hard and weighed down her shoulders throughout the day. The house in Marksbury Road echoed with silence. Her parents both did their best to paste on a brave face and compensate by telling her all they'd done, but Maisie was right, there was nothing for her to rush home for and poor old Phyllis needed them, so it had to be worth it.

* * *

When wearing their uniforms, Cordelia and Rita were as dedicated to their profession as anyone, but were up for some fun and when Bridget outlined their plan, they giggled with excitement and said they would do all they could to help.

They arranged to meet down in the cellar where the two nurses had set up an ancillary medical unit for use when the bombing started – whenever that was likely to be. There had been a raid on the second of June, though thankfully confined to the aircraft factories in North Bristol, but perhaps a harbinger of what was to come.

Everyone in the tobacco factory was putting in extra effort beyond the job they were paid for. Girls and women who'd opted to fire-watch spent their lunchtimes up on the roof and after work filling buckets with sand, manhandling stirrup pumps and attending talks about the basic pyrotechnics of an incendiary bomb.

Besides hospital-type beds, the factory cellar, a vast affair with a low ceiling held up by rows of sturdy metal pillars, had been kitted out with metal bunk beds. There were tables, chairs, books and a gramophone complete with a pile of records.

Maisie sifted through them looking for a title and singer she might recognise but her search proved fruitless. She frowned and read one out. 'What's *Cavillera Rusticana*?'

'A piece of classic music,' Bridget responded.

'And this one. *Dream of Olwen*?'

'Another classic,' said Bridget.

'Doctor Meredith thought classic music would be best,' explained one of the nurses. 'He said it was the kind of music that calms the savage breast.'

Maisie giggled. 'And there's a lot of breasts in this place, though I don't know whether they're that savage.'

'Don't worry,' said Cordelia in svelte tones as warm as her looks. 'I've got some dance music and so's Rita. Now this is what you need.'

Both nurses handed them a brown paper carrier bag each.

Bridget peered inside. The apron and headdress were as white as the ones the two nurses were wearing, but the dresses were darker.

On seeing their puzzlement, Cordelia explained. 'They're St John's Ambulance uniforms. Doctor Meredith is commander in chief and we're members too. He doesn't have any nurse working in his department unless she's a member of St John Ambulance. If you're not one when you first start, you are by the time you leave.'

Bridget suddenly got cold feet. Surely they would be found out. 'But won't they notice that our uniforms are different,' she asked.

Cordelia's stiff headdress rustled like paper tissue when she shook her head. 'No. St John's Ambulance nurses are helping out. Even the WVS are helping out, pushing trolleys and wheelchairs and simple medical stuff. All hands to the pumps, as Churchill would say – if he was here, that is.'

'And try not to ladder the stockings. Even black stockings are hard to come by,' warned Rita.

Although still a little reluctant, Bridget agreed to go with Maisie, who seemed very excited by the whole thing.

5

BRIDGET AND MAISIE

It was just after seven when Bridget and Maisie, giggling but nervous, caught a tram to the hospital.

Their black stockings were amazingly silky and both admitted to liking the feel of them beneath their starched dresses and aprons. Their headdresses, billowy white things and stiffly starched, were tucked into a couple of brown paper carrier bags. Bridget carried a third carrier bag containing a box of chocolates and a silk scarf in green and blue bought by Aggie with the money she had collected.

Bridget had gasped on seeing it. 'It's beautiful.'

Maisie had been insightful. 'Where did you get that? Must 'ave taken four months clothing ration.'

Aggie had tapped the side of her nose. 'Never you mind.'

'Black market,' Maisie had whispered to Bridget, who had winced but made no comment.

Their uniforms were hidden beneath their coats and although it was the first week of June and should be blessed with sunshine, it was raining and a cold wind was blowing.

Bridget sensed Maisie's nervousness matched her own. In the fading twilight, her attention was drawn to the dark silhouette of St Mary Redcliffe Church, a building rich with history and coupled with her own personal experience.

What a wonderful day it had been, seeing Lyndon O'Neill dumbstruck at the sight of Admiral Penn's tomb. He'd been further impressed when she'd confirmed that he was indeed the father of William Penn, a founding father of the United States.

It had all begun with her cutting her finger on a tobacco leaf, a visit to the medical unit to get a plaster, the very special visitors, and most of all him. He'd introduced himself as Lyndon O'Neill the third. From there on, the pace of their acquaintanceship had made her dizzy. At his request, she'd showed him round the city. He'd promised to see her again before he went back to the States, but he didn't. He'd also promised to write to her, which he did, though nowadays it was far more intermittent than it had been.

'I want to do a real job,' he'd written. 'Pa is fine about me joining him overseeing the plantation, learning all there is to learn. Ma is not so keen. She wants me to finish college, but I can't. I'm bored. There's so much happening in Europe and nothing much over here.'

Bridget had read and reread the letter until the corners were curling. She'd heard nothing since. Each morning, she awaited the arrival of the postman. A letter had to be due. It had been so long.

She forced herself to talk of the here and now. 'I wonder if Phyllis has heard from Robert.'

'We'll soon find out. I'll ask 'er.'

'Don't you dare. Just ask her how she's feeling.'

Maisie glanced at her sideways. 'Doing a lot of thinking, I shouldn't wonder. I mean to say, she don't need to stay with that creep if there's no baby.'

Bridget's face went blank. The same thought had occurred to her, but mentioning it seemed callous, and as for Maisie calling him a creep... usually she would reprimand her, but it was Maisie being her blunt self.

Both knew about Phyllis's fleeting liaison with her typing teacher, who'd been the complete opposite of Robert. Phyllis's head had most definitely been turned. She'd been starry-eyed about bettering herself, learning how to type and ended up totally smitten and very pregnant.

'Well, let's hope for the best,' said Bridget in her soft, singsong voice of careful pronunciation.

'She might not want 'im to come back. I wouldn't blame 'er. Didn't like 'im much at all. Shame she 'ad to marry 'im. As fer 'is mother—'

'Maisie! What's done is done and...' It was no good. Bridget couldn't think of how best to end the conversation; outspoken as ever, Maisie had hit the nail firmly on the head.

Nipping smartly off the tram, they found a spot out of the wind, though a fraction of it still found them.

'Blimey, I can feel a right draught around my stocking tops,' giggled Maisie.

Bridget giggled too. 'Maisie, surely we don't have to do this. It's crazy!'

'Anything goes! Come on. It'll be fun.'

The veils flapped like swans about to take flight.

Maisie began to lose patience. 'How the 'ell do these fix on?'

'Like this,' instructed Bridget. 'They're a bit like the veils the nuns wear, though shorter. It's been pressed to form a triangle. Let the pointed bit trail down the back and grab hold of the two ends – then pin it like mad!'

After stuffing their coats into the carrier bags, heads down in case they were challenged, they charged up the steps into the

King Edward the Seventh Memorial Building which formed part of Bristol Royal Infirmary.

A chalk board in the foyer listed the wards and patients' names. Their eyes scanned the list and saw that Mrs Harvey was on the third floor.

'Here goes,' hissed Maisie and led the way, her little chin jutting forward, her step resolute and the brown paper carrier bag bumping against her leg.

The stone floors and bare walls echoed from many footsteps. Staff in a variety of different uniforms – including St John Ambulance, rushed around everywhere.

Despite Bridget's misgivings, it seemed they were just two of very many, all brought in to help with the escalating crisis.

'Can't see any wounded soldiers 'ere,' stated Maisie.

'Over the other side,' said a WVS lady pushing along an elderly lady in a wheelchair. 'All the general cases have been moved over here.'

They grabbed the lift, an ancient affair with an inner and outer grille which took some strength to get open.

The lift made a clunking noise as it hit the right floor. Gripping the grille with both hands, they tugged it open and tumbled out.

With an air of knowing where she was going, Maisie led the way through busy people pushing wheelchairs or trolleys, bedpans or trays of cups and saucers.

Maisie slowed, glanced over her shoulder and nodded. They were outside Ward C.

Bridget perused the clock above the pair of double doors to the ward. It was five minutes to eight. Visiting time would be over soon.

'We'll have to 'ang around,' said Maisie.

'What if somebody asks us for a bedpan,' hissed Bridget.

'We'll toss a penny if that 'appens,' said Maisie. 'Heads I do it, tails you do it.'

'Great,' muttered Bridget.

Though Bridget was scared to death, it was obvious Maisie was enjoying this.

They lingered round a trolley some way along the corridor, shifting the enamel receptacles that had been left on there from one side to another, as if it really served a useful purpose. For the most part, nobody gave them a glance; they were just two more nurses doing their bit.

The minute hand of the clock juddered as it measured the seconds and minutes. Finally, a bell sounded. Visiting hour was over.

'Here goes,' murmured Maisie.

The two girls exchanged nervous looks, before turning their backs on the door. They must allow all the visitors to leave before they went in. They looked like nurses and had to behave as such.

Again and again, the doors opened, some visitors pulling on gloves as they headed swiftly towards the stairs or the lift.

'Oh no.' Bridget took a deep breath and flattened herself to the wall.

'Let that be a lesson to her,' spat Hilda Harvey, her thick soles clomping off along the corridor. 'And I don't want her having any ideas about going back to work.'

'Not to worry,' Tom Harvey suggested, scurrying behind her like a Jack Russell, afraid of being left behind.

'Not to worry? Not to worry?' Her voice was as shrill as sharp fingernails scratching grooves in a glass pane. 'It's not her that has to worry. It's me! My poor Robert. Who knows where he might be? And who's there to worry about him and pluck up the courage to give him the grim news? Me! Just me!'

Maisie's dark eyes met those of Bridget's. 'If I was Phyllis, I'd cut my losses and head for the hills. Get out of that bed in there, pack my bag and go anywhere else but back with that old cow.'

'You mean join up?'

'She could, couldn't she?'

Bridget nodded. 'She could indeed.'

Once the Harveys had disappeared, Bridget and Maisie breathed a sigh of relief, then, grasping their courage with both hands, they headed into the ward.

There were about ten beds on either side, each provided with a folding screen that could go all around the bed if need be. The lights had been turned down low, leaving one single bulb throwing a pool of light onto a desk in the middle of the ward. At present it was unoccupied. Bridget decided it was the domain of the ward sister.

A voice came from the other end of the ward. 'Now just lie there whilst I take your blood pressure, Mrs Ferguson. Then I'll give you these aspirin to help dull the pain. All right?'

Judging by the groaning and anguished entreaties to stay and hold her hand, Mrs Ferguson was far from all right. The ward sister remained behind the green-curtained privacy of the folding screen.

Maisie nudged Bridget. 'Come on,' she whispered.

Heart thudding against her ribcage, Bridget followed.

They slowed their steps, hardly breathing in case the ward sister left the patient's bedside and came their way.

'I need a bedpan,' whined a pain driven voice.

'Lie quietly, Mrs Ferguson. I'll get you one right away.'

A shadow fell upon the end of the ward and there was a brushing sound as one of a set of double doors was pulled open. Hopefully the sluice where the bedpans were kept and emptied had to be out through those doors.

Shivering in her shoes, Bridget held back whilst Maisie went forward on tiptoe, scanning the lines of beds up ahead.

Not too far in, Maisie stopped, crooked her finger and jerked her head to where Phyllis, eyes closed and fists tightly clenched lay beneath a dark grey coverlet.

Light on her feet, Maisie was swiftly beside the bed.

Bridget followed.

In a trice Maisie had soundlessly wheeled the screens around the bed. 'Phyllis?'

Suddenly aware she was not alone, Phyllis's eyes flashed wide open. 'You two! Whatever are you doing 'ere?'

Maisie pressed a finger to her lips. 'Shhh.'

Phyllis's jaw dropped and her eyes were wide with surprise. 'Since when did you become nurses?'

Maisie giggled. 'Only relatives are allowed to visit, so your old mate Maisie put 'er thinking cap on. We came in disguise, thanks to Bridget's mates in the medical unit at Wills helping us out with a couple of spare uniforms. Like the stockings?' Grinning from ear to ear, she lifted her skirt and extended her leg high enough to expose the white flesh between stocking top and the leg of her knickers.

Phyllis expressed a weak smile and shook her head. 'You're a right one, Maisie Miles.'

Although shocked at Phyllis's appearance, the self-satisfied look remained on Maisie's face and she held back comments that might hurt. Phyllis looked a shadow of her old self. Her naturally pale skin was a sickly white and her red hair seemed to have lost its bounce. 'So how are you?' she asked in a hoarse whisper that she forced to sound cheerful.

'You heard I lost the baby. It was a little girl. I named her Alice.' Her voice was steady, but her eyes were sad. She gulped in an effort to collect herself.

'We know,' said Maisie and went on to explain about one of the women in the bread queue being related to Sally Grey. 'We phoned to find out 'ow you were and what ward you were in - relatives only they said. Saw the 'arveys on their way out. She was givin' the old man 'ell.' Maisie grimaced.

Phyllis scowled. 'I'm glad he came with 'er. He's not a bad bloke at all. But 'er...!' The dark scowl deepened. 'That old cow blames me for losing the baby, as though I did it on purpose.' Her eyes filled with tears and sobs choked whatever she'd been about to say. 'All she's worried about is how sad Robert's going to be, never mind me.'

Maisie pulled a face. 'Could be worse if 'e ever found out it weren't his baby.'

A warning look from Bridget shut her up, though Phyllis appeared not to notice.

'You've heard nothing from Robert?' asked Bridget.

Phyllis shook her head and frowned. 'Nothing at all. I shouldn't think he'll be back for the funeral and neither will I.' She gulped. 'The doctor said I'm to stay in for two weeks, so his mother's taken charge. I suppose I can't grumble, seeing as she's going to pay for it all.'

All three fell to silence. Having anyone die was always difficult to cope with, doubly so when it concerned a baby.

Bridget handed Phyllis the chocolates and silk scarf bought with the whip round at work.

'Hope you like it.'

Phyllis smiled, touched the soft fabric with her finger tips and told them to thank everyone.

The sound of footsteps preceded a loudly voiced question from roughly halfway down the ward. 'What's going on here? Who pulled those screens across?'

Within minutes, a portion of screen was pulled back.

The ward sister sighed.

Phyllis's eyelashes fluttered as the sister efficiently but gently tucked in the bedding at one side.

'That's it, Mrs Harvey. You go back to sleep. Whoever drew the screen was right to do so. You need your rest. I'll draw it back across so nobody can disturb you.'

The small rubber wheels squealed as she pulled the screen back round Phyllis's bed. Once her privacy was regained, Phyllis's eyes flashed open and Maisie and Bridget came out from beneath the bed.

"Phew,' said Maisie, pulling the stiff linen headdress from her head. 'That was close.'

Bridget was speechless. She kept asking herself why she had allowed Maisie to talk her into such a madcap scheme. What happened next made her glad that she had.

'Bridget,' whispered Phyllis. 'There's a bag in the bedside locker.' Her voice caught in her throat. 'Take it. I won't be having any babies for a long time.'

Bridget frowned. She couldn't work out what was going on.

Phyllis jerked her chin and whispered, 'Go on.'

Quietly, so the ward sister didn't hear, Bridget did as asked, pausing before she opened it, waiting for a signal from Phyllis to go ahead.

Phyllis's eyes met hers and Bridget slid the contents out onto the bed. They lay there, two flannelette nightdresses, one folded neatly on top of the other and Phyllis's throat tightened at the sight of them. They were the ones she had bought on her way to the bakers. Just the sight of them brought tears to her eyes. She pushed them towards Bridget. 'You take charge of them, Bridget, until one of us has need of them; you, me or even our Maisie.'

Even Maisie looked dumbstruck and her eyes too brimmed with tears.

Head bent, a single tear ran down Bridget's face as she stroked the fabric, imagining a living baby Alice snuffling and asleep in its warmth.

'We'll have a coffee in Carwardines when I get out of here,' whispered Phyllis, a suggestion met with tearful nods. 'Can't say when, but sometime...'

Without saying another word, it was taken for granted that it was time to go.

The pair of them leaned against the screen, pulled back a corner of material and peered out. The ticking of a clock somewhere passed like dripping water as they waited for the right moment. Eventually it came. The long-suffering Mrs Ferguson yet again demanded attention from the far end of the ward. There was no time to say or wave goodbye. They took their cue and ran on tiptoe, out through the doors and along the corridor to the lift. The only sound as they went down in the lift was of cables and metalwork clanging in sequence.

The ground-floor reception area had emptied of would-be visitors. A crowd of nurses wrapped in woollen cloaks were going off duty. Grabbing the opportunity to fit in, Maisie and Bridget tagged on behind.

Outside, they paused. It was still light and they once again found a secluded spot where they could change.

'What will you do with the nightgowns?' asked Maisie as they made their way to catch a tram.

At first, Bridget felt confused about how she should respond. She didn't really want the nightgowns. 'I doubt I'll ever use them,' she said at last. 'I'm not sure I'll ever get wed.'

Maisie regarded her querulously. 'I'll put 'em in me case if you like.'

For a moment, Bridget regarded the ground thoughtfully. 'No. I'll take care of them..'

'Until one of us needs them,' murmured Maisie.

'Yes,' returned Bridget. 'Until one of us needs them.'

6

MAISIE

Dear Maisie,

I was over the moon when I read your letter and wish I was with you living in that pub, or at least having a drink at the bar.

Thinking of you a lot and how you'd laugh to see me in shorts and frying an egg on a piece of old tin. No fire needed! It's that hot.

Don't know when I'll get some leave but hope it won't be too long. The eighth army couldn't do without me!

Anyway, can't wait until the day comes when I see you again. Hope you and your mates are keeping safe.

Please wait for me.

Love, Sid.

Maisie smiled and felt quite pleased that she'd written to Sid and told him about her new circumstances. The letter had taken a while to get there and his response had taken a seemingly shorter time to get back. As though he'd been waiting for her to write, she thought, and that was nice.

Funny how his cheeky grin was still implanted in her mind and she still recalled his saucy comments and his attempt to put his arm round her when they'd gone to the pictures together following them meeting in the queue outside.

'You all right to 'elp out tonight then,' asked Aggie.

'Yeah,' said Maisie, folding the letter and sliding it into her pocket.

'Got no young man to meet up with, then?'

'No need to. Got one already in me pocket,' said Maisie and laughed at her own joke.

Friday night in the Llandoger Trow was always busy, the bar full of men thirsting for a drink after a long week at work, sailors and dock labourers smelling of salt, plus a sprinkling of women, some sitting whilst their men drank, others eyeing up men that looked free and out for some fun – at a price of course.

One after another, tankards were filled, the dimpled glass turning from clear to a rich and yeasty brown.

'Busy night,' said Maisie, nodding to the sea of demanding faces all trying to get the attention of those serving.

There was an art to pulling a pint and Aggie had taught her well. The first few pints she'd found easy to pull, but her left arm had ached like mad by the end of the evening. Now, her muscles having built up, she didn't have that problem, but joked, chatted and took the money.

'I'll 'ave the arms of a navvy with all this pint pulling,' Maisie murmured to herself.

Aggie heard her. 'In time you'll 'ave arms like mine.'

'You've got bloody big ears,' Maisie said to her.

'Matches me gob,' returned Aggie.

Maisie laughed.

'Two pints 'ere, love.'

Two empty glasses were refilled. In the process of handing over the customer's change, the wide, lopsided door of the bar was opened. A gush of warm evening air still touched by lingering sunlight filtered in, diffusing the acrid human smells of working clothes, sweat and strong beer. Maisie was vaguely aware of a tall, rangy figure, broad shoulders thrusting against dark clothes, the peak of his cap pulled low over his eyes. Like a lot of young men, he headed straight for the youngest and prettiest barmaid, which of course happened to be Maisie.

Just as she made ready to ask him what he wanted, he swept the cap from his head and said loudly rather than shouted, 'Make way for a sailor!'

There was raucous laughter, coupled with the odd comment of 'What do 'e mean by that?'

Maisie gasped and was out from behind the bar and shoving through the crowd until she at last threw her arms round her brother's neck. 'Alf! I didn't know you were back.'

His grin was broad and as beguiling as ever. 'Why, did you think one of them subs might 'ave got me?'

Her frown was as fierce as her voice, though the latter was laced with laughter and a great relief she couldn't admit to. 'They wouldn't dare. They'd 'ave me to deal with if they tried that one.'

Although he laughed, a dark look clouded his eyes, enough of a message for her to realise there'd been some pretty scary moments out there on the ocean waves. 'Little sister, I can always count on you to punch above your weight.'

'Watch it, Alfie Miles!'

He pretended pain when she delivered a hefty punch to his shoulder. He eyed the navy blue dress she was wearing, the make-up, the wiry curls that refused to be confined in a snood or wound into a modern style. 'You're looking as though you're off out. Got a date, 'ave you?'

She wasn't one for blushing but did feel her cheeks warming ever so slightly. 'Yeah. With all this lot,' she said, indicating the crowded bar.

'Not time to chat with yer old brother then.' He shook his head and made a face as though he was deeply offended.

Maisie made a groaning noise. 'Bloody 'ell, Alf. Why didn't you send me a telegram or somethin'?'

''Tain't that easy out at sea in the middle of a war.'

She shook her head in regret. 'Course it ain't. Sorry, Alf. How long you got?'

'About three days. Depends how long it takes to turn the ship round.'

'That's not long. Can't you get a bit longer? There's a bed 'ere if you need one. Aggie's got loads of empty rooms.'

He shook his head. 'No chance.'

It had been some time since they'd been together and there was so much catching up to do. The sight of her brother filled her eyes and brought her to a decision. 'I'll ask Aggie if we can 'ave an hour.'

The expression on his finely chiselled face, more tanned since he'd been at sea, was a joy to behold. 'That would be great.'

Aggie almost pushed them out the door. 'Make the most of it. You ain't seen each other for ages. I can manage.'

* * *

They headed along the old city streets, where the upper storeys of black and white timbered houses threw shadows into the evening sunlight.

As they walked, they talked – nineteen to the dozen, as Aggie would say, Maisie asking Alf about the places he'd visited, what it was like being on the ship, including the danger. She sensed he only told her the better things so she wouldn't worry. Alf asked her what it was like living above the old pub.

'Creepy but nice. Do you know that Long John Silver's place

in *Treasure Island* was based on the Llandoger? Bridget told me. Bridget knows everything – well, about books and history she does.' She laughed in a disparaging manner. 'Though not much about men. Can't ever see 'er marrying. Might do though if that Yank ever comes back.'

Alf latched on to her talk of the American and told her how he'd visited the ports of New England, taking on armaments. 'Even propellers for Spitfires – and there's them saying they ain't gettin' involved in this war – and there they are, making money from it hand over fist.'

The warm glow of the sun filtered through the gaps between ancient buildings as they made their way through Mary le Port Street which was narrow and dated from the Middle Ages. A covered stone walkway connected one side of the street with the other.

'Long way from York Street,' commented Alf, his eyes glancing off the shop windows.

'Good,' returned Maisie with a shiver. 'I wouldn't want to be back there.'

They stopped for a beer in a small pub that wasn't too crowded. A thin man in a dark suit was playing something soft and vaguely classic on a piano.

'Well, that ain't too out of tune,' Maisie remarked.

'No. It isn't.'

Between sips of sweet cider, Maisie prattled on but stopped when she realised that Alf was no longer contributing anything to the conversation. She looked up into his face. 'Cat got yer tongue?'

He raised his eyes from the surface of his beer. His amiable countenance had turned serious. 'Have you heard anything from the old man?'

Suddenly it seemed as though the last of the evening sunlight had gone and her own expression followed suit, her smile gone and a flash of concern in her eyes.

She hesitated before shaking her head.

Alf frowned. 'You don't seem that sure.'

Maisie lowered her eyes and thought back to when she'd accompanied Bridget to buy presents and had espied a reflection in the plate glass window.

Brother and sister had always been close, so thus it was that Alf noticed her ongoing hesitation. 'What is it?'

'I thought I saw him.'

'To speak to?'

She shook her head. 'No. It was only a glimpse.'

Alf ran his fingers through his hair, a deep frown creasing his brows. 'He's not around York Street. I collected a few things from there. The landlord's let it to a widow and her son.'

Maisie nodded. 'That can only be a good thing.'

There was hesitance in Alf's expression. She knew him well enough to realise that he was holding something back. 'What is it?'

His sky blue eyes met her midnight dark ones. He took a deep swig of beer and slumped back in his chair, hands plunged deeply into his pockets. His look was troubled. 'Eddie Bridgeman will be after 'im. 'E don't forgive easily.'

Maisie frowned. 'But he's in prison – ain't he?'

A cold shiver ran through her body when he shook his head.

''Fraid not. The word is 'e used some bigwig lawyer to plead 'is case. It's become government policy to transfer criminals from prison to the army. Eddie was only convicted of receiving and a bit of thieving. Nothing violent. Of course being Eddie...'

Maisie sat forward in her chair. 'He's out of prison?'

Alf nodded. 'Yeah. Didn't keep 'is part of the bargain though. Got let off on ill health grounds, though rumour 'as it that it wasn't 'im that was examined at the 'ospital, that 'e paid some-body else to pretend to be 'im. Only hearsay, mind, but it worked. Eddie's out! He's expected to do some kind of war work, like being an ARP or something.' He sighed. 'Can't see that 'appening.'

Maisie was inclined to agree with him, but all of that paled into insignificance against what really worried her. 'He'll be after Frank.'

'That's right.'

Her eyes, now filled with fear, met his again. 'He'll be asking around, after anyone who might know where he is.'

Alf nodded.

'Including me.'

Alf nodded again. 'Be careful, sis. Be bloody careful.'

'Thank God I left York Street.'

Alf glugged back the last of his beer. 'Thank God we both did.'

7

BRIDGET AND MAISIE

It was a week or so after Bridget and Maisie had sneaked into the hospital and Alf Miles had gone back to join his ship, that both were on their way to the red-brick factory in East Street where millions of Woodbines were made every year.

Jostled by the increasing crowd of women and girls, all keen to get into work, Bridget waved at Maisie and Maisie waved back. Despite there being a war on, it was just another ordinary working day for the tobacco girls. Crowds of women and girls, some looking tired out due to the fact that they were doing fire watches and other part-time war work, swelled as they filtered from side streets and progressed further into East Street and closer to the factory.

The aim was to clock in by eight fifteen and everyone allowed enough time to get in, clock their card, then make their way to where they worked via the cloakroom where they could hang up their things. Today they were brought to a standstill. A group of women had formed a barrier at the top of the steps, waving pamphlets and shouting over the heads of the puzzled workforce. The voices were strident, their actions close to menacing.

'Women are meant to be wives and mothers as ordained by God. They are not meant to wear a uniform and enter the armed forces. It is their God-given duty to stay at home, to be there for the warrior's return. For women to join the armed forces is a sin against God. They will be tempted, as Eve was in the Garden of Eden, with sins of the flesh. I urge you ladies, stay in your homes, stay in your jobs until you are married; refuse to wear khaki, navy or air force blue... Your job is to maintain the Home Front, keep your husband happy and raise a family.'

'Stupid cows! This ain't a church, it's a factory,' muttered Aggie Hill, never one to mince her words and big enough to topple the lot of them if she cared to barrel through.

'What are they up to?' asked a very put-out Maisie.

Bridget was tall enough to see six solid women in thick tweeds and stout shoes, waving leaflets and shouting at the tops of their voices. 'Don't want us to join up by the sound of it,' Bridget suggested.

The grumbles of disapproval from the girls round her changed to shouts of derision.

'You're working for Hitler by the sound of it,' an angry voice shouted.

Others joined in. 'Get out of our way. We've got work to do.'

Shorter than Bridget but undeterred, Maisie managed to poke her nose through. The women causing the mayhem wore tweed suits and their plain features were animated and unadorned with lipstick or powder.

'Come on, girls. Push them out of the way,' Maisie shouted. In her head, she was ticking away the minutes and the money that went with them if she was late.

'You sure they ain't Salvation Army,' asked a girl with glasses who worked in the wages department.

'No. They ain't got any tambourines,' declared Maisie in a loud voice

'Just as well,' added Aggie. 'I ain't that musical anyways.'

Their amused response was more than laughter; it was a battle cry. These women were standing between them and making a living. The labour force of W. D. &. H. O. Wills heaved forward en masse. Leaflets held aloft in gloved hands waved like flags and hats balanced on primly primped hair went flying.

Although they toppled and were being buffeted by a crowd growing angrier by the minute, the women's voices still rang out.

'Stay home,' shouted one far more shrill than the others. 'Join British Urban Mothers and keep your husband happy.'

'Keepin' my old man 'appy means I end up on me back and it nearly always ends up in a bigger family,' shouted one woman. The comment was met with raucous laughter.

Maisie frowned. 'British Urban Mothers?' She burst into laughter. 'B.U.M! Well, I for one ain't joining anything with a name like that!'

The word was savoured with outright laughter but no matter the mockery, the staid women in the stiff suits and hair didn't budge.

Bridget blanched as a leaflet was thrust in her face, a paper cut glancing off her nose.

'Look.' Maisie dug her elbow into Bridget's side. 'Isn't that Phyllis's mother-in-law?'

The bane of dear old Phyllis's life stood taller than all the other women. She also shouted the loudest. Waving aloft a bunch of leaflets, she held her ground in front of the pair of double doors leading to the factory. Three women had taken up position to either side of her, waving their leaflets in gloved hands, repeating everything Hilda Harvey shouted. 'I urge you sisters, not to take the unwomanly path of serving alongside men.'

'Unwomanly path,' repeated the others.

'Women are not meant to be soldiers or to serve alongside soldiers. Their task is to keep the home fires burning, to tend to their home and bring their children up to be good Christians.'

'Good Christians. Not soldiers,' repeated Hilda's colleagues.

Maisie stuck out her chin and shouldered her way forward until she was glaring up into Hilda Harvey's face. 'Some of us can fight as well as any man – especially where I comes from,' she added, warming to the occasion and the audience of friends round her. 'And if we're needed to wear a uniform and fight, then we will.'

A chorus of agreement erupted.

Unperturbed and with one hand on her hat, Hilda carried on. 'Great temptations happen when men and women are thrown together. Fornication! Wickedness!'

Some of the women behind Maisie burst into ribald laughter. 'You're right about that. It 'appens in 'ere all the time.'

Gossip had always been rife in the factory about romances going on between them that shouldn't be carrying on. More so in war when husbands were away fighting. Despite the rhetoric of officialdom, people feared that today might be all they had, that there would be no future.

Clinging tightly to her hat, Hilda continued. 'Desist from going into pubs, from dancing close to male bodies, from watching American pictures and, most of all, refuse to put on a uniform...'

Aggie Hill had decided that enough was enough and rallied her troops. 'We lose money if we don't clock on in time,' she shouted. 'Come on, girls. Follow me.'

Hilda Harvey finally lost the battle to hold onto her hat as Aggie's arm swept her aside. She and the rest of the women were knocked over like a set of wooden skittles. Like a human tidal wave, the women surged past them and into the factory, an unstoppable mass more concerned with earning a living for their families than adhering to any high-minded oratory by women they regarded as living in the past and a very different world to the one they lived in. Besides that, they would do everything they needed to do to achieve a final victory.

'If you might only stop and listen...' Hilda shouted after them.

'What, and lose quarter of an hour's money? Not on your nelly!'

Nobody wanted to do that if they could help it. On the dot of five fifteen they would surge in the other direction, the tide going out more quickly than it had surged in.

The atmosphere in the stripping room was uncommonly warm and there was a lot of laughter as they went over what had happened on the front steps.

'Well, that old trout was certainly full of herself,' remarked Aggie.

A grinning Maisie, pink faced and somewhat pleased with herself, enlightened her. 'That was Phyllis's mother-in-law. Wonder if she's noticed what British Urban Mothers stands for. Bum!' She giggled every time she thought of it.

Aggie's face dropped. Phyllis had been one of her 'chicks', a girl straight from school she'd taken under her wing. 'And she's livin' with 'er? Poor kid. Must be like being in 'Orfield Prison.' She tutted and shook her head at the thought of the exuberant Phyllis incarcerated in something like the sprawling brick building hidden behind high walls and fronted by the very green Horfield Common. 'Still,' she added with a chuckle. 'She must 'ave been cock-a-hoop when you two went visiting at the hospital. And dressed as nurses. You two will cop it one day you will. Is she 'ome now?'

Bridget pulled out her stool and dragged a heap of fresh

tobacco leaves towards her. 'I did go round there. Mrs Harvey answered the door and told me Phyllis was lying down and couldn't be disturbed.'

Aggie was hanging onto what Bridget was saying. 'But you didn't believe 'er.'

Bridget shook her head and bent back to her work. One memory above all others from that particular day was still vivid in her mind. As she'd opened the garden gate, she'd glimpsed a black-edged card in the window, the curtains behind it pulled tightly shut so not a chink of light slipped through. Her eyes had misted at the sight of it; she knew it would say 'Alice'.

Hilda Harvey had answered the door and, as expected, was far from friendly.

Swallowing the memory, Bridget went back to telling her friends what had transpired.

'I asked her if Bridget was going back to live with her mother seeing as Robert hadn't come back. Goodness, I should have kept quiet. She went wild. Told me that Robert was coming home and that it was Phyllis's duty to stay put and wait for him despite losing the baby.'

Aggie patted her back. 'Never mind, pet. Something will turn up.' She paused as a thought crossed her strong features. 'Ain't that in one of the books you told me about?'

'Yes,' said Bridget, head bent over her work. 'Mr McCawber. He was always in trouble and of the opinion that something would turn up.' She sighed. 'I hope it does for Phyllis.'

The baskets were waiting to be filled with stripped leaves and as she carried out her daily task, Bridget's thoughts kept going back to her visit to the Harvey house in Bedminster Road. On her way back towards the garden gate, she'd heard raised voices, followed by one of pleading and it occurred to her that Aggie wasn't far off the mark with her comment that Phyllis might just as well be in Horfield Prison. She also knew full well what Mrs Harvey thought of the girls who worked in the tobacco factory. She'd overheard her say so to Phyllis on her wedding day.

'Only common girls work at the tobacco factory. You're marrying my Robert. The likes of them are best forgotten. I wouldn't have invited them if I'd had my way. But there. It's Robert's wedding.' She ground her teeth at the memory.

Aggie shouted at Maisie to climb onto a table and turn up the volume on the wireless set which hung from a bracket on the wall. The sound was always turned low until first the news came on, followed by an announcement from the Ministry of Food, which in turn was followed by music.

'*The government has decided that bread will not be rationed and neither will fish and chips...*'

A great cheer rang throughout the room and tobacco leaves flew like patriotic flags through the air.

'*On another note, it is expected that meat rationing is on the horizon and clothes rationing will come in some time soon...*'

Grumbles followed and advice was freely given.

'Grab what you can, then, whilst you can!'

'Buy a sewing machine – if you can find one.'

Clothes were already becoming scarce in the shops and things looked to be getting tighter. Rationing was taking a hold and women were making do with whatever materials they could get. Buying a new outfit was almost out of the question – unless you had a lot of money. Those with spare cash had bought what they could before and just after Christmas. Judging by this announcement, it seemed their foresight had paid off.

In an effort to lighten the mood, Bridget picked up a magazine and began to read it out loud. '*Have you seen the gaily coloured ribbed stockings? Ribbing has a wonderful shapely and slimming effect on your leg, and the bright colours make them gay and smart...*'

'Swelt me bob,' cried Maisie, a very Bristolian comment, and climbed back up onto the table, raised her skirt and did silly poses that showed off her legs – like everyone else, her stockings were darned but good enough for work. *'Bright colours will make them gay and smart...'* she trilled.

The dour atmosphere burst with hoots of laughter until the doors swung open and the foreman marched in. Since becoming a company ARP in charge of setting up incendiary watch on the roof, Clifford Morgan marched around as though he was a sergeant major with a battalion of hardened men under his command. The truth was that most of his 'men' were 'women' and at times the truth seemed to hit his wobbly jowls, a disconcerted frown creasing his pink brow as he looked over his troops.

'Milligan. You're on duty tonight. The first four hours. Miles. It's time you did your bit too.'

'I am doing my bit,' Maisie replied tartly. 'I've been up on the roof at The Llandoger. Bit rickety up there, I can tell you.'

'I don't care about that. You're needed 'ere.'

Maisie tossed her head. 'I don't fink the Germans will ever come.'

The foreman drew in his jowls and his thick forehead puckered over his bulbous nose. 'Oh, so you know more than Mr Churchill, do you?'

'No, but I won't believe it until it 'appens.'

8

'Marvin! So good to see you again.'

The tall man with the iron grey hair and tanned face bent over her hand and kissed the fingertips of Betty Jane O'Neill and exchanged the look of two people who had known each other for a very long time. 'Betty Jane, I could have sworn you were only a few years younger than me. Now I'm thinking it's more than a few – maybe ten or even twenty. You haven't changed a bit.'

His tone was as sweet as honey and his smile spoke volumes. There were shared memories in that look and also the affirmation of what they were back then and what they were to each other now.

Betty Jane O'Neill laughed and fluttered her eyelashes as though she was the girl she'd once been, the one who'd been courted by Marvin James Rixey, a man who no longer owned cotton plantations but had divested his interests into factories, utilities and international shipping. He was rich and powerful and of the same social strata as she was cut from. For a time, it seemed they might marry, but then she'd let emotions get in the way, but that was back then. Over the years, love for her husband,

Lyndon's father, had cooled. Status now meant more to her than charm. She had ambition for her son to build anew on his father's empire, to elevate both the family and the fortune to the very peak of Virginian society – New York too for that matter. Marvin had a daughter and she had a son. Betty Jane planned to unite both their families and their wealth.

'I'd like you to meet my son, Lyndon.'

Lyndon stepped forward at the waving of her fingers. The hand that gripped his was hard and square. 'How do you do, sir. Pleased to meet you again, though I can't quite recall the last time we met.'

'Some time ago, too long in fact.' Marvin looked beyond Lyndon to Betty Jane. 'If I recall, you came to Gilda's birthday party. You do remember Gilda, though she was only eight at the time?'

Lyndon smiled affably as a flute of champagne warmed to his fingertips. 'I vaguely recall a girl wearing a pink gingham dress and braids down to her shoulders. She had a way about her.' The truth was that he remembered her as an only child spoilt and overindulged by her widowed father. In ball games, she sulked if she wasn't the winner and snatched back toys that others dared play with, insisting that they were all hers and nobody had any right to touch them.

'That's my girl,' exclaimed Marvin with unfettered pride. 'The pink gingham and braids have gone, but she still has a way about her. Come on, let me introduce you. If you'll excuse us, Betty Jane.'

Betty Jane's smile remained fixed as she watched her wonderful son walking side by side with the man who had first made her heart skip a beat. Lyndon wasn't to know that she'd contrived to arrange this meeting, to tell her old lover of her son's obsession with a girl from some goddamned provincial city in

England. It was a relationship she was determined to break. 'I firmly believe in like marrying like, Marvin. And besides,' she'd said, the light of ambition glowing in her eyes. 'Think of it. The Rixey wealth and the O'Neill wealth combined.'

He'd agreed with her. 'If your son and my daughter see fit to get fixed, I wouldn't stand in their way.' A cunning look had crossed his face. 'She's as ambitious as her old man, perhaps even a bit more ruthless.' Gilda Rixey looked what she was, sleek and polished from her head to her toes. She was a thoroughbred meant to adorn the arm of a rich husband. She had been through all the right schools. She'd also spent two years at Berkeley before she'd flung it aside, declaring that pursuing knowledge or a career would gain her nothing more than what she already had.

Betty Jane appeared to sip her drink, but champagne nor any other alcoholic drink passed her lips when she was plotting something she wanted badly – and furthering the family fortune was top of the list

Lyndon's thoughts were still in England and, with his father's backing, he fostered the idea that he might go back over to learn more about cigarette and cigar making – and to see Bridget of course. He knew his mother well enough to know that she was plotting something.

He crossed the impeccable lawn in front of Grosvenor House, the grand New York home named after a plantation the Rixeys used to own in Georgia. Liveried servants, the darkness of their faces emphasised by the whiteness of their jackets and gloves, glided silently and deferentially amongst the guests, their footsteps seeming barely to bend the blades of grass they crossed.

He heard Gilda's laughter before he saw her, the sound coming from within an encirclement of attentive young men. Each one appeared to be trying to impress her with their straight As at college, their prowess on the sports field, their certainty that the world of business, or whatever other field they pursued, could not possibly last without them.

'Gilda, my darling. Look who I've got with me.'

The circle of admirers broke at the sound of Marvin Rixey's voice, as though he were Moses himself and they were as obliged as the Red Sea to part before him.

Gilda had shoulder-length blonde hair that fell 'peek a boo' style over one side of her face. Her dress was white and covered in red polka dots, her slim waist cinched in with a red satin belt. Everything about her shouted impeccable taste and an expensive price tag. Her smile was wide, her teeth white and her eyes flashed with interest the moment she spotted the handsome Lyndon O'Neill but dimmed rapidly with a cold guardedness.

'Now come along you two. You must have lots to talk about.' Marvin guided both of them away from his daughter's entourage of young men. 'Lyndon is the son I never had.' His expression suddenly turned regretful. His heartfelt sigh swiftly was followed by a loving kiss on his daughter's forehead. 'But I've got my beautiful daughter.'

Hamming it up, thought Lyndon and looked down into his drink. To his mind, the grizzle-necked, rotund cotton magnate had seen too many second-rate theatre companies and second-rate actors.

Gilda caressed her father's arm and smiled up at him adoringly. 'Daddy has had to settle for me and me alone.'

'Give me grandchildren, my darling. They'll make up for it.'

'I dare say,' she replied, black lashes fluttering over light blue eyes.

Surmising where this was going, Lyndon looked down into his drink. So Marvin Rixey was looking for a stud, was he? Lyndon wasn't so much embarrassed as annoyed.

Gilda carried on in the same vein. 'Daddy, just in case you've forgotten, it takes two to make the next generation and the right husband hasn't yet come along.'

'I do know that, my dear,' said her father.

Lyndon fancied he saw connivance in the affectionate look that passed between them before Gilda turned and smiled beguilingly.

'Lyndon, darling, shall we take a promenade and you can tell me all that you've been up to since the last time I saw you?'

She slipped her arm through his. The warmth through the thin fabric of her sleeve was like an electric shock that planted a wary thought in his head; Gilda was out of the same mould as his mother.

The next hour or so was spent in pleasant enough conversation, but he sensed collusion with his family, that the social gathering of today and the following evening would ultimately lead to dinner for two.

'Play along with it,' his father counselled when it was just the two of them talking man to man. 'Just to keep your mother happy.'

He saw the wisdom in those words and for now would concur. The only girl who had piqued his interest was on the other side of the Atlantic.

* * *

After the guests had left, Gilda rejoined her father, smiled warmly up at him and slipped her arm through his.

'Drinks,' he said to a passing waiter.

Drinks were poured and given.

'Well,' he said, his gaze riveted on his beautiful daughter who in his eyes was the Venus who had sprung from his loins. 'Can you imagine a family alliance with that young man?'

She smiled coquettishly up at him. 'So that's what this is all about.'

Her father's smile matched her own. 'Exactly. He's young and handsome. You're extraordinarily beautiful.'

'You're biased, Daddy. What you mean is we both have a considerable fortune, but it could bear bigger fruit when combined – and I don't mean children. Money. The result would be colossal.'

'Correct.' He raised his hands one foot apart at first, then brought them together. 'A fresh injection of capital could ultimately lead to Rixey Incorporated becoming a global force.'

She kissed her father's cheek. 'Daddy, I'm a girl after your own heart. I'll do what's best for the family and the firm. Anyway, he's quite cute.' She stroked his cheek with one well-manicured finger.

'That's my girl,' he said and laughed. 'You're a chip of this old block and that's for sure.' He paused and turned to her. 'Do you think you can snare him?'

'Daddy,' she returned with an air of outright rebuke and a fluttering of eyelashes. 'You could put it a little more subtly.'

'I stand chastised, but can't help being blunt. Can you get him to fall in love with you?'

Gilda tilted her head as though she was considering the possibilities. 'Now let me see.' She took a sip of her drink before a smile lit up her lips and eyes with catlike endeavour. 'Of course I can. It's as easy as falling off a log.'

9

BRIDGET

Bridget Milligan stood side by side with her mother looking out of the living-room window. The sound of rattling milk bottles signalled the imminent arrival of the milkman. Once he was close enough, they would also hear the clanging of garden gates and the subtle difference between full milk bottles being dumped on the doorstep and empties clattering into metal crates.

The milkman didn't matter. Mother and daughter were both awaiting the sound of the postman whistling his way along Marksbury Road. Her siblings wrote at least once a fortnight from South Molton. The eldest girls, Ruby and Katy, had turned out to be prolific letter writers, but the youngest girls were still having theirs written for them. They'd all smiled and shook their heads at the one-line messages on the postcards Sean and Michael managed to send between them, their words sparse but full of enthusiasm for their new life.

Patrick Milligan appeared at the door dividing the kitchen from the living room with a spatula in his hand. 'Me best girls, don't you know the postman won't get here any quicker?' The smell of fried bread came with him. 'Your breakfasts are nearly ready,' he added.

'Keep it warm,' said his wife, grateful that she had a man who could cook. It wasn't beneath him to do a spot of dusting either.

Like her mother, Bridget was edgy. Receiving letters from Devon was one thing, but she badly wanted one from America. Her vow to be a spinster after witnessing her mother miscarrying had gone out of the window on meeting Lyndon O'Neill. The look, sound and smell of that dreadful morning, the aftermath of burning the bloodied remains on the fire would never go away entirely, but his arrival had muddied the waters. Something had shifted inside her.

Although it wasn't much past seven o'clock, the sky beyond the window above the rows of uniform houses was already as blue as Bridget's eyes. Her brandy brown hair nestled on her shoulders. Later, once she arrived at the tobacco factory, she would hide its glossy glory beneath a headscarf. But that was for later, after the postman had clanged the garden gate, marched up the garden path and posted a letter through the letterbox.

Her mother sighed. 'He's taking his time, so he is. P'raps we should be having that breakfast your father's frying.'

Bridget shook her head and kept her gaze fixed on the scene beyond the window. 'I'm not hungry.'

Unseen by her, the eyes of her mother flickered with concern. Mary began folding some items of laundry ready for ironing. Pain shot through her. There were only adult clothes amongst the sheets, pillowcases and towels, no children's clothes. She forced herself to look on the bright side. 'No news today, but I must admit them last letters they wrote were lovely. I never knew our Katy and Ruby could write so well. They sound happy.' She swallowed down the feeling of regret that they didn't appear to be missing her and went on to mention the boys. 'Typical of Sean and Michael to say so little. They could write three times as much on the postcard if they set their minds to it. Still, that's boys for you.' She gave a little laugh, but Bridget wasn't fooled. She knew very well it was the two youngest she was worried about. Her mother hesitated before mentioning them. 'I wish the little ones could write for themselves, but...' she shrugged, and Bridget knew she was worrying that the letters from the two youngest might not be reliable seeing as they were being written by the adults they were staying with. 'Still, I suppose they must be nice enough if the local evacuation committee have billeted them there.'

She didn't sound convinced. Bridget eyed her mother's worried face and did her best to reassure. 'Tell you what, I'll write to the boys and ask them to go along and check on them.'

Her mother slapped the sheet she'd just folded on the top of the pile. 'I thought of that, but they're living on a farm so must be some distance away.'

'I know the boys are older, but they do go to the same village school and must see Molly and Mary at some point in the day.'

She was relieved on seeing a little spark of brightness on features that so closely mirrored hers. The passing years had been kind to Mary Milligan despite being the mother of seven children. Every one of the grey hairs had been earned, and although they softened the original colour, her mother's hair was still lustrous.

She felt her mother's eyes on her. 'Don't be too disappointed if your young American doesn't write, me darling. This war...'

Bridget swallowed the tight feeling that rose in her throat. 'I just think that today's the day,' she said.

Her mother eyed her sidelong. She would do anything in her power to prevent her daughter being hurt and, to her mind, that meant doing what she could to end the relationship before it could go any further and cause real harm. 'Maybe you can stay pen friends seeing as he's so interested in Bristol.'

Bridget heard the warning in her mother's voice, the suggestion that it might be wiser if she settled for less. 'We'll keep writing,' returned Bridget. 'Until such time as he does manage to get back here.'

Mary Milligan clamped her mouth tightly shut. There were so many things she could have said, but on second thoughts perhaps some hope should remain for the young in these troubled times. Resigning herself to the hurt she felt sure would come, she went back into the kitchen, where the greasy smell of the frying pan drowned the fresh air coming in through the back door and kitchen window.

Bridget kept her eyes peeled. She'd seen the pity in her parents' eyes, heard the warning that he wasn't of their class, that he'd already forgotten her and that his family might not – no – *would* not approve of their son being involved with a girl from a lowly background and a different country. All the same, she couldn't get him out of her mind and she truly believed she would see him again – it was just a case of when.

Her father came in from the kitchen, along with the smell of slices of bread frying in the fat scraped from the beef dripping saved from the Sunday roast. Every bit of fat was laboriously scraped and saved, used for frying and even in cakes and pastry for savoury and sweet pies alike.

Having eaten two pieces of fried bread, he pushed the bits of clock he was working on to one side of the table. He'd begun mending clocks not long after his return from the Great War of 1914–18 and was good at it. Of late, he'd mentioned opening a proper repair shop giving him more room to spread out the wheels and cogs, screws, casings and pendulums. 'Once the war is over,' he'd proclaimed.

It was his custom before beginning his daily work to settle himself in the brown armchair closest to the window, the best place for reading his newspaper. He glanced at his daughter before redirecting his attention to the headlines. 'That postman isn't going to come any quicker, no matter how much you want him to, and there's no guarantee he'll be posting through our letterbox,' he remarked.

Bridget sensed him regarding her through the dense smoke that twisted and turned from the bowl of his pipe. Her mother read tea leaves. Her father read minds, or at least observed people very intently.

Her mother had read the tea leaves a while back, not long after Lyndon had departed on a transatlantic liner for New York, and foretold that there was no future in the relationship. He wouldn't be back; he wouldn't be in touch.

Bridget's instinct told her otherwise, and anyway there had been something odd about the way her mother had carried out that reading, holding the cup in both hands and taking her time before making a pronouncement. She'd also been too quick to discard the leaves as though unwilling to accept what they were telling her.

'Do you think America will come into the war?' she asked her father.

He frowned over the bowl of his pipe as he tamped in more tobacco. 'They did the last time, though late in the day. This time...' He sighed. 'Who knows what might happen. Anyways, don't dwell on the fellah.'

'We're just pen friends,' she said adamantly, though deep down she wanted so much more.

'Aye,' he said thoughtfully, the newspaper – made of thinner paper nowadays – cracked as he attempted to flatten it. 'A tickle under the heart,' he added, without raising his eyes from the news, most of which was not good.

The sound of whistling joined that of early-morning bird-song, a sure sign that Dan the postman was on his way. This morning he was whistling 'It's a Long Way to Tipperary...'

She was aware of her father leaning forward, watching with interest as Dan pushed open the gate and whistled his way up the garden path. 'I don't know how he does it,' he said. 'Gets to the sorting office at four, then traipses round the streets carrying that heavy sack. No wonder he's got one shoulder higher than the other. Then it's the second post and after that I know for sure that he does four hours fire-watching. Barely time left to close his eyes.'

Neither do you, Pa, she wanted to say, knowing he didn't sleep well what with his gammy leg, the result of an injury during his Merchant Navy service during the Great War. He also put in some time with the ARP unit, traipsing up and down the streets here-about, checking that nobody was showing a chink of light.

The garden gate of number twenty-two, a tubular thing of painted metal, clanged open on its strong spring. Dan was barely halfway up the garden path when Bridget sprang into the hall-way, grabbing the letter with both hands before it hit the coconut mat behind the front door.

The bright morning turned even brighter as she checked the handwriting and postmark before sliding it into her overall pocket. Her headscarf went into the other pocket as she went to collect her handbag.

At the sound of the mailbox, her mother came running in from the kitchen and her father looked over the top of his paper.

'Is there anything from Devon?' asked her mother.

Bridget shook her head. 'No. It's for me.' Her voice trembled with excitement. 'It's from him.'

It wasn't difficult to interpret the look that passed between her parents, disappointment that there was no word from Devon, and worry.

'Never mind. Perhaps we'll get something from the kids tomorrow.' Bridget kissed her cheek. 'Definitely tomorrow.'

* * *

At the sound of the slamming door followed by the clanging of the metal gate, Mary Milligan sat down on the sofa opposite her husband. The furniture took up most of the space in the square living room, which could barely contain the whole family when home together. A fitted dresser, something all the houses in the street had, took up most of one wall and a round mirror over the fireplace reflected the light from the window.

'Another letter turns up like a bad penny,' Bridget's mother said and sounded bitter.

Patrick Milligan looked up from his newspaper and felt overcome with love. The worry in her eyes matched his own. 'Tis only the letter, not the man himself. We should be thankful for that, Mary me darling.'

A soft frown beetled between her brows. 'I suppose. I'd been looking forward to grandchildren and worrying our Bridie wasn't interested in courting. Then this American came along.' She shook her head disconsolately. 'Why ever did she have to go and fall for a young man from the other side of the ocean?'

Patrick got up from his chair and wound his arm round her shoulders. 'Now, now, Mary me girl. We're worrying about something that's not happened.'

Mary smiled weakly.

Patrick still saw his wife as the girl he'd first met in Cork and still loved her to bits. Though he never mentioned it, he recalled every detail of the last miscarriage, more specifically the bundling of the foetus in newspaper, the smell and the smoke as it had slowly been consumed by flames on the bonfire in the garden. 'How are you feeling, Mary?'

Mary knew her husband well. 'You're trying to change the subject.'

'Nonsense.'

She gave him a direct look as sharp as a knife. Sometimes he felt she knew every thought in his mind.

'Mary, he's on the other side of the Atlantic. How can she get hurt? They're never likely to meet ever again.'

'He'll hurt her, I'm sure he will.'

The piece of waste land immediately opposite the crowded Milligan house was known locally as 'the tip' and was dominated by a green gasometer. The smell from it resembled rotten eggs, but that was the price to be paid for something that kept the gas stove alight and made coke as a by-product – a bright burn in the grate during the dark days of winter. Initially the gasometer had stood alone, but in the closing months of 1939 had been joined by two concrete air-raid shelters. Her father had baulked at the news of them being built so close to the gasometer.

'A direct hit and the whole lot will go up in flames.'

Being early, the rush of girls and women heading for the factories and shops of Bedminster had not yet happened, a fact Bridget was thankful for. She had time enough to read her letter so headed for a sunny gap not overshadowed by either the smelly gasometer or grim-looking shelters.

For a minute she just looked at her name and address, caressing the writing with her eyes and then with her fingers. The lightweight paper fluttered in her hands at the same rate as her pulse, racing as though there were hurdles to jump and streams to ford. There would indeed be obstacles, and her instinct told her they would be quite formidable.

She opened the letter. Her eyes devoured the date – 14 June – two weeks ago. She read on.

Hi there, Bridget,

Loved your last letter describing how famous statues in the city have been boarded up or moved to a safer place – we wouldn't want Queen Victoria getting bombed, would we? Here's hoping the old girl is content with her new quarters.

There's a lot of disagreement over here as to whether we should get involved in this war. According to my father, we already are. A number of American companies are making items stated to be machine parts, which are in fact propellers for fighter planes.

My father sits on the fence with regard to getting involved, mostly I think to placate my mother, who is definitely against getting involved. No big deal. They rarely agree about anything.

I'm off up to New York shortly. My mother has a few social engagements lined up and wants me to accompany her. We're also meeting family, uncles, aunts and cousins from Georgia that I haven't seen since childhood. It will be nice to see them, though I fear my mother has an ulterior motive. She keeps mentioning the daughter of a friend from way back who she reckons would be a good match. I keep trying to tell her that I'm not ready to get hitched. Strikes me that I shall need to be on my guard.

Have you got a steady boyfriend? It wouldn't surprise me if you did. You're better than pretty. Beautiful even.

I understand the tobacco is still arriving safely, though not in such quantities as required. Wish I could too. All of me! There was talk of me coming over there to get some hands-on experience in the factory.

W. D. &. H. O. Wills like members of their family to work their way up and gain some experience of what it's like on the factory floor. I suggested to my dad that I could do the same. He thought it a good idea. My mother nearly fainted and reminded us both that there was a war on and neutral vessels are fair game!

I've told everyone about visiting St Mary Redcliffe Church and the tomb of Admiral Penn, father of our own William Penn, founder of Pennsylvania and a founding father of the US constitution.

Bye for now, sweet Bridget, and keep safe.

Lyndon.

The warmth of the summer day suddenly turned ice cold. His mother was trying to marry him off? Although she'd always told herself that she never wanted to fall in love, marry and have children, those convictions now seemed hollow. She feared that, like Phyllis, he might not be able to resist persuasion from his parents.

With this in mind, she made herself a promise; if she heard nothing else from him, then that was it. She would banish him from her thoughts and get on with her life.

10

PHYLLIS

June came and went and as there was still no word from Robert, Phyllis became more restless. Letters had been sent, but none returned.

Phyllis's suggestion that she should go home to her mother was met with outright fury.

'Your place is here. You're his wife.'

'If he comes home.'

It was entirely the wrong thing to say. Phyllis felt the intensity of her mother-in-law's sharp glance over the click clack of her knitting needles. More wool from an ancient pullover was in the process of becoming a scarf or a pair of socks.

'That's a wicked thing to say.'

Phyllis barely held her temper but stabbed at the lisle stocking she was in the process of darning – yet again. 'I'm not being wicked. We may have to face up to the facts – whatever they may be.'

In a rare moment of feeling sorry for Robert's parents – especially his father – she'd agreed to stay with them. Tom Harvey had been heartbroken enough that there had been no news from his son but he'd been even more devastated at the loss of the baby. He'd told her about the funeral.

'At least it was a sunny day,' he'd said, mopping at his eyes with an oversized handkerchief. 'Alice had a nice bit of sunshine and lovely flowers. Hilda saw to that.'

She'd imagined that funeral, Hilda standing stony-faced at the head of the grave, her own mother pushed to the sidelines. Tom would have been crying. She knew that was so even though she hadn't been there, confined to hospital for the requisite two weeks.

Her mother had visited on her return from hospital when she was still in bed, alone with her tears and the weakness she'd suffered for a few days after returning home.

Hilda had insisted her mother didn't stay for long. 'She's still weak.'

Her mother had been sympathetic but had also agreed with Hilda. 'I do have things to do. I'm going out tonight and Hilda is right, you do need the rest.'

It was only after she'd gone that it had occurred to Phyllis she'd been wearing lipstick. Still, that was some weeks ago and she hadn't exactly been herself.

A light had gone out in Tom Harvey's eyes. Phyllis noticed it, even if his wife didn't. He was in mourning for a son lost and a grandchild that had failed to be born. Despite his personal grief, he continually asked Phyllis if she was all right, if she wanted anything – a cup of tea perhaps, a pillow for her back. She always thanked him and said that she was fine and could she get him a cup of tea.

The past two months felt like a lifetime. From the very first Hilda Harvey had made it obvious that Phyllis was to blame for losing the baby. Phyllis had almost got used to her whining and moaning, putting up with it for Tom's sake.

A whole army had been pulled out of France at the end of May and, as Churchill had stated, the battle for France was over. The battle of Britain was about to begin. There had already been air raids in London and other places. So far, Bristol had got off lightly, hit-and-run raids mostly aimed at the aircraft factories and the docks. The city was still intact.

Hilda Harvey stabbed with renewed energy at her knitting. 'Robert will be home soon. I'm sure of it.'

Tom Harvey went back to staring down at his newspaper. It occurred to Phyllis he'd been looking at the same page for the last half an hour.

'As for you, Tom Harvey, well, your attitude is only to be expected. Putting ideas about joining up into Robert's head...'

Tom Harvey looked astounded, as though she'd shot him straight through the heart.

Hilda carried on. 'Him keen as mustard to go off and fight. I tell you, what did he know about fighting? I suggested he could have applied for something in a reserved occupation, something where he could use his brains, not his brawn. That's what he should have done. At least he would have been here for his daughter – not that it counts for much now.'

Phyllis stared into the empty fire grate aware of an angry glare flying in her direction. 'Well, he wasn't here,' Phyllis said at last, resigned to the fact that Hilda Harvey would never forgive her for marrying her son and certainly never forgive her for losing the baby!

With silent detachment, Tom Harvey got up from his chair, his face grey, his shoulders hunched. 'In the absence of anything stronger, I think we could all do with a cup of tea.'

Phyllis was about to say, yes please, but Hilda Harvey, red spots on her pale cheeks laid into him.

'Oh yes, that's you all over, Tom Harvey! Let's all have a cup of tea. A cup of tea makes it all right. Don't think of Robert. Don't think of me.'

Tom Harvey regularly looked downtrodden and henpecked, but Phyllis perceived that tonight he looked thoroughly beaten as he headed for the kitchen.

Unable to stand it a minute longer, Phyllis laid the darning to one side and got to her feet. 'I'll see if he needs a hand with the tea.'

Despite their departure, the carping voice continued unabated. 'I'm sure he's capable of making a cup of tea. Even someone as useless as him is capable of doing that.'

It struck Phyllis that her mother-in-law could stand in for an air raid siren if need be.

She shot through the kitchen door and pulled it closed behind her, glad to have a barrier between her and Robert's mother. A gas flame licked at the base of the kettle. Cups and saucers were set on a Bakelite tray.

'You've been a bit down today,' she said, then stopped, suddenly aware that something was very wrong.

Tom Harvey was stood with his back to her, staring out to where the setting sun bathed the garden in a golden light. Like the sunlight, his shoulders appeared to be shimmering gently with noticeable regularity.

As though suddenly realising she was there, she heard his intake of breath, then saw him swipe at his eyes before turning round to face her. His face was streaked with tears.

Her heart went out to him. She took a step forward. 'What is it? What's the matter?'

He used his finger to lift the remaining wetness from one cheek, then the other and looked at her as though making up his mind to tell her the problem. Coming to an instant decision, he took a brown envelope from his pocket. 'It's a telegram and came this morning before I went to work. It's addressed to you, but you know how Hilda is, she would have insisted on opening it, so I shoved it in my pocket and took it with me.' He shook his head and his big sad eyes were again filled with fresh tears that he barely kept in check. 'It's been burning a hole in my pocket all day.' He shook his head. 'I'm sorry. I should have mentioned it sooner.'

It was as though her fingertips had turned to ice, the coldness travelling up her arms, into her shoulders and the rest of her body. It was official of course. War Office. Black lettering. The numbness was as strong in her mind as in her body. So many regrets whirled round in her head like the waltzer in the winter fairground that came to the 'Cut' before Christmas each year.

She finally remembered that she wasn't the only one in the kitchen. Tom Harvey stood with his head bowed and his hands in his pockets. Phyllis took hold of the telegram in one hand and began to open it with the other. Despite everything, she hoped it would say that Robert had been held up, even that he had been taken a prisoner of war. Her freedom was too high a price to pay for a man's life.

The words swam before her eyes, but three, just three jumped out at her.

Missing presumed dead.

She read it for a second time, then a third when it hit her. She was indeed free, but instead of elation she felt a great surge of guilt. *No! I did not wish for this*, she told herself.

A sickly feeling rose in her stomach. She reached for the kitchen table, the pattern on the oilcloth covering whirling and dancing before her eyes.

She passed the telegram to her father-in-law.

He held it close to his face and, just as she had, read it more than once. Finally his hand fell away, the telegram still grasped tightly in his fingers. 'What am I going to tell Hilda?'

Phyllis heard the despair in his voice and saw the helpless look on his face.

Suddenly the kitchen door was tugged open and there was Hilda in her lace-up shoes, as tightly restrained as the rest of her. 'I thought I was going to get a cup of tea.' She frowned, looked from daughter-in-law to husband and back again before spotting the telegram. 'What is it? What's that?'

Phyllis bent her head and folded her arms as though she was hugging herself. She didn't want to be here. She didn't want to know what would be said next.

Tom's eyes fluttered nervously and his jaw dropped, his jowls turning to jelly before he finally cleared his throat. 'It's Robert. He's reported missing in action, presumed dead.'

11

BRIDGET

It was a Saturday afternoon and it seemed the whole world had descended on Castle Street and its surrounding areas, even though the shop windows were nowhere near as interesting as they used to be. The fact that the sun was shining had a lot to do with it, plus most people had finished working at midday and were out to enjoy themselves, though frugally thanks to the war.

Maisie and Bridget were having a coffee and, as usual, Maisie was bemoaning her teacake being spread with margarine rather than butter.

'Wouldn't mind if they 'ad a bit of jam,' she grumbled.

It was at that point that the door opened and Phyllis and the fresh summer air rushed in together.

'My goodness! At long last,' cried Bridget.

Warm hugs were followed by comments about how each was looking and what they were wearing.

Phyllis admired the yellow cotton dress Maisie was wearing and the blue blouse and spotted skirt that Bridget told her had been made with her mother's help.

'From a pair of curtains, would you believe.' said Bridget, showing obvious pride in her mother's sewing skill.

'I made this belt,' Maisie said, her thumbs inside the creamy-coloured belt encircling her tiny waist. 'From cardboard and string.' She went on to describe cutting out the piece of cardboard from a box into a long strip and winding it round and round with pieces of string more often used for tying up parcels.

Bridget offered to order Phyllis a cup of coffee and Maisie offered her half her teacake. Both were declined.

'I can't hang about. I hoped I might find you here.' She glanced nervously over her shoulder at the crowds milling along the pavement outside. 'I managed to lose my mother-in-law, but I swear she's got the nose of a bloodhound. She won't be long hunting me down.'

The three of them sat heads close together. Phyllis smelt of fresh talcum powder. In old times she'd smelt of perfume, but everyone was being careful with the little they had.

She took a deep breath, hating to have to speak the terrible truth she was about to impart. 'I've had a telegram. Robert is missing in action, presumed killed.'

'Oh, Phyllis.' Bridget patted her friend's white gloved hand.

'Oh, God,' murmured Maisie, equally taken aback by Phyllis's bad news, though being Maisie, her mind raced forward. 'So what will you do now? Come back to work? Move back in with your mother?'

Bridget welcomed the thought of it being the three of them again. 'That would be wonderful.'

Phyllis started and half rose from her chair. Amongst the crowd, she detected Hilda Harvey's hat bobbing around like a dinghy at sea. 'I need more time to talk to you, but not here. She's out there looking for me.'

Alarmed by her friend's agitation, Bridget thought quickly. 'I've got Friday off. How about I come along then?'

Pushing a tangle of red hair swiftly behind her ear, Phyllis nodded and got to her feet. 'Please. I really need somebody to talk to.'

She was gone in a flash, leaving Maisie and Bridget speechless.

Bridget, for one, had thought the circumstances of their visit to the hospital might have been just the beginning of a happier life for Phyllis. She shook her head. 'Poor Phyllis. She's lost a baby and a husband.'

Maisie set her cup back into its saucer with an air of triumphant finality. 'On the good side, she might also be losing her in-laws.'

Bridget threw her a disapproving look.

'I don't mean that the way it sounds,' said Maisie. 'There has to be some good to come out of this. Poor cow. She's 'ad it rough. 'Ope 'er mother takes 'er back in.'

Bridget frowned. 'I'm betting things aren't so straightforward. Phyllis looked worried, but I'll help her in any way I can.'

* * *

When Friday morning came, Bridget strode off along the road wearing a pretty dress and a straw hat with cherries bouncing on the brim.

Her secret hope was that Hilda Harvey wouldn't be at home, but if she was, she wanted to hold her head high.

Hedges, bushes, borders and blooms in the front garden of the Harvey house were planted in rigid straight lines. Heavy net curtains hung at the curved bay window, an impenetrable barrier between the world within and the one beyond the square-cut privet hedging. Not a weed showed between the rose bushes and the lawn looked newly mowed, each stem of grass of the same height and proportion as its neighbour.

She studied the dimpled glass in the upper portion of the door, a sunray design of red, green and orange. It was as uncompromising in its design as the front garden, just like Mrs Harvey come to that.

Bridget pressed the bell. The living-room curtain twitched and just for a moment she was sure of Hilda Harvey's pinched features, noting it was her and letting the curtain drop back into place.

The door was not going to be answered.

Taking a few steps back, Bridget glanced up at the bedroom windows. If she remembered rightly, Phyllis had one of those front rooms. The windowpanes reflected the green and trees opposite, nothing of what was inside, then suddenly there was movement.

Phyllis waved. Her lips moved. 'Wait!' She pointed across the road to the group of trees between the house, the road and the banks of the Malago, the narrow brook that ran there before disappearing beneath the road.

Bridget turned to look. She immediately understood what Phyllis was saying. Hide behind the trees and wait.

The hinges of the garden gate were well oiled but still she slammed it shut, determined that Mrs Harvey would know that she'd left.

Bridget set off across the road to the patch of green grass and the clutch of leafy sycamores. The heels of her white sandals sank into the soft grass, but she ignored it, accepting it as a small price to pay for meeting up again with her old friend. Asking her to wait must mean that at some point Phyllis expected her mother-in-law to go out.

There was a dip between the trees and a path down to the water worn smooth by kids fishing for tiddlers and tadpoles. That and the trees were enough to hide her from the house. Only somebody who had continued to watch would know that she was here.

It seemed like an hour, but possibly only half an hour before she glimpsed the stiffly upright figure of Hilda Harvey stalking off staring determinedly ahead.

Bridget stepped cautiously from behind the tree and watched until the feathers of Hilda Harvey's hat had finally bobbed out of sight.

The grass was springy underfoot as she left the cover of the trees and made her way to the open green immediately opposite the house. All she had to do was cross the road and knock again... unless...

It was suddenly as though the house had come alive and exactly what Bridget had hoped for happened.

'Phyllis!' Her heart jumped with joy.

The two old friends broke into a run until they collided, hugged tightly enough to break ribs and cried warm tears into each other's hair.

'You look very well,' said Bridget, as they held each other at arms' length, hands clutching shoulders, smiling faces streaked with tears.

'So do you,' returned Phyllis. 'Nice dress, though I did think you looked good in that nurse's uniform. As for Maisie showing off those stockings...'

They laughed together, just as they used to laugh, as though there had been no gap in their friendship and everything was as it used to be.

Bridget glanced towards the house. 'Will she be long coming back?'

Cheeks pink and eyes sparkling, Phyllis shook her head. Loosened by the breeze, wisps of hair escaped from the dull black snood Phyllis was wearing. 'She's gone to a British Urban Mothers meeting.'

Bridget laughed. 'Bum, as dear Maisie pointed out.'

'That's our Maisie,' Phyllis laughed. 'Hilda wouldn't have noticed that. Anyway, its title is pretty short, but the meeting's likely to be long. We've got at least an hour and a half.'

'Shall I come inside?'

Phyllis baulked at the idea. 'That's the last thing you want to do. If she catches us... Besides,' she laughed nervously, 'I can't stand being in there and you won't much like it either. Anyway,' she said, her face suddenly brightening, 'I'm not staying here.' Her smile vanished again as swiftly as it had arrived. 'Robert is missing, presumed dead. I think he is, but his mother... well... you know what she's like. She insists on me staying until he gets home. But I won't. I can't!' She turned her head and looked to where bright green leaves were deepening with summer. She tapped the black snood. 'I made this when I got the telegram.' She turned back to face Bridget, her expression confused, her sad eyes apologetic. 'The trouble is I don't feel that sorry, Bridget. I know I should, but I just can't seem to.' She shook her head. 'I feel guilty that I'm not grieving, honest I do, but I lost the baby and that was hard enough.'

Bridget could tell there was a lot Phyllis wanted to say, things she could say to a friend that she couldn't possibly say to anyone else. 'Go on. Tell me more.'

Phyllis swallowed. 'I feel sorry for 'im, Bridget. I wouldn't wish anyone to die, but...' She took a deep breath and her narrowed eyes widened. 'I don't mean to be selfish, but these last months livin' with 'is mother 'ave been 'ell. Hell,' she said on realising that she'd drifted back into a strong dialect, aitches dropped and words ending in 'r' sounding as though they ended in 'l'. During these long, dreary months, she'd borrowed a book of elocution from the library, read it from cover to cover, and dipped into it again and again. She reminded herself that she would have to pay a fine when she took it back. For some reason she didn't want to admit it to Bridget of all people. For her own reasons, Bridget had long modulated her voice into a cross between melodic brogue and clear articulation. Phyllis had never said so, but she'd much admired it. '

'How's his mother taking it?' Bridget asked, imagining Hilda Harvey entertaining a greater bitterness than the one she already owned on a day-to-day basis.

Phyllis shook her head in a despairing fashion that stabbed Bridget to the core. Even in her worst moments when the real father of her child had abandoned her, she'd still shown some of the old exuberance. 'She's refusing to believe it. Reckons the War Office employs a load of idiots who can barely read and write, let alone keep tabs on whether soldiers are alive or dead.'

Bridget blanched. 'They wouldn't be doing the job if that was the case.'

Phyllis sighed deeply. 'You know enough of her to realise she thinks nobody can do anything right.' She glanced up at Bridget from beneath pale lashes, unadorned with make-up. The rest of her face was unadorned too, unusually for Phyllis who had loved her make-up and looking glamorous.

It was hard to know what to say next. Wives who cared for their husbands would normally be weeping a river by now. Phyllis was just despairing, her eyes flitting around as though seeking some path of escape.

Phyllis fixed her with a very direct look. 'I can't help feeling the way I do, Bridget. I was frogmarched into this marriage.'

Bridget was loath to remind her that she'd been expecting the child of another man and Robert had been her lifeline to respectability.

Phyllis seemed to read her mind. 'I know what you're thinking, and you're absolutely right. I didn't marry because I loved him.' She stared at the ground, pursed her lips and folded her arms as though shielding herself from any condemnation. 'I've put up with livin' with that old cow all the time Robert's been away.' Strands of Phyllis's auburn hair escaped from the snood as she shook her head in exasperation. Her eyes suddenly flashed at her in the old endearing way Bridget remembered. 'But I swear, Bridget, that if I 'ave to stay put for much longer, I'll either throw meself out of the window or drown 'er in the Malago.'

Bridget knew enough about Hilda Harvey's character to understand, but couldn't help laughing. 'Marry me, marry my mother. That's what Robert should have said.'

'It sometimes feels like that,' said Phyllis, and Bridget's laughter vanished.

'So what will you do?'

A garden gate suddenly chose that moment to swing on its hinges and make a loud squeaking sound. Phyllis gulped, melted closer to the tree trunk and glanced nervously over her shoulder. She emitted a great sigh of relief on realising that the sound belonged to the gate of a house further along, but the moment seemed to galvanise her. She spun back to face Bridget, a fiery determination in her eyes.

'I intend to get away as quickly and as far away as I can. That's where I need your help. I need a job and a place to stay.'

Bridget shrugged awkwardly. 'We do have a bit more room now...' She went on to explain about the young ones being evacuated, something she hadn't had time to do in the hospital.

'I don't want to stay round 'ere,' Phyllis exclaimed, eyeing the house across the way with dismal contempt. 'I thought I might get a flat once I get a job. I'm still getting army pay until it's proved one way or another and then it'll be a widow's pension.' She bent her head. 'Hilda's taken charge of the book until it's time to draw. She keeps it in a writing bureau. I don't 'ave a key, but a kitchen knife should do the trick. Then I'm off. I still need to get a job. I need to save. I think a girl should save.'

'You've got to come back to Wills's,' Bridget responded brightly. 'They'll welcome you back with open arms.'

Phyllis shook her head. 'It would be the first place she'd look for me. I also need to live away from here.'

'Or she'll drag you back?'

She nodded gravely. 'As far as she's concerned, Robert is only lost, in which case everyone's got to wait until 'e gets back. Forever if necessary. That includes me.'

Bridget could hardly believe what she was hearing. 'That is so unfair.'

Phyllis nodded. 'That's the reason I have to get a job and somewhere to stay in another part of Bristol.'

'That shouldn't be a problem, what with able-bodied men – and women – being called up. Firms are crying out for replacements. Have you anything in mind?'

Phyllis sighed. 'Not really. I've been thinking of joining up, though not yet. I need time to think.'

There was silence between them as they thought it through. The warm breeze rustled their hair just as vigorously as it did the leaves on the trees.

'I'll ask around,' Bridget said at last. The silence descended again before Bridget said, 'I'm sorry about the baby.'

Phyllis only shrugged. 'It couldn't be helped.'

'No, of course not.'

Bridget smoothed her hands over her hips, loving the feel of the material, the way it fitted her so well. The dress had been huge, bought by her mother from a jumble sale and cut down to size. The colour suited her complexion and just for the moment she preferred thinking of its feel and its provenance rather than reading Phyllis's mind.

'Do you think you'll ever have children?' Phyllis asked.

Bridget was taken unawares. It was suddenly as though her tongue had swollen and was too big to wrap itself around any suitable words.

Their eyes met. Bridget breathed a heavy sigh before responding. 'To tell you the truth, I don't know. I've seen what my mother went through. I don't mind telling you that it's put me off.'

'Oh, Bridget. I didn't know that. I think you'd make a wonderful wife and mother, but it's your decision. Don't ever let anyone push you into anything. You're better than that.'

'And you were better than Robert,' stated Bridget.

Phyllis shrugged. 'I was weak. Stupid. You're not stupid, Bridget. Not like me. Robert never took no for an answer.'

Bridget considered what she might have done in the circumstances but, she wasn't Phyllis. They were great friends but different in character. In a way she thought Phyllis braver and perhaps also a bit more exciting than her. Phyllis had always come across as daring; her fling with Alan Stalybridge proved that. Bridget recalled her saying how much more passionate he'd been than Robert.

Bridget kept her own counsel and merely said, 'I remember you voicing reservations about whether you cared enough for Robert.'

'I did,' said Phyllis with a helpless spreading of her hands. 'Everybody said I couldn't go wrong with Robert. I got persuaded into it.' Her expression was both sad and confused. 'But then... of course, there was Alan. I wish he hadn't gone off. But there you are, he did and Robert was there.' She shrugged and there was pleading in her eyes. 'I had to do what had to be done, but...' She studied the intertwining of her fingers as she tried to put all that she felt and what she had not felt into words. 'I slept with Alan before I was married and it was marvellous.' Her face shone with enthusiasm, then fell as she recounted her wedding night. 'It was so different with Robert. So cold. But that's all in the past. At least I know how it should be now, don't I.' Her eyes shone and she hugged herself. 'And I want to find that again.'

Bridget felt her face warming and left her silence open to interpretation. To judge her would be unfair. For now at least she needed comfort. 'So it's a new life on all fronts,' Bridget said at last.

Phyllis nodded. 'I thought about moving in with me mum, but Hilda would be round there all the time, keeping an eye on what I was doing.' She folded her arms, threw back her head and looked up at the sky. 'I can imagine it now: Hilda banging on the door and my mother doing her best to persuade me to wait until I knew for sure whether Robert was dead or alive.' She shook her head. 'I can't wait, Bridget. I'm young and I've got a life to lead.'

Phyllis had always had a bit of a selfish streak, but Bridget realised this wasn't about selfishness. Once she'd known she was pregnant, Phyllis had taken the best path for the baby, even if it meant being tied to a man she didn't love. Now she was being honest about her marriage, not wanting to hurt anyone but looking to the future, trying to work out where the world might be going and how best to make her way in it.

'Carpe diem,' Bridget said softly.

'Eh?'

'Seize the day,' said Bridget. 'It means that we must live in the moment. Like the hymn, *Oh God our help in ages past, our hope for years to come...*'

Silence descended until the sound of a ringing doorbell from across the street startled them.

'Mrs Harvey?' Bridget suggested.

Phyllis took on a contemptuous look. 'Unlike me, she has a key.' She threw Bridget a telling glance. 'Me and the milkman have to ring the bell. He's the one ringing the bell. She's left the money in a teapot. I've left the door on the catch so I'd better go over and deal with it. I'll see you again.' She half ran across the road, and called over her shoulder, 'And if you hear of any jobs going, let me know, but don't call round, I'll call on you.'

12

FRANK MILES

Frank Miles couldn't believe his luck when he took up with a widow who ran a boarding house in Ford Street. At first he'd been just another lodger renting a room, but once he'd told her a sob story about his wife dying and his children abandoning him to take off on their own selfish lives, he earned her sympathy. He achieved even more when he gave her a few bob extra rent from money he'd stolen from a pub that hadn't locked the doors and windows as well as they could have done. Not that he told her that. 'A bit from what I've saved just to show how much I appreciate your hospitality.' Once that was done, his feet were well and truly under the table.

The widow was named Vera Thompson and was roughly his age and too fat for his liking, but what did that matter as long as he had a roof over his head and was fed big stews that stuck to his stomach?

The great thing was that she was fairly new to Bristol and wasn't in the know as to who he really was and what he did. He made a big play on being a widower – which was true – and further elaborated on his story, saying that his son had moved a loose woman into the family home and told him he had to go – which was not true. He even told her that he'd spent time at sea for years, hence his profuse beard of gingery hair that hid the lower part of his face. The silly old bag had believed him. It still made him smile to think how easily he'd pulled the wool over her eyes.

The boarding house was far enough away from York Street for him to be considered a stranger, but close enough for him to keep an ear to the ground. Although uneducated, he was streetwise and fully aware that news travelled quickly from one pub to another, so he made a point of only drinking in one where he was not known. At the same time, he had to continue to lie low. The last thing he wanted was for Eddie Bridgeman to find out where he was. He'd heard a rumour he was already out of prison and looking for him, but he reckoned he'd covered his tracks well.

Frank was not known to do gainful employment and thus the last place anyone was likely to look for him was anywhere that called for honest work. The secret, he decided, was to land a job that nobody else wanted. War work was well paid, but also controlled by government, and governments were something best stayed away from. Because of the demand, many hard-working folks had left their peacetime jobs for others that were better paid. As a result, there were very many less salubrious jobs crying out for willing hands to fill in the gaps. With that in mind, he found a job with a slaughterhouse situated on the outskirts of the city and close to open countryside. His job was to load bones, hooves and horns onto a small lorry and deliver to one of the rendering yards in St Phillip's.

Although the delivery point was close to his old stomping ground, he figured how to do it safely. The employees at the rendering yard wore scarves over the lower part of their faces to help them cope with their stinking environment. Frank covered his own face just before entering the yard, which made him as unrecognisable as everyone else.

Few pleasantries were exchanged between the men working at the renderers and lorry drivers. All the gruff men in the yard wanted to do was to unload and tumble the bones onto heaps that heaved with rats and flies before they were taken by wheelbarrow and tipped into great vats. In peacetime, the resultant liquid was used to make soap; in war, the bulk of it was used to produce glycerine for armaments. Drivers were known to want their loads turned round as quickly as possible so they could get out, strip their masks from their faces and breathe in the fresher air outside. The men in the yard wanted to do much the same and envied those who had the option of driving away.

Frank kept his head down at the slaughterhouse. He wasn't interested in passing the time of day with fellow workers who, for the most part, were older and had lived in the country or the edge of the city for most of their lives. Working in isolation gave him the time he needed to think about his future and a better way to make money. Ultimately, he might get back to where he was, but with his fear of Eddie Bridgeman, he needed to stay put – at least in the short term.

Obsessed with improving his lot and keeping himself to himself, he gave the appearance of being a hard worker and attracted the attention of his employer.

Clifford Venables managed the slaughterhouse and prided himself on being a good judge of character who firmly believed in rewarding hard graft. He watched as Frank roped a sheet of canvas over his load prior to delivering it to the rendering yard. At the moment when Frank was about to open the driver's door, Clifford thrust open the metal framed window of his office and shouted down, 'Miles. I want a word with you.'

Frank blinked up at the big red face, the bushy eyebrows, the treble chin sitting like a layer of cushions above too tight a shirt collar. What had he done? He had a sudden urge to ask one of his work colleagues if they'd heard a rumour he was being sacked. Like everyone else, he did take the odd piece of offal back to the boarding house and Mrs Thompson's gushing thanks. But there was nobody else in the yard he could ask, the loaders having gone off to where a herd of lowing cattle awaited their fate.

The metal stairs leading up to the manager's office rang like a bell with each footstep.

Venables invited him in, sitting like a huge pile of blubber behind a ramshackle desk.

Frank played the part of the respectful employee, sweeping his cap from his head and standing with it in front of him, clasped in both hands. He stood silently and waited, discreetly studying the man in front of him. Clifford Venables didn't just have a triple chin. His fat arms pressed against his shirtsleeves and his body barely fitted into his chair. Perspiration beaded his forehead. Not for nothing was he called Fat Cliff.

Like a sudden cut in that fleshy face, his small mouth opened and shut as he began to speak. 'I've been watching you, Miles.'

Frank froze.

'You're a hard worker. Keeps yer head down and gets on with the job. You know Jack Parker dropped dead yesterday, did you?'

Frank said that he did and wondered where this was leading. Jack had been eighty and had worked part-time, a dour man who had less to do with his workmates than Frank did.

'How do you fancy taking over his rounds, delivering meat to them butchers' shops that like us to take their bones away to the renderers?'

This was not at all what he'd expected. He was overjoyed as he thought of the extra bits of meat he might be able to lay his hands on. Vera was complaining all the time about how the rationing didn't go far and that without a bit of offal there'd be nothing worth eating. Now what if he could get a bit of decent meat as well?

'I think I can manage that,' Frank said with undisguised confidence.

Fat Cliff pointed a warning finger. 'Just you take care everything ordered gets delivered. We don't want anything going astray, do we?'

'Of course not, Mr Clifford.'

Of course not? Frank was already reckoning on a bit of that meat finding its way into Vera's oven – or better still, he could sell it on – if there was enough of it, that was.

Frank scratched his head as he made his way back to the yard, the metal steps clanging with each descending footstep; his plan was not yet fully formed. It needed a bit more thinking about. What he did know beyond doubt was that there was a good chance to make some serious money. There had to be a way, he thought. Surely not all those butchers were honest, and if they weren't...?

That evening, Vera ladled out a bowl of meaty stew. Flour being in short supply, she told him how she'd thickened it with rolled oats.

'Mind you,' she added. 'It's the bones that give it the flavour. Amazing how much meat came off them bones you brought home for me. So handy you being able to get them so fresh.'

Frank's spoon paused halfway to his mouth. He'd been thinking of heading for the pub tonight where he could laugh and talk with other working blokes and not have to hear all this ongoing chatter about rationing and cooking. Yet something in what she said gave him pause for thought.

He grinned. 'Might be able to get you a bit of extra – not just bones. Liver, kidneys, hearts and stuff...'

She wrinkled her nose. 'Offal? Be nice if you could get a breast of lamb or some nice ox tail. Be even better if you could get a bit of meat for roasting.'

'Might be able to.' He tapped the side of his nose. 'Things are lookin' up fer me, old girl. Now,' he stood up and rattled the few coins he had left in his pockets. 'I've only got enough for a couple of pints...'

'Don't you worry about that,' said Vera with a beaming expression. 'I'm sure I can stand you a few pints, seeing as you brought 'ome them bones. I'm one of the lucky ones. Think how many are going without a decent bit of meat on the table and not everybody can afford black-market prices. Here's half a crown. Am much grateful, Frank. Much grateful indeed.'

And a lot of other people would also be grateful thought Frank as he whistled his way to the pub. Many a woman would appreciate the bits and pieces he got from the slaughterhouse. His mind turned to the lorryload of bones and bits and bobs. A lot of them still had plenty of meat on too – which gave him an idea, one that could make him a decent bit of extra money.

13

MAISIE

Nerves were on edge, what with the men away and news coming from all over the country about air raids. So far, Bristol had escaped lightly, but London especially had received a bit of a bashing. The girls and women who worked in the stripping room were readying themselves. A tea urn was in place in the cellar that had been so ably converted for use as an air-raid shelter, along with blankets, chairs, camp beds and tins of food.

'Right, that's our stomachs taken care of, but we need something else to take our minds off things,' declared Aggie. 'Let's club together and buy a few more records.'

Aggie's persuasive methods were quite formidable and it wasn't long before coins rattled into the leather shoulder bag she wore round her neck.

' So, we've got the gramophone sitting ready and waiting for us down in the cellar – sorry – air-raid shelter. Trouble is the only records that came with it are "March of the Chocolate Soldiers" on one side and "In a Monastery Garden" on the other.'

'And that's all we've got?' exclaimed Edith Jones who spent

most of the day singing along with anything that came on the wireless. 'I can afford a tanner to 'elp with that,' she said.

Aggie shook the leather satchel and fixed Edith with a piercing look. 'Two bob would 'elp a bit more. Otherwise it's that one of Jeanette MacDonald and Nelson Eddy singing "Indian Love Call" and "Rose Marie". Plus, a bit of tea dance music from the twenties. They're the cheapest.'

The resultant groans and mutterings about twenties music being dead and buried were followed by a hunt in purses for extra coinage, though Edith, who had four kids and a husband who'd scarpered the moment he'd received his call-up papers, still showed some reluctance.

Maisie had lived with Aggie long enough at the Llandoger to guess what would happen next. Aggie had a big body and a big heart. She saw her pat Edith's shoulder. 'Sixpence will be enough if that's all you've got.'

Everybody knew Edith Jones was finding it hard, four mouths to feed and no husband to bring money into the house. It was well known that her mother was supposed to look after them and queue up for rations. It was also rumoured that the kids often went short because their grandmother exchanged some of the ration coupons for black-market gin. Actually Maisie knew it was more than a rumour; she'd seen her staggering along the road, her shopping bag lighter than it should be.

Still, she thought, *that's their business.*

'Here you go,' Maisie said, her copper pennies greasily warm in her palm before she sent them tumbling into Aggie's bag.

Once everyone had been coerced for a second time, Aggie's face was a picture of satisfaction as she gave the heavy bag a good shake.

'That's a bit more like it.' She called for a piece of paper and a pencil as she surveyed the upturned faces. 'What's it to be then? What records do we buy?'

'George Formby.'

The younger women grimaced and groaned until Aggie made comment.

'Now, now. We've got to allow for all tastes...'

'And *old* tastes,' somebody grumbled.

Bridget suddenly engaged with the discussion and suggested Benny Goodman. 'Music you can dance to.'

Her suggestion was met with instant approval by many of the younger women.

Maisie tried to recall music she'd heard on Aggie's wireless at the Llandoger. 'How about that Vera Lynn. I likes the songs she sings.'

It was agreed that a bit of crooning would soothe their souls and who better to provide it than Vera Lynn.

At lunchtime, Aggie enlisted Bridget and Maisie's help to count out the takings. Coppers, shillings, sixpences, florins and half crowns were separated and placed in neat piles on the table. Later while they ate, talk was ongoing about what records would be bought.

'I'm looking forward to listening to them,' exclaimed Edith Jones.

Looks of condemnation flew in her direction.

She looked from one disbelieving face to another and spread her hands in a helpless fashion. 'What 'ave I said?'

Bridget enlightened her. 'We're going to be playing those records to hide the sound of the bombs dropping – just in case you've forgotten there's a war on.'

Edith looked shocked, even a little frightened. 'I'm trying not to think of it! Got enough on me mind what with finding enough grub for the kids.' The legs of her chair scraped the floor as she got to her feet. 'I'd better be going. Got to buy a few pork bones for dinner tonight.'

Maisie sensed her embarrassment and felt sorry for the poor woman. She looked washed out. It couldn't be easy, she thought, coping with four kids, no husband and a gin-sodden mother. 'Must be a bit of a struggle feeding her kids,' she remarked as she scraped the last of the cottage pie from her plate.

She smelt a hint of lavender water and cigarettes as Aggie leaned forward, her voice no more than a whisper. 'I knows for a fact that she buys the pinky fruit and whatever veg the barrow boys have got left on their carts that nobody else wants – stumps of cabbage, turnips and half black potatoes. As for meat, I 'ear it's mostly bones – and not just pork bones,' she said, her voice dropping that bit lower. 'Gets a bit of horse meat from the knacker's yard over in St Phillip's.'

Maisie felt instantly sorry for her. It wasn't easy being poor and hard done by, and she certainly knew all about that. Frank Miles had ruled his household with a heavy hand. It hadn't helped that she wasn't his natural daughter. What money did come into the house had been spent on booze and cigarettes. Feeding her and her half-brother, Alf, had not been a top priority.

As a child it was sometimes Maisie's task to use her waif-like appearance to go along to the knacker's yard and get meat for a rock-bottom price. She'd seen the dead, old and worn-out horses taken in there, their meat usually destined for pet food. That was before the war. For anyone that desperate, horse meat was as sweet as beef and far cheaper. At present, in the midst of war, it slipped beneath the rationing regime – if you could get it. The authorities were beginning to latch on. Horse meat was becoming more sought after, a handy alternative to short-term deprivation and long-term starvation.

Bridget forked over the last bit of food on her plate. The

cabbage was a bit watery, the meat a little gristly; like everyone else, the canteen cooks were finding it hard to maintain standards.

'So what did Phyllis 'ave to say,' Maisie asked once it was just the two of them left at the dining table. 'Shame I couldn't 'ave got a day off too.'

Bridget cradled her teacup. 'Now that she's heard about Robert, she doesn't see any reason to stay, but, of course, her mother-in-law won't have it that Robert might never come back. She's insistent that Phyllis stays with them until he comes marching back through the door.'

'Won't be doin' that if 'e's dead,' spluttered Maisie. 'That woman's mad. I'm sure of it.'

'Phyllis has made her mind up. She's determined to get out from under their roof.'

'Back to her mother?'

To Bridget's mind, it seemed the best option, yet she couldn't help thinking Phyllis had been a bit reticent when she'd suggested it. 'I could offer her a bed at my house, what with the kids being evacuated, but it would only be temporary. They're not going to be away forever.'

Maisie agreed with her. 'Plus Hilda will be round knocking on the door and demanding she comes back and waits for Robert.'

'Exactly. Even coming back here to work could be difficult. Phyllis needs to get away until Mrs Harvey has accepted that her son is never going to come home – well – not unless he's just lost.'

'So poor old Phyllis needs our help,' said Maisie, then glanced up at the hands of the clock hanging on the canteen wall. Smoke from a hundred cigarettes was still rising, tea was still being drunk and food scraped greedily from plates. A number of women made the canteen lunch their main meal of the day, preferring to feed their families on an evening and go without themselves.

Intending to mull over what could be done to help, Bridget picked up her handbag. 'I've got to pick up tonight's dinner. How about you come with me and we can chat about it without anyone else around?'

Maisie gulped back the last of her suet pudding, custard and jam and almost choked. 'All in a good cause,' she remarked.

Like Bridget, she was missing Phyllis's bubbling personality and could imagine what it must be like living with the Harvey family. She herself couldn't have stood it, so if there was anything she could do to help, she would do it.

After stacking their dishes onto a trolley, they headed for the cloakroom to relieve themselves before the arduous duty of standing in the queue with ration book in hand.

'Barely time to pull me knickers up,' said Maisie.

In order that they wouldn't be late back to work, they ran along East Street and crossed the road, past the National Provincial Bank and joined a crocodile of women all waiting in the queue for whatever the butcher might have.

During peacetime, Bert Stanley, the pork butcher, had a blue neon light flashing in his window depicting a laughing pig. Since the outbreak of war, it was no longer blue or flashing thanks to the blackout and the drive to save energy. *Less smoke from your chimney, less coal being wasted.*

Breathless and pink-faced, they came to a standstill. Both of them scrutinised the length of the queue and assessed the likelihood of them being late back at work. They decided they could just about do it.

Maisie took off her turban and let her hair bounce free. It was still as curly as when she was younger but longer now and lying silkily on her shoulders. She wiped the scarf across the nape of her neck and took a deep breath.

A contingent of British Urban Mothers suddenly appeared carrying a banner held aloft, which read:

BRITISH URBAN MOTHERS ARE NOT SOLDIERS

Hilda Harvey was marching along at their head, and they were singing a familiar tune, the words changed to fit in with the creed they were attempting to establish.

Bridget and Maisie stared at the heavy-footed women with their tweed suits and feathered hats until they were out of sight.

Other women in the queue called them traitors.

'Reminds me of Moseley's Blackshirts,' said one of them. 'Should be locked up.'

Maisie shook her head. 'Poor Phyllis. I wouldn't swap places with 'er for all the tea in China. Who does Hilda Harvey think she is, telling women they've no right putting on a uniform? I think Churchill might 'ave something to say about that. The woman's mad.'

'And enough to drive anyone she lives with mad,' stated Bridget. 'I really think that if Phyllis doesn't escape her clutches soon, she'll go mad herself.'

In an odd way, Phyllis's dreary lifestyle reminded Maisie of her days growing up in York Street and her stomach tightened. Neglect had been the order of the day which wasn't so with Phyllis. Phyllis was like a puppet having no movement of her own but Hilda Harvey pulling the strings.

'You're right. We have to help her.'

Bridget felt a sense of relief that she was no longer the only one privy to Phyllis's plans. She sighed. 'Seems such a shame though.'

Maisie eyed Bridget's profile, the classic nose, the arched eyebrows, the pink perfectly formed lips and all presented without a trace of make-up. She had a serene beauty, a clear but gentle voice. Nothing was too much trouble and she seemed to love everybody and would do anything for anyone. The one thing Maisie couldn't quite understand was why she didn't have a regular boyfriend. She excused herself not having one because she was that much younger than Bridget. Phyllis had ribbed Bridget about not going out on many dates, though she had back-pedalled a bit when Lyndon O'Neill had come along. Even she had been taken aback at Bridget's sudden enthusiasm for a man who lived so far away.

'How about if Phyllis joins up,' Maisie said with wide-eyed enthusiasm and gurgling laughter. 'That really would set the cat among the pigeons. We both know how the old witch feels about women in uniform.'

'It's an option in the long term, but for now she needs to sort herself out. She wants somewhere to stay and work.'

Maisie flipped her shoulders in a casual manner. 'A job shouldn't be a problem. Wills's would take 'er back like a shot.'

Bridget shook her head as they took another few shuffling steps forward in the queue. 'She won't come back into the factory. She needs to get as far away from Hilda Harvey as possible. I did think she might be able to get a job at Edwards and Ringers, but then thought Hilda might trace her there. You know... once working in a tobacco factory, still working in a tobacco factory.'

Maisie narrowed her eyes as she considered the possibilities. Phyllis had made a very big mistake and had paid for it. She deserved to be helped and Maisie was willing to do that. Bridget and Phyllis had befriended her when she'd first begun working at the tobacco factory. They'd been very kind and drew her into their little group without a moment's hesitation. She'd loved being one of the Three Ms, but now it was only the two of them, her and Bridget. Phyllis had left a surprisingly big gap.

She frowned and began to chew at an escaped strand of hair. 'Out of the area, out of the tobacco industry. Shame she can't find a place in an office – that's what she wanted to do,' mused Maisie.

Bridget sighed and shook her head. 'I think anything would do for now. I've had a few ideas. She could go into service at some country house or something, but an employer would ask for references, and letters would be going backwards and forwards. At present, she's still registered for rations and suchlike at her in-laws' address.'

'And her mother-in-law would intercept her letters,' said Maisie with outright certainty.

Bridget nodded sadly.

Maisie shoved her hands into her overall pockets. 'It ain't 'ard to weigh up that old cow.' She looked up suddenly, eyeing the queue in front of them that seemed to be slow moving forward and that worried her. She didn't like being late for anything, and certainly not arriving late back at work. 'When do you reckon we'll get to be served?'

Bridget eyed the women in front of them, some still with their curlers in, some without teeth and small children clinging to their sides. One of them looked pregnant and fit to drop at any minute – she hoped it wouldn't be any time imminent. All the women looked tired, ground down already with too much work and too much queuing. She felt sorry for those wearing shabby coats and wrinkled stockings, but for all their careworn expressions and worn-out clothes, they stood as guardians at the head of the queue, throwing dirty looks if anyone dared push their way forward. 'Not long. Anyway, my mother ordered hers first thing this morning when she heard the pig boat had come in from

Ireland, dashed along at an ungodly hour and ordered three pigs' tails.'

'Do you like them?' asked Maisie, surprised that anyone did.

'They're a bit greasy. I think my mother was forgetting that the kids are down in North Devon. She reckons that pigs' tails grease their insides so they grow that much quicker. I prefer pork bones. No greasy skin on those.'

Maisie jumped at the mention of pigs' tails, bones and greasy skin. 'I've got an idea,' she said suddenly just as they reached the counter.

Bridget got out the family ration book, opened it flat and offered it to the butcher.

Recognising her as Mary Milligan's daughter, Bert Stanley leaned forward, held his hand across his mouth and whispered to Bridget, 'Tell yer mum that I've got some liver, lights and caul out back if she fancies making some faggots.'

Bridget had long surmised that Bert rather liked her mother, his wide smile exposing broken teeth the moment she came into the shop.

'I'll tell her,' said Bridget.

'All right is she? Not ill or anything?'

'No,' Bridget replied. 'She's got a lot of writing to do. My younger brothers and sisters have been evacuated.'

'Ah!' he said, tossing his head as though he understood completely. 'You look just like 'er,' he added.

Bridget avoided meeting the twinkle in his eyes, enough to confirm that he really did have a thing about her mother.

Maisie was getting fidgety. 'Can you 'urry up? We can't afford to be late getting back to work. Our money will get docked, so if you please, mate...'

Taken aback by her outright comment, Bert threw her a disparaging look. 'Right you are,' he said, clenching his jaw.

The pigs' tails were wrapped up in white paper and placed into a brown paper carrier bag. The tails were regarded as offal so off ration, but there was also a shoulder of lamb – enough to make three meals.

Bridget paid up and headed out, wanting to laugh at Bert's face in response to Maisie's cheek, but holding it in until they were outside.

'Well, that was telling him,' said Bridget, laughter bubbling up with her words.

'Needed a bit of a gee up,' pronounced Maisie.

'He likes my mum,' said Bridget.

'Oh.' Maisie understood. She'd only met Bridget's mum briefly, though long enough to see she was a good-looking woman and that Bridget very much resembled her.

They strode quickly, the string of the carrier bag cutting into her hand, Bridget asked Maisie what was this idea she had in mind.

Maisie dug her hands into the pockets of her overall and tossed her head, causing a couple of bluish black curls to escape from under her turban.

The big black hands on the huge clock hanging above the factory entrance juddered to the next Roman numeral. They didn't have much time, so they quickened their steps.

Bridget turned to her. 'Well?'

Maisie took a deep breath. 'Firstly, she don't want Mrs Harvey to know where she is. Secondly, she don't want any employer asking too many questions...'

'As few as possible,' Bridget corrected. 'And it has to be quick. She needs to go to whatever place is hiring and start the job right away – if that's possible.'

'Course it's possible!' Maisie looked so pleased with herself that she smiled at everyone as they trotted along to the cloakroom. Then she turned back to Bridget. 'Ain't gonna leave that meat 'ere are you?'

'Bet your life I'm not! Although it's not prime beef, it'll be gone if I don't take care of it.'

Maisie knew this was so. Rationing was beginning to bite and just a few ounces of meat per person per week were hardly enough to fill some people's gullets, let alone their stomach. The black market was beginning to flourish and so was thieving – even at W. D. &. H. O. Wills. Warnings had been given. Anyone caught would lose their job and was likely to be prosecuted. Following a few light-fingered occurrences, everyone now took their shopping back to their workstation and shoved it under the table. Even the most basic of offal had become a precious commodity.

'So what is it you've got in mind,' an intrigued Bridget asked Maisie.

'Soap factory. There's better conditions in the munitions factories, so even though soap production is down, they are in need of workers.'

Soap was becoming as precious as pearls, but Bridget had to admit to some surprise. 'It's not the best of places.'

'Beggars can't be choosers. Anyway, Hilda Harvey wouldn't think of finding her there.' Maisie's quick mind had moved on. 'We needs to find 'er somewhere to live. There's a chance of a room at my old place in York Street.'

Bridget was hesitant. She knew enough of Maisie's family to fear complications. 'What about your father?'

Maisie winced and her jaw tightened. 'He's out of prison but not back there; daren't go back there. Too scared of Eddie Bridgeman tracking 'im down. A widow with a grown son away fighting is renting it. No doubt she could do with a bit of extra rent.'

Bridget's face lit up. 'Maisie Miles, you're a genius.'

'I think so too,' said Maisie, giving a haughty toss of her head.

* * *

That morning after Bridget had left for work, Mary Milligan picked the letter up from the doormat and knew it was from him. A letter had arrived in June which Bridget had been privy too and here was another in July. He was sending one a month.

Mary frowned at the letter. It was noticeable that Bridget no longer loitered by the front door waiting for the postman. Neither had she expressed hope that her American boyfriend would write to her again so soon. It seemed as though her obsession with the young man was at long last over.

'You could be right, Patrick. She's lost interest. I certainly hope she has.'

Patrick patted his wife's shoulder. 'There you are then. Keep it in case she asks. We don't know what that last letter said. Seems to me it could have said something that disappointed her.'

'You could have asked her, Patrick. She opens up to you.'

He shook his head. 'Some things are best left private.'

They loved all their children and only wanted the best for every one of them. At times, Patrick thought that his eldest daughter was spending too much time at home looking after her mother and her siblings.

'You need to go out more. Fine yourself a young man,' he'd said to her, but his recommendation had resulted in nothing more than a weak and quite secretive smile.

Bridget's mother did as he asked, placing the letter in the box she kept for official things like her children's birth certificates, her marriage certificates and insurance policies.

This morning of all mornings something much more important had arrived that made her heart leap with happiness. With the assistance of the evacuation committee, they were to visit their children in South Molton. Train tickets had been booked for all three of them for she'd insisted that her oldest daughter would not be left out.

* * *

Lyndon O'Neill gritted his teeth. His mother had invited Gilda for one of her afternoon tea parties – though champagne was also on offer along with strawberries and cream and cakes bursting with cream. Britain might be suffering severe food rationing, but the USA certainly was not.

He headed for a neglected gazebo away from the textured lawns where unpruned roses had been allowed to run wild. He needed to think.

The smell of woodsmoke came from the other side of the red brick wall where the gardener grew luscious soft fruits, as sweet and juicy as could be. A blackbird sang in the branches of an apple tree that dipped over the wall. It was the only sound, the only living thing around.

'Darling.'

The blackbird stopped singing. Gilda had arrived. She was wearing a white linen dress that ran to creases across her flat stomach. Her hair was controlled with a red spotted band.

'Are you hiding from me?' she said to him whilst sliding her arm through his. Her bright red lips smiled up at him and her ice blue eyes fixed on his.

'The garden party was crowding me.'

'Me too, darling.'

He tensed as her lips brushed his face.

'And now it's just the two of us.' Her voice was husky and her body was too close. 'There's no one around.' She pressed her body against him. 'You know I'm a very modern girl. What I mean is, we don't need to wait until we're married. We can do it right here and now. There's nobody back here, is there?'

He stiffened – more so when her hand glided downwards – a natural reaction of course, but not one he had any intention of getting out of hand. He grabbed her hand, pushed her away. Disappointment on her face then a pouting of lips.

'Darling. I never took you for being shy.'

His jaw tightened. 'I'm not interested, Gilda. Our parents have got it all wrong. You've got it all wrong.'

The corners of her lips turned downwards and the hard look in her eyes turned to anger. Men NEVER turned her down. She wasn't used to it.

The pretty smile and bubbling laughter that was so much part of her persona was nowhere to be seen. There was now an ugliness to her face that Lyndon perceived as the real Gilda, the other one just being for show, no different than putting on a fresh dress or applying lipstick to cracked lips.

'Don't you like girls, Lyndon? Is that it? Prefer all boys together, do you?'

He shook his head. His laugh was one of disbelief.

'You haven't changed a bit, Gilda. Still spoilt and thinking you can have anything you want, getting angry if you can't. Well you can't have me, Gilda, and you're not having me.'

With that, he once again thrust away the hands that reached for him, turned, stalked off and vowed to get as far away from family and country as possible.

14

PHYLLIS

It was late afternoon when Phyllis dared to tell Hilda Harvey where she was going – or at least the bit about visiting her mother.

Hilda fixed her with a disbelieving stare. 'Are you sure that's as far as you're going? Wouldn't be calling in on that common Irish girl whilst you're at it?'

Phyllis boiled inside. She fully accepted that Hilda was snobby, but there was no excuse for her being nasty. However, she held her temper.

'Of course not. I haven't seen my mother for such a long time.'

Although Hilda grunted acceptance, Phyllis couldn't help feeling nervous. She wouldn't put it past her to come marching out behind her, complete with her stiff hat, stiff face and stupid banner.

Once everyone had finished eating, Phyllis began collecting the dishes and taking them into the kitchen. Her heart was racing, her thoughts fixed on a future in a different place, unrestricted by anyone telling her what to do.

Absorbed and somewhat excited, she washed some of the tea

plates more than once and spent longer than usual wiping each item and putting it away. She had a lot of thinking to do and whatever was going to happen next scared her.

Back in the living room, her mother-in-law sat knitting in one chair, her father-in-law reading his newspaper in the opposite chair. They were, she thought, like bookends, two of a kind, though, in actuality, they grated on each other. One was amiable whilst the other never saw the good in anyone – with the exception of her son.

'I'm off then.'

Hilda Harvey said nothing, but bent her head more stiffly over the ever clicking knitting needles.

The last time Phyllis had seen her mother, it had been at the Harvey house. Their conversation had been stilted because Hilda had remained in the room, her beady eyes flickering from one to another, readily leaping on anything with which she disagreed and making comment where none was invited.

Her mother had looked uncommonly well on that visit. Bright red lipstick and skilfully applied make-up, hair fashionably styled and instead of the more familiar comfortable shoes, she'd been wearing black suede court shoes, the heels far higher than she normally wore. After she'd left, Hilda had muttered something about mutton being dressed as lamb. Phyllis had ignored the remark.

'I'll be off now,' she said again. It was difficult not to rush out of the house as fast as her court shoes could carry her.

Hilda made one of her disapproving noises, no recognisable words, just a noise.

Phyllis tried again. 'I'm sure she's looking forward to a bit of company. She's all by herself nowadays without me there.'

Hilda muttered and, although quietly spoken, Phyllis was sure she heard her say, 'I doubt it.'

'Excuse me?'

Hilda Harvey stopped knitting and glared at her. Her lips pursed in a fierce pout, wrinkles sprouting like sunrays round her mouth. 'Never mind your mother. What about Robert? What if he comes home? You should be here for him.'

Phyllis slung a blue and green silk scarf into her handbag. It was bright and cheerful and Bridget had said it brought out the colour of her hair and her eyes. Robert hadn't liked it, all the more reason for choosing it, she thought defiantly. 'I'm only going to visit my mother,' she said, her words carefully controlled through clenched teeth. 'And let's face it, there's no chance of him walkin' through the front door in the next hour or so, is there?'

Hilda's face turned a darker shade of puce. 'Oh, you would like to think that, wouldn't you, hussy that you are! Don't think I don't know why you married my son. You got yourself in the family way pretty quick in my opinion, and who's to say that it was my Robert's baby? I've come across girls like you before, any port in a storm! Taking advantage of a respectable young man...' Hilda Harvey's eyes blazed as she spluttered the last words.

Phyllis blushed all the way to the roots of her hair. 'That's a terrible thing to say.' She grabbed her cardigan and her handbag, her bright red hair falling forward to hide her guilt.

Tom Harvey put down his paper. 'Now, now, Hilda. Phyllis is right. That's not a very nice thing to say.'

His wife turned her malevolent glare on him. 'That's it, Tom Harvey. Take her part. You never take mine.'

'Your comment's unfounded, Hilda. Consider her feelings.'

His attempt to calm things went unheeded.

'How do you think I feel! And how's our Robert going to feel. That's you all over, thinking only of yourself.'

Normally Phyllis's father-in-law was cowed into submission, but today was an exception. 'I've had enough of this. I'll come to the garden gate with you, Phyllis. I need to get out there anyway and see about deadheading the roses.'

There was kindness in his voice, though his wife's acid tongue was not yet stilled and she screamed after her.

'It's your fault you lost the baby. Be in no doubt I'll tell him that. You just see if I don't.'

The words followed them out of the house like poison-tipped arrows.

When they got to the front gate, Tom Harvey's courage began to fail and he made excuses. 'She's upset about Robert.' He shook his head. 'She'll never accept that he might be dead. And what with the baby...' When he shrugged, Phyllis felt a great urge to reach out and pat his shoulder. 'I just wish we heard one way or the other, though if he is dead...' His voice trailed away and the moment of showing sympathy was gone. She didn't want to hear the rest of what he'd been about to say, that if Robert failed to return, her mother-in-law would likely become more difficult than she was already. It served to make Phyllis even more determined to escape.

'I won't be late,' she said before striding off down the road, though she wished she could stay out all night.

Once away from the forbidding house and with tears stinging her eyes, she ran all the way to Marksbury Road and the house where she'd grown up. Before opening the garden gate, she stopped and wiped at her eyes. Despite everything, she wanted to look her best. She didn't want pity, but she was in need of support. Her friends Maisie and Bridget were doing their best to sort something out for her. Much as she would prefer to live once again in her childhood home, there was the likelihood of being continually badgered by her mother-in-law. She had to consider all options.

The tensions she lived with every day lessened as she walked up the garden path. A warm feeling replaced the chillness of the Harvey household. The privet hedge was still the same, the lilac was flowering in a flood of purple to one side of the path, its scent heavy on the air.

Her intention was for this to be a short visit, long enough to share her plans for the future with her mother. A little time spent here, and then she was off to visit Bridget.

She glanced at her wristwatch, a Christmas present from Robert some years back. It was a little before five. *Give Bridget time to get home from work,* she thought to herself.

Thinking of Bridget being at work brought a pang of jealousy. Oh how she wished she was still at work too, that she'd never had ambitions to learn to type, then perhaps she would not have met Alan Stalybridge who had taught her to type before seducing her, fleeing to London and leaving her pregnant and with no option but to marry Robert as swiftly as possible. All in the past now. Forget it. The future beckoned and the first step was to visit her mother.

It seemed strange to knock at the front door that she had known since childhood, but Robert had insisted there was no reason to retain a key. The possessive tone of his pronouncement echoed through her mind. *'You're my wife now. There's no point in having a key to your mother's house. Your home is with me.'*

Phyllis brushed the last of the wetness from her eyes and blew her nose before her mother opened the front door. She looked surprised to see her. Whilst pregnant, Hilda Harvey had discouraged her from visiting anyone – even her own mother. A whole list of the things women shouldn't do shunted like a lumbering goods train through Phyllis's mind.

An expectant mother should not be seen outdoors once she begins to show.

No woman should continue to work once she was married.

And the latest in defiance of the powers that be, no woman, single or otherwise, should join the armed forces. Her mother-in-law was still leading the charge on that one, marching through Bedminster with banner held high, passing out leaflets and shouting slogans.

'Hello, stranger. What are you doing here?' her mother said.

'I needed some fresh air and to talk to you. If you don't mind that is,' Phyllis asked, slightly surprised at the appearance of the woman standing before her. Her mother's eyebrows were more finely arched than usual, obviously plucked into shape. Her lips were red and she was wearing rouge.

Slim shoulders shrugged and she smiled. 'I suppose you'd better come in.' Her tone was breezy enough but tinged with nervousness.

A wave of nostalgia flooded over Phyllis as she entered the house where she'd grown up. Everything was much as it had always been; the flooring was still a mixture of green carpet and beige and brown linoleum vaguely resembling faded wooden blocks. The furniture was still brown Rexine, plain but service-able, though the cushion covers seemed new. The wooden mantel clock struck the hour, a tinkling sound that served to enhance the feeling of having returned home.

Her mother jumped at the sound and for a moment her gaze stayed fixed on the clock's enamel face.

'So how are you?' her mother asked, dragging her eyes back from clock to daughter. She planted a peck on her cheek and hugged her.

In the midst of her hug, Phyllis noticed the smell of face powder and a hint of perfume, items her mother had rarely worn.

'I'm fine.'

'Cup of tea?'

'Yes please.'

Any news about Robert?'

'I'm still getting his army pay. They haven't issued a widow's pension just yet.'

'Oh well, where there's hope...'

Phyllis cringed. 'It takes a little time to swap over. They told me two weeks.'

Her mother jerked her chin in acknowledgement. 'And how's his mother?'

Phyllis gritted her teeth. 'She won't accept that he's dead.'

'Well, I suppose it's difficult to confirm...' Her mother suddenly noticed her tears. 'Oh darling. I'm so sorry.'

Phyllis pulled out her handkerchief. Smears of mascara transferred onto its whiteness as she dabbed at her eyes. 'I can stand that. It's Hilda I can't stand. I have to get out of there before she drives me totally mad.'

'My poor girl!'

Suddenly Phyllis felt like the little girl she used to be, safe in her mother's arms no matter what had happened in the world outside.

Her mother patted her back as an avalanche of tears ran down her face. 'There, there,' she said, her voice warm and moist against Phyllis's ear. She straightened and smiled. 'Now give your nose a good blow. I reckon you're just about ready for a cup of tea.'

Phyllis smiled through her tears but couldn't accept that a cup of tea was the antidote to how she was feeling. She watched as water gushed from the kitchen tap into the kettle and a blue flame erupted from the gas stove once a match was applied to a burner.

Phyllis drew up a chair to the kitchen table, which was covered in a patterned oilcloth in order not to mark the polished wood. She traced the pattern, the flowers spilling through green trelliswork, the red and white checked background.

Back turned, her mother continued to warm the teapot, place cups and saucers onto a tray and milk into a jug.

Phyllis's eyes remained downcast. 'The thing is, I don't think Robert will be coming home. I think he's dead.'

'But you don't know for sure,' said her mother as she placed the tray on the table, her eyes flickering between the pot and the kettle, not once settling her gaze on her daughter.

Phyllis shook her head. 'I wish I did. His mother doesn't believe he's dead and no matter how much time passes, whether it's five, ten or twenty years, I don't think she'll ever accept it. Robert's father is worried that she might tip over the edge once we do know for sure, but in the meantime, he placates her.'

'I see. And what about you. What are your intentions?'

'I want to carry on living. I need to accept what's happened and sort my life out.'

She willed her mother's eyes to meet hers, saw them flutter but continue to carry on with what she was doing.

'There's no sugar by the way,' her mother said as she spooned tea into a brown glazed teapot, added boiling water then picked up a tablespoon and gave it a good stir. 'Quite honestly I'm getting used to drinking tea without it and have lost a few pounds. It's definitely possible to live without sugar in tea.'

'You do look slimmer.' Phyllis said as she followed her mother who carried the tray through to the living room. She had noticed that she was wearing a black dress with a roll-neck collar, a sparkling brooch pinned at the shoulder. She looked far more elegant than Phyllis could ever remember, the change enhanced by lipstick, powder and eye make-up, even at this time of day. She'd never known her do that; indeed, she'd condemned Phyllis for wearing make-up and making herself look too dressy. Phyllis thought of how in the past her copper-coloured hair, which was only a little less bright than Phyllis's own, had been hidden beneath a tartan scarf. Not so now, today it was swept up in one of the latest styles.

A sudden realisation struck; her mother had managed very well without her, even happily by the looks of it. Better than me, she thought. That morning she'd looked in the mirror and saw herself looking strained and unhappy. So much had happened and she badly wanted to turn the clock back and have everything as it once was.

Her mother jerked her chin high and her head higher. Phyllis sensed some kind of decision had been reached.

'I'm glad you came round. We weren't able to 'ave much of a conversation with your mother-in-law listening.'

'There's no privacy that's for sure.'

Her mother's expression was unreadable as she poured out the tea. She bit nervously at her bottom lip. It was as if she was holding something back, something that she was finding difficulty putting into words.

A sip of tea accompanied by one eyebrow was creased in a questioning manner.

'How come you're speaking different?'

Phyllis jerked her head up in surprise. Inside, she felt secretly pleased that her mother had noticed but did feel a little embarrassed admitting what she'd done. 'I borrowed a book on elocution from the library. There's not much else to do at the Harveys' except unpick old jumpers and hold up my hands whilst Hilda winds wool into skeins and then balls.'

She took another sip of her tea, aware that her mother was still looking at her, a pleasant smile on her face.

'You sound really posh. I've always wanted you to be posh. I thought that by marrying Robert that you would become posh.

Oh well…' Her expression soured before she smiled and said, 'I'm sad about Robert. It must be difficult for you. I must say, I wouldn't want to live under the same roof as his mother.'

'It isn't easy.'

'And what now?' Her mother returned her cup to the saucer with an air of finality, her eyes finally meeting Phyllis's.

Phyllis also returned her cup to the saucer and heaved her shoulders in a deep breath. 'I'm going to move out and get a job.'

'Really? Well, going back to Wills's shouldn't be a problem, but where will you live?'

There was something oddly brittle in her mother's voice that was totally unexpected.

'I did think about coming back here.'

Her mother's eyes were downcast. 'I'm not sure about that. This is the first place Mrs Harvey will look for you.'

Phyllis nodded. 'I know.' She felt unnerved and fancied that although her mother expressed sympathy there was some other reason for her hesitance. 'You're quite right,' said Phyllis. 'I can't go back to Wills's for the same reason. I don't want her turning up there and shouting the odds.'

'Fancy another cuppa?'

Phyllis nodded. 'Yes.' She watched as her teacup was refilled, the brew far weaker than it had been before the outbreak of war, the tea leaves used more than once. Her mother, like everyone else, was being careful.

'Is there anything lined up on the job front?'

'I'm making enquiries. I'm sure something will turn up,' she declared as positively as she knew how. The fact was she needed help from her friends and hoped they would come up with something.

Her mother lit up a cigarette and offered one to Phyllis. She took one purely because smoking was a substitute for words.

'Well! Sounds as though you've got everything in hand.'

Phyllis nodded, flicked ash into an ashtray. 'Bridget has promised to make enquiries. I'll find something, and even if I don't, well, I can always join up, can't I?'

'I never thought you'd consider that.'

Phyllis waited for her mother to suggest something else. The cigarette went to her mother's mouth, out again. Another puff, more smoke, lips pursed, slack, then pursed again. There was something nervous about her smoking, as though she had something to say but hadn't quite made up her mind what it was.

It wasn't often the two of them sat quietly and thoughtfully like this, but it did give Phyllis chance to study her mother more closely. Something was going on here that she didn't quite understand. Never had Stella Mason looked so glamorous. Wearing make-up and high-heeled shoes went against everything she'd railed against. And now, here she was, looking like the woman she'd not wanted her daughter to be.

There came the sudden sound of a fingernail tapping nervously at the bone china teacup – one of the best ones usually kept for special occasions. Each fingernail was painted bright red. When had her mother begun painting her fingernails? What had happened to change her?

Dragging her gaze away, Phyllis forced the truth from her mouth, all the pent-up anxiety now coming out in the open. 'If I'm not widowed and he does come home, I want a divorce, in which case I can then move back in with you, Mum. Then it's nothing more to do with my mother-in-law. She can't stop me from doing anything,' she proclaimed defiantly.

Lashes caked with mascara brushed her mother's flushed cheeks and for a moment she seemed loath to look up.

'The truth is... I've got news of my own to tell you.' A deep sigh sent her mother's breasts heaving against the black dress and above the cinched-in waist. She inhaled the half-smoked cigarette. The truth poured out with the smoke. 'I'm getting married.'

Phyllis's jaw dropped. The smart dress, the make-up and the modern hairstyle suddenly all made sense. If Phyllis had ever been the centre of her mother's world, she certainly wasn't now. All this had been done for a man.

Her throat felt tight but she managed to ask the pertinent question. 'Who are you marrying?'

'Well...' That fluttering of lashes again like a young girl admitting she'd fallen in love for the first time ever. 'He's a Canadian. You recall meeting your cousin, my nephew?'

Phyllis uttered a faintly discernible response. Yes, she did.

'Well, it's his commanding officer. The darling boy took his dear old aunt...' she laughed at her little joke. She certainly didn't look like anyone's aunt. 'He introduced us and, well, from there on... we kind of clicked.'

Stunned by the unexpected revelation, Phyllis woke up to the fact that this woman was not just her mother, but a curvaceous woman who men found attractive. 'I didn't know you were lonely.'

Dimples appeared in the pinkness of her mother's cheeks. 'Neither did I until I met Matt. Matthew Horsley. Colonel Matthew Horsley.'

Phyllis took a deep breath before asking when the wedding would take place.

'Some time in the New Year,' said her mother. 'You will be invited of course. Let me know your new address as soon as you have one.'

Phyllis's gaze and mind wandered. Going home had only been a small hope, what with Hilda being so close at hand. But that particular door had now been well and truly closed.

'Is he a widower?' In Phyllis's opinion, the best husband for her widowed mother had to be a widower, someone of similar experience.

Her mother adopted a shifty look, her sparkling earrings catching the light as she turned to face the window, fingers tightly laced as though she were holding something she couldn't afford to drop. 'Actually, he's divorced.'

'I see. And kids? Has he got kids?'

'A son and a daughter. Both grown up.'

When Phyllis clenched her jaw, her mother noticed. Her face reddened.

'And you can take that look off yer face. I am not making a fool of myself!'

'Being divorced isn't the same as being widowed.'

'Well, that's a bit condescending of you. Anyway, I'm old enough to know my own mind!' An angrier pink coloured her mother's cheeks.

Phyllis pursed her lips as an old saying she dare not voice came to mind. *There's no fool like an old fool.* She held back. Many women over forty were certainly past their best. Her mother wasn't one of them.

'Where will you live?'

'Here until he gets stationed elsewhere. He's local at the moment, but if he does get posted, I'll get a place close to him, so, you see, you can't stay here. It wouldn't be for the long term, and anyway, I wouldn't want Hilda charging round here and shouting the odds – especially once she knows I've got a fancy man that stays here on occasion. The old cow wouldn't hesitate reporting me to the council for subletting, or worse still calling me a whore or accusing me of running a... a... house of ill repute,' she said at last.

Phyllis had to admit that she was right, but her mother's revelation about getting married had come as a shock.

They sat silently with their own thoughts, the tea tray and two cold cups of tea between them.

'I'm sorry,' her mother said at last. 'It must be a shock to you, but there you are. I've got my life and you've got yours.'

Phyllis noticed the tears shimmering at the outer edges of her mother's eyes.

'Oh, Mum,' she said, throwing her arms round her. 'You're right. Of course you have. Be happy, Mum. Be very happy.'

15

BRIDGET

Bridget's parents had been told at the very beginning when the children had been evacuated that visiting rights were encouraged though somewhat limited thanks to travel difficulties. Servicemen had priority over civilian passengers so parents like the Milligans were asked for their forbearance.

The invitation and travel passes were therefore greeted with great excitement.

'A whole week,' squealed Bridget's mother, then burst into tears.

There was both excitement and envy when Bridget broke the news to Maisie and the other girls in the stripping room.

'Lucky cow!'

'Take me in yer suitcase.'

'We could all do with a week in the country – and in August!'

After the headaches and worry about Phyllis and her own disappointment on not hearing from Lyndon, Bridget too found herself looking forward to getting away.

'I feel a bit guilty leaving Phyllis at this moment in time,' she said, wistfully pushing aside the remains of the scone and jam she'd chosen at tea break that morning.

'Never you mind. I'll take care of her,' said Maisie. Her gaze settled on the untouched half of Bridget's scone. 'Might need to keep me strength up though.'

Bridget pushed the plate across. 'You have it. I'll have the holiday.'

* * *

It was August, hot and sunny, the train steaming through fields of ripening corn and wheat, fully leafed trees nodding at a cloudless summer sky.

They had to catch two trains to their destination and, when finally arriving, found a small black Ford saloon was waiting to collect them.

'Blimey. Gonna get us all in that little thing?' murmured her father.

Bridget might have laughed out loud if it hadn't been for the memory it invoked of the chauffeur-driven Bentley Lyndon O'Neill had picked her up in when she'd shown him round Bristol.

'Suitcases and all?' Patrick said incredulously to the driver.

'I'll tie 'em on top,' returned the man.

'Hope I can get my leg in,' said Bridget's father, eyeing the small car. 'It won't bend, you see.' He tapped it so the driver was in no doubt that it was not flesh and blood.

'Get in the back with yer Missus and stick it across.'

The solution was delivered in a blunt though kindly manner. Countrymen, Bridget surmised, were pragmatic, adept at overcoming obstacles, no matter what they were.

The sound of rumbling came from the car roof once they left

the smooth surface of the road and were trundling down a rutted track.

The Milligans listened, exchanged ho-hum sort of looks and hoped for the best, firstly that the luggage would still be there on arrival, and secondly that Winter's Leap would live up to Sean and Michael's description.

The track eventually widened and joined a narrow lane that was straight for a time. When it finally turned a bend, there was the house named Winter's Leap.

'Bit more than a farmhouse,' remarked Bridget in breathless admiration as she leaned forward in the little cramped car to get a better view.

Bridget felt mounting excitement. This was the first time in her life she had ever been on holiday. Summer holidays for such a large family meant a day at Weston-super-Mare, Portishead or Clevedon on the summer excursions laid on by the Great Western Railway from Bristol Temple Meads. But this!

'Quite a place,' declared Bridget's father, head tilted back as he took in the weathered stone portico, the mullioned windows and what was left of aged gargoyles long distorted by time and weather.

Bridget's mother agreed and Bridget found herself holding her breath. It was a stunning place even though the cowshed and other farm buildings were not too distant, their smell hanging in the air.

'It's all gettin' on a bit,' said their driver as he unloaded their luggage.

'It's Elizabethan,' Bridget said at last on seeing the date of 1549 carved above the door.

Her remark emboldened their driver. 'See them windows?' He pointed to row upon row of tiny panes glittering like diamonds in the dying rays of the setting sun. 'Pretty ain't they,' he added.

Bridget detected pride in his voice.

'Do you live here?' she asked.

He laughed and pushed his battered hat further back onto his head. 'Bugger me, no!' He instantly apologised. ''Scuse me language, ladies.' He tapped the brim of his hat in a respectful manner. 'Name's Charlie Bond. I only works 'ere I do. I lives in one of the cottages over t'other side of the field thereabouts.' He waved his arm vaguely to some place beyond a stone wall on the other side of which was a pile of steaming manure. 'Oh,' he said suddenly, pointing elsewhere. 'That's the boss,' he said, lowering his voice, then louder, 'I got 'em, Mr Cottrell. 'Ere they are.'

His pronouncement was directed to a rangy man who took big strides across the yard, wielding a long stick over the backs of a dozen or so cows before coming through a five-bar gate. Leather gaiters were buckled round his lower legs and his shirtsleeves were folded up, exposing black-haired arms and hands the size of shovels. His feet were caked with mud and the brim of a hat, equally as battered as that of Charlie Bond, hung low over his eyes.

'Cows are ready and heavy to give. Get to it, Charlie.'

Without so much as a wave, Charlie was gone. The Milligans were left standing, their luggage on the hard ground in front of them.

He offered his hand to Patrick. 'Us and the vicar are members of the evacuation committee. Everybody's got to help out in these difficult times.'

'We can't thank you enough for having us stay here a whole week. It's much appreciated, Mr Cottrell,' said Patrick.

'Those of us who can accommodate people should do so,' returned Mr Cottrell and nodded at the house. 'It's certainly big enough. And call me Archie.'

Patrick Milligan went on to introduce Mary Milligan and then Bridget.

'Don't be surprised if you catch my daughter staring up at this old place and snooping into a few corners. She's keen on history. Always has been.'

'She's welcome to have a look round. It's good to see some interest in the old place.'

Like the house, Archie Cottrell looked as though he'd been here forever and, due to the colour of his clothes, built of the same solid grey stone. What struck Bridget most was that he was well spoken when she'd fully expected him to have the same accent as Charlie.

'The boys are on their way back,' he pronounced.

He didn't say from where and nobody asked. Mary Milligan's face lit up like an electric light bulb.

'Oh Patrick,' she said. 'I'm so looking forward to seeing them.'

Bridget's father returned her happy smile. 'It'll be grand! Really grand!'

Archie jerked his head towards the house, a signal for them to follow him. 'My wife's readied the rooms. Tea, cakes and sandwiches have been laid on. We thought you'd be hungry after your journey. And just to let you know, your youngest two are coming to live here.'

Mary Milligan grabbed her husband's arm and looked up at him in alarm.

'No need for you to concern yourself. Just matters arising. That's all.'

With perfect timing, a figure beckoned them from the doorway, one hand resting on one of the stone pillars holding up the canopy.

Archie jerked his chin in that direction. 'My wife. Rose.'

'Get yerselves in 'ere. Tea's brewing and you'll be wanting to get yourselves settled.' Although meant as a welcome, it sounded more like an order. Unlike her husband, Mrs Cottrell's accent was exactly as expected from a Somerset farmer's wife. 'I'll take that, me girl.' Without giving Bridget's mother time to protest, her suitcase, which had been weighing her down, was taken from her hand.

There was nothing fragile about Mrs Cottrell. Her look was forthright and her movements swift as she took them up the stairs, the suitcase carried as though it was light as a feather.

Mrs Cottrell pushed open a door and addressed Bridget's parents. 'This room's yours.'

Bridget was as taken aback as her parents by the size of their bedroom and the four-poster bed with thick curtains. A large bay window, its glass set in leaden diamonds, looked out over the front yard, the barns and fields beyond.

'My youngest girls! They are all right, aren't they?' Her face was filled with alarm.

Rose Cottrell was kindly but firm and her joviality was undiminished. 'No need to worry. It was decided they'd be better 'ere than with the sisters. We'll explain it all later. Now then, bath and lavatory is at the end of the landing.'

Mrs Cottrell turned to Bridget and, in a very businesslike manner, ordered her to follow up a set of winding stairs.

At the top, she found herself in a room full of sunshine nestled beneath the eaves. From the dormer window, she found herself looking down into a walled garden which she surmised was at the back of the house. Beyond that, she espied what seemed at first like flashes of lightning, though on reflection that seemed impossible. The day was fine, not a cloud in the sky. On leaning further into the window, she saw another flash and knew it was the result of sunlight bouncing off the glass roof of a large greenhouse.

Mrs Cottrell told her that she'd have to use the same bathroom as her parents. 'There's no bathroom up yer, but two bathrooms on the next one down. Your family got one and mine the other. Unpack and come on down when you're ready. You must be starving after your journey.'

Without waiting for any thanks, the door closed in a decisive and no-nonsense way just like Mrs Cottrell herself.

Bridget looked round the room in breathless delight. It was a beautiful room, the walls dappled with sunlight. Every so often, she perceived a flitting shadow and worked out that it was a bird flying backwards and forwards from the eaves.

Her stomach growled with hunger and she was looking forward to something to eat and drink. Unpacking wouldn't take long. Not wishing to be overburdened on such a long train journey, she'd packed only the barest essentials.

Once it was done, she knelt on the window seat, pushed open the lattice window and took a big breath of fresh air. It tasted as sweet as water. From some distance off, she heard the sound of a tractor, from the front of the house that of cows lowing in the milking shed. Away from the farmyard, the smell was of ripe corn and earth warmed by the sun, and the leaves of fresh vegetables gently baking to deep green. To that was added the perfume of roses, sweet peas and wildflowers. She drank it all in as her eyes detected the colours of the countryside. Everything seemed so much brighter and she wondered if her brain was only fooled into thinking colours here were more vibrant than in the city.

A sudden movement down in the walled garden caught her attention, as did the smell of tobacco smoke from a lit cigarette. She sat herself on the window seat, stretched her neck and located dark blue amongst the multitudes of green.

A man was leaning against the warm bricks of the wall and wore an RAF uniform. His attention did not seem particularly focused on anything, perhaps the fruit bushes, perhaps the beds of regimented vegetables. He was rangy, like Mr Cottrell. Father and son, she decided and kept staring, watching this figure that seemed in a world of his own.

Perhaps it was pollen, or perhaps the old air of the house, but something tickled her nose and she sneezed.

He heard her and looked up to her window, instantly seeming to know the direction the sneeze had come from.

Her first inclination was to duck back inside; her second, perhaps out of curiosity or sheer defiance, was to stay put.

A cool breeze ruffled his hair, moved on and did the same to hers. He lifted one hand in acknowledgement. She returned the gesture, though not until she'd retained his features to memory: a strong face, deep-set blue eyes possessing the same brightness as that of his father, and hair the colour of hazelnuts – not quite blonde but not quite brown either.

A quick wash of her face and hands and she descended the stairs to the next floor. From the ground floor came the sound of Mrs Cottrell inviting her parents to come into the dining room and their politely spoken responses.

'And here's your girl,' said Mrs Cottrell as Bridget came down the stairs from the first floor to the ground floor where the kitchen and other reception rooms were situated. 'Now come on with you. Get something of this tea inside you before the boys arrive or they'll eat the lot.'

'I can't eat a thing until they're here,' admitted Bridget's mother, her face bright with joy and one hand placed reverentially over her heart, as though it was beating its way out of her chest.

'I think you should,' said Bridget's father.

'It looks too good to eat,' proclaimed Bridget.

Not since before the war had either Bridget or her parents

seen such a spread: home-made bread, a fruit cake, apple tart, fresh raspberries, a jug of cream, bright yellow butter and a dish – not just a jar – but a dish of home-made jam.

'First off, a nice cup of tea,' said Mrs Cottrell as the pot was tilted and a stronger-looking brew than they'd seen for ages was poured into a series of cups. 'Oh. By the way, call me Kate. We don't stand on no ceremonies 'round 'ere.'

The food was delicious, the tea welcomed. The conversation was pretty one-sided, Mrs Cottrell telling them all about the history of the house and how it was handed down from one generation to another. 'Built in the time of Queen Elizabeth,' she said. 'One of Archie's ancestors assisted Drake fending off the Spanish Armada. Got given the land and built 'imself a house. Been in the family ever since.'

Running footsteps, then excited laughter heralded the arrival of Sean and Michael.

Bridget's mother sprang to her feet, a little cry of delight escaping her lips and tears filling her eyes. 'My boys! My darling boys!'

The two of them crashed into their parents' open arms and greeted their sister with almost as much enthusiasm.

Bridget's father shook his head. 'I don't believe it of you two.'

The boys looked up at him, perturbed that they might have done something wrong.

'You've grown,' he said, ruffling each head, which resulted in them laughing out loud.

'Oh, Dad. Of course we 'ave!' the pair of them responded.

'Dad, I'm fourteen next year,' said Sean, unhanding himself from his mother's feverish embrace. 'I've decided I want to work on a farm.'

His father only just managed to stop himself from ruffling his son's hair again, a sad smile curving his lips. His eldest son was growing up, and this war was hastening the process. 'Is that right, me boy. Well, let's see if you still feel the same next year before you make your mind up.'

Bridget's mother tried to speak as she brushed the tears from her eyes. 'Don't wish the time away,' she finally managed to say.

'Used up all those crayons and paints yet?' Bridget asked them.

Acting as he'd seen grown men do, Sean shoved his hands into his trousers. They were long trousers and looked new. Just the sight of them brought a lump to his mother's throat.

'We didn't really 'ave much use for them so gave them to Molly and Mary. They don't get to do much else when they're not in school. They're in town and that funny old pair...'

Kate Cottrell noted the sudden alarm on the faces of Bridget's parents. 'Sean. Michael. Look to the food and fill yer bellies,' she ordered. Her voice was firm and her face serious. Whatever it was she wanted to declare about the youngest girls' billet, she wanted it said in private.

Michael didn't wait to be told twice. Sean sauntered after him. He was on the verge of manhood and keen to fulfil the part as quickly as possible.

Kate Cottrell directed a calmly reassuring look at Bridget's parents. 'There's nothing to worry about. Everything's been sorted.'

Although her guests looked concerned, Kate Cottrell turned her attention back to thirteen-year-old Sean and ten-year-old Michael.

'Get your boots off before you makes a start,' cried Kate Cottrell.

The boys duly obeyed, went outside, left their boots beneath the frowning presence of the stone porch and raced back in to help themselves.

Nobody was aware that somebody else had entered the room until a brandy-deep voice said, 'I've still got mine on, Ma.'

'Go on with you,' said Kate Cottrell, reddening and clucking like a proud mother hen. She almost glowed at the visitors, so bright with joy was her face. 'My son, James,' she introduced with pride.

An instant shock shot through Bridget as her calm blue eyes met those of the young man she'd seen smoking a cigarette in the walled garden. At a distance, the resemblance hadn't been so obvious, but close up...it could be him! It could be Lyndon come all the way across the Atlantic to surprise her. His smile was Lyndon's smile and so too were his features: dark blonde hair, sun-touched in places; sky blue eyes; the same lethargic cheerfulness playing about his lips. Even the way he moved and held himself matched the same self-confidence, no doubt inherited from his father, but also reminiscent of the way Lyndon had strolled, as though the world was his for the taking.

She stared, aware of a strange buzzing in her head until realising the buzzing was words and he was speaking to her.

'I heard you sneeze,' she heard him say. 'Hay fever I expect, though only short term. The countryside can get you like that at first.'

'Yes.' Her response was almost breathless.

'James,' he said.

His hand was warm and totally encompassing her own.

She was aware of him shaking her parents' hands, mentioning the children, asking if they'd had a good journey down – so much longer nowadays. Trains were slower, names of stations removed.

'Not always easy to tell if you're on the right train,' said a smiling James. 'Never mind the enemy being foxed without signs, how about the natives?'

Bridget laughed, at the same time seeing an approving look on her mother's face, even greater joy on hearing that her sons had been missing home but enjoying the countryside.

'The older girls too,' added Kate Cottrell. 'The vicarage has a very big garden.' Her joviality diminished somewhat when she added that the two youngest girls would soon be sorted out. 'They should never 'ave been placed with them two...' An odd look passed between her and her son. 'But there,' she said, regaining her exuberance. 'They'll be 'appy 'ere with their brothers.'

James handed Bridget a cup of tea. 'Fancy a slice of apple cake with that? We use our own cooked fruit – or at least my mother does. I don't cook. Do you?'

She said that she did, though not so much lately with the children all being down here. It was hard not to be tongue-tied, but she couldn't help it. A train journey to Devon and she'd found a dead spit of Lyndon O'Neill standing here in an old manor house.

'Will the girls be here soon?' she heard her mother say. Satisfied that her boys were being well looked after, she needed to know how the others were doing.

'Think they're 'ere,' said Kate Cottrell, one ear cocked towards the door that led into the angular hallway of flagstone floor and old paintings of fat cows, sheep and sprawling landscapes.

'My mother's got amazing hearing,' said a bemused James when Bridget's father exclaimed that he hadn't heard a thing.

What sounded like wheels and horse's hooves became loud enough for everyone to hear and preceded the arrival of the vicar. A big man with a bushy beard, he filled the doorway, his chest like a barrel beneath the glaring white of his dog collar and the ruff that was his beard. 'Hello one and all,' he bellowed.

He was introduced as the Reverend Roger Roebuck.

'That's my name,' he said jovially. 'Though the boys mostly

refer to me as Roy Rogers on account of the horse-drawn buggy – saves petrol, you see.'

The girls who had followed him into the room, let out little screams of delight on seeing their parents, the youngest hugging their mother's legs, the older ones smiling up at their father and proceeding to tell him something of their day: of paddling in a brook and the fact that one of their friends had been caught stealing apples from an orchard; of a pig that had rampaged through the town chased by a gang of men shouting out for Percy to come back.

'That was its name,' cried a thrilled-sounding Ruby, less overcome by emotion as her sisters. 'Percy the Pig!'

The youngest two, Molly and Mary, remained with their faces buried in their mother's dress, clutching her with half-buried fists.

'They didn't like living with them funny old women,' said a solemn-faced Katy who was only slightly older than her younger sisters but sounded older. 'One of them had whiskers.'

The Cottrells exchanged a look with the vicar.

Bridget's mother plastered her hands on their heads, pressing them ever closer into her skirt. Over their heads, she exchanged a worried look with Bridget's father.

As sharp of sight as she was of hearing, Kate Cottrell patted Bridget's mother's arm and told her everything would be all right. 'They're looking forward to coming here. I've got their things and told Molly and Mary that they'll be staying here from now on,' she said in response to their enquiring looks.

'I don't know,' Bridget's mother said hesitantly. 'Perhaps we should take them home...'

'And split the family,' her husband pointed out.

She lowered her eyes and clasped the two youngest even

closer, too tightly perhaps because they began to fidget, aware their siblings were here, plus the feast set out on the table.

'We've got room,' Kate Cottrell said reassuringly.

The vicar smiled benignly at the visitors from the city. 'I'll give you the details later.'

Kate Cottrell again took charge. 'Soon enough, soon enough. Now come on you lot. There's food waiting to be eaten.' Kate Cottrell was one of those women who showed love and affection through food, her creed being that a well-fed child – or adult for that matter – was a happy one. 'Let's take our cups of tea into the front parlour.'

Her invitation was given in a forthright, uncompromising manner to Bridget's worried-looking parents. The vicar went too; Bridget and James knew they were not required.

'Left to our own devices,' said James. There was a twinkle in his eyes and a blithe smile played round his lips. Both turned Bridget's legs to water.

'Look at me. I've got a jam tart.'

Little Molly, who a moment ago had clung to her mother for dear life, was now on her second jam tart, the stickiness from the first one smeared round her mouth.

'I likes this farm,' said Mary.

Bridget was tempted to ask her whether she was missing her parents. Of course she was, so why ask? Mentioning it would only exacerbate the moment when they would be once again separated from their parents. London was being bombed. It was only a matter of time before Bristol received the same treatment. Sad as it might be and difficult to live with, they were safer here in the country.

Being slightly older, it was Ruby and Katy who had adjusted best out of the four girls. The younger two stood close to each other, barely an inch between them, their eyes scrutinising their surroundings with reserved interest.

Bridget felt emotional watching them, seeing small differences in their appearance and the fact that they seemed closer as a result of their isolation, separated from the rest of their siblings. The presence of their two brothers, especially the more mature Sean, also helped to bring them out of themselves.

'It seems the youngsters have acquired a country appetite. I would say it might not be a bad idea to grab another slice of cake before this lot have gobbled it all up.'

Bridget started. Engrossed in what the youngsters were up to, she'd almost forgotten that James was there.

'I think I might be in the RAF when I grows up,' declared Michael.

'Do you now,' said a smiling James. 'Better eat some more cake then to help you grow big and strong.'

'Oh yeah,' said her disbelieving brother. 'I s'pose you're gonna say next that I needs to eat loads of carrots to improve me eyesight.'

'The more the merrier,' said James, shaking his head and adopting a serious expression. 'A pilot flying at night needs good eyesight to see where he's going. It's not much good having a pilot who can only fly in daylight.'

Michael's jaw dropped as he swallowed this fact.

'Better get and take another piece of this carrot cake before it's all gone,' said Sean with a grin.

'Good oh!' said James. 'Carrot cake as well as apple cake. We are lucky.'

Bridget recalled a newsreel at the cinema and a pilot being asked how he managed flying at night. His answer had been that he ate plenty of carrots and that was the reason why. She smiled.

It was obvious the boys greatly respected James and that he in return gave them his time.

Sean declared that when he was old enough, he would never leave the country, wouldn't join the air force but would drive a tractor.

'That's what I wants to do,' he declared.

'That's it, Sean,' said James, ruffling her brother's hair. 'Do something you love.'

He exchanged a slight smile with Bridget before again addressing the boys.

'My,' he said, tilting his head so he could more easily see out of the window. 'There's a few sunny hours left before the sun goes down and you're all off to bed. Sean, you're the eldest in the family. How about you all show your sister here round the farm. She's come a long way and I bet she needs to stretch her legs.'

Sean swallowed the last of the sandwich he'd been eating. He addressed James in a man-to-man way that made Bridget want to cry. 'You coming too, Pilot Officer Cottrell?'

James saluted. 'You bet I am.'

Touched by the orange glow of evening sunshine, they trooped outside, Sean walking beside Bridget and James, a subtle signal that he belonged in their company now, his childhood just about left behind.

Michael led the girls ahead of them, pointing out the fields, the names of cows, chasing the chickens that came pecking round their feet.

Before long, the girls were bounding into fields, picking flowers, throwing sticks for the dogs and patting the pony Michael told them was named Brandy that nuzzled their hands as they fed it bunches of wildflowers.

Ruby stopped some way ahead of them and asked if she could

go into the pony's field. Her younger sisters gathered round, all seemingly keen to do the same.

'Only if your brothers go in with you. Where's Michael?'

'Up here.'

The shout came from the middle branches of an oak tree.

James addressed Sean, 'Get your brother down. Both of you go into the field with your sisters. They're not used to farm animals, and Brandy can get uppity when strangers are around.'

'Kids,' exclaimed Sean with a disgusted toss of his head.

Bridget hid what would have been a loud laugh with her hand. 'He sounds like my dad.'

'He's growing up,' returned James.

Bridget had not fully recovered from finding herself faced with a man who bore such a close resemblance to Lyndon. As they walked, she studied him anew. She wanted to dispel this sudden unwieldiness in her heart, the feeling that she'd been knocked off balance or had fallen into a dream, similar to that endured by Alice when she'd followed the white rabbit and fallen down the well.

James's shirtsleeves were rolled up past his elbows, exposing lower arms as brawny as his father's and just as hairy.

Fronds of grass, red poppies, cornflowers and golden rod flicked against her legs. She picked one, chewed its end and contemplated what to say to fill the silence between them, anything to cope with this strange occurrence.

'I like silence,' James said suddenly. 'It gives you chance to breathe. To think.'

'Away from the airfield and bombing raids,' she replied, glad that he was the one who'd broken the silence.

He laughed. 'Truth be told, Bridget, I haven't been on a bombing raid yet, but I do know how to get there.' He went on to tell her that despite the incursions and air raids on London, there had not been much in the way of retaliation. 'But there will be,' he added, his light laugh reduced to a wavering smile. 'We'll get to fly over Germany and drop bombs, not just leaflets. So what do you do?'

'I'm just a factory girl.'

That's how she began. Funnily enough, she felt no shame about telling him what she did and the fact they lived in a council house.

He remarked on the little he knew about Bristol, so she told him.

There was something surreal about telling the same things she'd told Lyndon, almost as though she was repeating it to the same man.

She added a bit about Southey the poet, of Humphrey Davy the man who'd invented a lamp for miners that would give them more safety working underground, of Isambard Kingdom Brunel's Clifton Suspension Bridge, of Samuel Plimsoll who had noted sailors losing their lives on overloaded ships and had devised a measuring device to prevent it happening.

When James failed to respond, she stopped abruptly and apologised. 'I do go on,' she said. 'Sorry.'

'Not at all. It makes a change to listen to a woman who's well read as well as attractive. One other thing, why do you stare at me as you do?'

'I'm sorry.'

'Don't be. Just tell me why it is? Do I remind you of someone?'

She blushed. Without an ounce of encouragement, she'd talked to him as though they'd known each other for longer than a couple of hours and hadn't realised she was staring at him. Of course she was. He looked like Lyndon, another golden haired young man with searching blue eyes.

'You remind me of someone. His name's Lyndon.'

She looked down at her hands.

'I look like him, act like him or both?'

She smiled and looked up at him from beneath her voluminous fringe. 'You definitely look like him. I don't know you well enough to know whether you act like him.'

'Then we need to work on us getting to know each other better.'

They stopped at a stile, watching Sean leading the pony by its forelock, the girls taking it in turn to ride on its back. Her youngest sisters, who had tearfully clung to their parents, were now whooping and laughing along with the rest of them.

'They look happy,' said Bridget. 'Your mother said they're moving into Winter's Leap.'

'One big happy family,' he said. 'Two coming here, the other two staying at the vicarage, though if there was room, my mother would have them here too. It's a kids' paradise.'

'Better than being with the Crawfords?'

For a moment it proved hard to judge his expression. His jaw tightened and then he held his fist in front of his mouth and coughed, as though smothering distasteful amusement.

'Sorry,' he said, removing his hand from his mouth and the vague smile that lingered there. 'What I was going to say that there are no Crawford sisters.' He paused. She sensed something out of the ordinary was about to be said – and it was. 'There's only Evelyn Crawford and her brother, Edward.'

Bridget frowned. 'I don't understand.'

They stopped in the shade of a tree whose branches draped over a stile. He offered her a cigarette. 'Edward was called up some months ago.'

'Not two sisters?'

His smile widened. 'Evelyn and Edward are pretty much the same build. Her dresses fitted him.'

'What?' Bridget's jaw dropped. 'Her brother Edward was dressing as a woman?'

James nodded. 'Got called up, didn't like the square bashing so deserted. His sister took him in, told everybody he was a long-lost sister.'

'Oh! The girls might have unwittingly noticed something, so the letters were written for them!'

'Right. Evelyn tried her best to keep them and her brother separate – just in case they let anything out.'

'Such as a woman taking a shave on a morning,' pronounced Bridget.

'Believe me, there's some that do,' laughed James.

She slapped him playfully on the arm. 'Then you've known some pretty strange women, James Cottrell.'

Their laughter came with heightened relaxation. Other comments followed; other small tales about their lives and experiences until it seemed they could talk to each other about anything.

'You'll be by yourselves tomorrow. My parents and I have a funeral to attend.' The smile that had been evident disappeared. 'Fred Davey died of wounds sustained at Dunkirk. We're going to the funeral. You can come if you like. My parents did mention it to yours and they're staying behind. I hear your father intends mending the old long case clock sitting in the hallway. I can't remember the last time it worked. Your mother's offered to cook lunch.'

'She'll probably need me to help.'

'That sounds reasonable, but you're welcome to come to church if you want to.'

* * *

Bridget had fully expected to stay and help her mother, but the racing clouds and warm breeze enticed her outside. Her mother suggested that if she wanted to go for a walk she should do so.

'I'm used to cooking for an army,' her mother reminded her. 'All the preparations are done, and I thank you for that. Now you go and explore. I know you want to.'

The sound of a pendulum ticking, then bonging as though it had escaped from its casing, sounded behind Bridget as she went out the open door.

School was now closed for the long summer break and all the children, having got over the excitement of seeing their parents again, had gone off to play amongst the hay ricks.

Bridget's feet were enticed along a footpath around the rim of a field. In the distance, she glimpsed a church tower surrounded by trees. It looked peaceful, sanctuary in the midst of war. She made her way towards it through a field of cow parsley and long grass that nodded in the breeze.

A low stone wall surrounded the churchyard where springy grass quivered in the slight breeze and was crushed under black-footed shoes.

It seemed to her as though the whole village had turned out to mourn this man's passing. A woman in a veil led the procession between gnarled gravestones, head bent, dabbing at her eyes, and trailed by three equally tearful children, one barely old enough for school.

Seeing them filled Bridget with sadness. With the exception of witnessing her mother's miscarriage, she had not been this close to grief or the remains of a family broken forever.

James, in his uniform, was easy to discern. Everyone else, with the exception of the widow and children, looked like so many black crows.

Tears stinging her eyes, and somehow touched with a

stranger's grief, Bridget turned on her heel and headed back for the farmhouse, her parents and her family.

* * *

During the rest of the week, the whole family helped out with the harvest, the smell of ripe corn and wheat warming the air. Bridget agreed with Sean and Michael that the best bit was riding on the very top of a cartload of hay bales which was pulled by a huge Shire horse with hairy legs and steaming breath.

James was always close by. His smile disappeared when she asked him about the funeral.

She remarked how sad it was.

To her surprise, James merely shrugged. 'At least he lived. He was loved. That's what it's all about; take the opportunities when you can. There's only today. Tomorrow won't always come.'

By the weekend, the last hay was baled and brought into the barn ready to provide winter feed for the animals.

They had an outside feast that night, a true ploughman's meal of cheese, fresh bread, butter and pickles with cider to wash it down.

Bridget never meant to get tipsy, not just with cider but with the confusion she was feeling inside. She danced with everyone, though mostly with James. Even when they weren't dancing, his fingertips found the curve of her spine, the length of her arm and that sensitive spot on her wrist.

Perhaps it was the cider, but she didn't object when James took hold of her hand and led her out into a night of stars.

He bent his head and whispered into her ear, 'The other guy – you can pretend I'm him if you like. In fact, I can be whoever you want me to be.'

She closed her eyes and let his words drift over her.

'Yes,' she said and felt she was made of water, fluid and running downhill fast.

His lips met hers, like velvet against her cheek, delicately brushing her throat with a touch as soft as eiderdown.

'I'm not drunk,' she said in a weak and oddly tearful voice. 'I'm not drunk.'

'Good,' he whispered back. 'I wouldn't want that.'

Her body was hot, skin on fire, so she didn't object when he began to unbutton her blouse and ease it gently from her shoulders, kissing each inch of her skin as it was slowly exposed. A shiver ran from her neck, through her breasts and down to her thighs. She tensed and reminded herself of what the consequences might be.

'I don't...' His mouth smothered her words. She was lost and filled with conflicting emotions. The funeral. The widow, no doubt wishing she could turn back time, but time and tide waited for no man – or woman. A fleeting moment in a life that could be snuffed out at any moment.

She found herself welcoming the coolness of the night air as the heat of the day retreated, the golden glow of sunlight replaced by the dewiness of silvery moonlight.

Once his fingers were caressing her inner thighs, she was lost and wanted to be lost. The city and everything she knew there was lost. His loins were hot against hers. James? Lyndon?

She tensed and uttered a slight cry when he entered her.

The thrusting stilled. 'I can stop. It's up to you.'

She flung her arms round his neck and whispered into his ear. 'Please. Please!'

Why? she asked herself afterwards. The answer was instant. Because there might never be a tomorrow.

16

PHYLLIS

'Well, if it ain't Bridget Milligan, back from 'er 'oliday in the country! Lucky cow!'

'Yes I was lucky,' returned Bridget. It wasn't easy not to blush.

The group of girls taunting her were from Knowle West, the large brick council estate some distance further on than Bedminster. Like Bridget, Maisie and their friends, they were a tight little circle who stuck up for each other and considered themselves tough.

Their tough tactics cut no ice with Maisie Miles. 'Take no notice. Their gobs are bigger than their brain.'

One girl, a bit braver than the others, rose from her chair, ready to challenge the diminutive girl from the Dings, until Aggie Hill's heavy hand landed on her shoulder, forcing her to sit back down.

'Kids all right?' Aggie asked.

Bridget said that they were. 'I helped with the haymaking. It was hard work, but I enjoyed it and Mum and Dad are happier now they know for sure that the kids are being taken care of with two lots of good people.'

'You look all the better for it. Nothing like a bit of fresh air to bring the bloom to yer cheeks.'

The threatening blush finally happened.

Maisie saw it and winked. 'And a sparkle in yer eyes.'

'It was lovely.' She went on to tell the amusing story of the Crawford brother deserting and pretending to be a woman.

Maisie wasn't fooled. 'But that ain't nothing to do with you blushing, is it?'

Bridget made no comment, but bent back to her work thinking about what had happened and whether such a moment would ever be revisited.

* * *

Phyllis arrived at Bridget's house after supper and together the two girls sat out on the doorstep, which had retained the warmth of the day.

'Here,' Bridget handed her the details Maisie had given her. The address of the soap factory and the manager was written at the top of the paper. 'They want somebody to wrap the tablets of soap and pack them.' At the bottom was the name of the widow now living in Maisie's old home in York Street. 'It's not the best job in the world or the best lodgings, but far enough away from your mother-in-law. It's the best we could do,' she added.

Bridget waited for Phyllis to respond, noted her thin shoulders, the slightly unkempt look to her hair. Before marrying, she'd been film-star glamorous, but now with all the problems she was dealing with, she looked as if she didn't care.

'You and Maisie are great mates,' Phyllis remarked. 'Don't know what I'd do without you both.'

Bridget sensed she was nervous about getting out from beneath Hilda Harvey's iron hand. 'I suppose it would be best to go back home with your mother and chance Hilda not turning up there.'

Phyllis shook her head and flicked her cigarette end into the dirt beneath the privet hedge separating the Milligans' garden from next door. 'There ain't no chance of that... there *isn't* any chance of that,' she corrected herself. She stared beyond the garden gate, her eyes wide with the lingering surprise she'd experienced at her mother's announcement. 'My mum's getting married again. She don't – *doesn't* – want me back cramping her style. It's as though she's lost twenty years. I don't blame her. I mean, everyone seems to be grabbing a slice of happiness before this war starts proper. But my mother...' She shook her head, face devoid of any understanding. 'In walked a Canadian colonel and my mum fell head over hills. Where he goes, she'll go. Eventually she'll have to give up the house.'

Bridget had intended telling Phyllis about James, but her old friend was too weighed down with her own problems. Phyllis had barely glanced at the piece of paper she still held in her hand.

'In all honesty it's the right thing to do. I've got to move on and live my own life. As soon as possible. Will you come with me?'

'You're my friend, of course I will,' said Bridget. 'The factory won't be open, but there's nothing to stop us going round to see about the accommodation. Perhaps we can have a drink afterwards.'

Phyllis got to her feet. 'Might as well now I'm out. I'm not keen on going home. Will it take you long to get ready?'

Bridget laughed. 'Two flicks of a lamb's tail. Just let me take my overall off, wash my face and brush my hair.'

* * *

They were both feeling nervous as they entered York Street, a cul-de-sac of poor-looking houses off Midland Road.

A cacophony of sound poured out of the stained-glass doors and windows of the pub at the corner of the street.

A drunk came out, saw them, smiled, then tugged politely at his cap before ambling away – thankfully in the opposite direction to the one they were going.

The yeasty smell of stale beer and sweaty drinkers were as nothing compared to the cloying, sweetish, sickly smell that assaulted their nostrils. Its source was a number of tall chimneys spewing slivers of whitish smoke, twisting and turning ever upwards.

'One of those is the soap factory,' said Bridget, eyeing them with misgiving.

Sash windows stared blindly out over a cobbled street where boys rolled marbles along the gutter and girls played hopscotch. Groups of gossiping women with careworn faces stared at them from dark doorways.

Phyllis fished Maisie's scribbled note from her bag and, after perusing the details, headed purposefully to number five.

They looked up at the façade fronting the pavement, noting that bricks that had once been red were now blackened by the cloying smoke of the nearby chimneys. The one redeeming feature was that the sole ground-floor window gleamed and the lace curtain hanging behind it was pristine white.

'Here goes,' said Bridget.

Phyllis lifted the cast-iron knocker and rapped it hard against the door.

A ginger cat chose that moment to curl its sinewy tail round their ankles.

Bridget bent down and tickled its head. 'Hello puss. Do you live here?'

As she straightened, the door opened and there was Mrs Proctor, the woman named on the note, a rounded figure with sparkling blue eyes and a large mole on one cheek. Her face creased when she smiled. 'Can I help you?'

Phyllis deferred to Bridget to explain why they were there.

'We heard you took in lodgers. My friend here needs somewhere to stay.'

The bright blue eyes looked Phyllis up and down and the smile widened. 'Are you married or single?'

'Single. My name's Phyllis Mason,' blurted Phyllis and trusted Bridget wouldn't contradict or look surprised. She'd forgotten to take off her wedding ring so hid her left hand behind her back.

Mrs Proctor's smile weakened and a slight furrow appeared between her brows. 'Well, me dear, I do prefer lady lodgers, but you should know that I don't allow gentlemen callers. Not even daytime or early evening.'

'I won't be having any,' Phyllis swiftly responded.

'Is this your cat?' Bridget asked, continuing to smile as though she hadn't heard what Mrs Proctor had said, the cat seemingly far more important.

Mrs Proctor's face lit up. 'Yes. That's Victoria. I named her after the old queen.' Her expression wavered with indecision. 'You like cats?' She appeared to be addressing both of them.

Phyllis showed her willingness by tickling between the cat's ears which Bridget now held in her arms. Victoria purred obligingly.

'She likes you,' said Mrs Proctor and chuckled. 'Well. I suppose you'd better come in. The room's upstairs at the back of the house. I won't say it's quiet because you can hear the goods trains in the marshalling yards. Not all the time, mind you, but just some of the time.'

Bridget set the cat down at her feet and watched as it skipped off along the passageway ahead of them, tail held high.

The house smelt of fresh paint. Maisie had described it as untouched by a paintbrush for years and that her brother had used an air rifle to shoot at the mice that poked their noses out of their holes.

Bridget took a deep breath. 'I smell fresh paint. Somebody's been busy.'

Mrs Proctor beamed with pleasure. 'My son painted the house from top to bottom before I moved in and before he got called up. My sister came over to give me a hand cleaning it before me and Victoria moved in. There were mice, but Victoria took care of them.'

The room for rent had cream-painted walls and the curtains at the window were a soft beige colour and scattered with pink roses. The bedding looked clean and there was also a washstand with a green tiled splashback and a matching jug and bowl.

'You can just see the privy roof down there,' said Mrs Proctor, holding back the net curtain so they could better see the pan tiled roof of the small lean-to set into the back of the house.

Mrs Proctor eyed the two young women. She'd never had red hair when she was young, yet in a strange way the tall young woman who'd introduced herself as Phyllis took her back to those times. It struck her that she was the type who tried to please everybody. She'd been like that and a fat lot of good it had done her.

She assessed the other young woman who had shown affection to Victoria as possessing great self-assurance and being stronger beneath the surface than showed above it.

Back in the Great War, she'd worked with many young women like these who had come from ordinary backgrounds and led ordinary lives. Once the war had begun in earnest, they'd found themselves in uniform, driving ambulances or becoming nurses tending badly wounded soldiers at the front line. She had been one of them and in doing so had truly believed that the war would change everything, even the differences between classes. Charles, father of her son, Sam, had been an officer and she a lowly nurse from Whitechapel who had been lucky enough to get the right training at the right time. She'd trusted people back then, including Charles and his sweet words. Now she was more wary, especially with regard to taking somebody under her roof.

The girl with the gentle face was smiling approvingly. The redhead moved round the room touching things, smoothing the eiderdown.

'Is anyone else lodging with you?' asked Bridget.

'No. There's three bedrooms. I've got one and my son uses the other when he's 'ome on leave. He's due tonight. There's a bath on the outside wall, though not to be used when my son's around of course. I don't mind 'elping you with the water – that's if I decide to let you 'ave the room.'

Phyllis exchanged a quick look with Bridget. 'What do you think?'

Bridget smiled approvingly. 'I think it will do you very well.'

Phyllis hesitated and took another look round and turned to Mrs Proctor. 'When can I move in?'

Mrs Proctor held up her hand, palm facing the two young women. 'Just a minute. I do need to know your circumstances.'

'Circumstances?'

'Why you want to live alone and do you have a job.'

'My mother's remarrying, so I need to find a place of my own and I've got an interview at the soap factory. That's why I need somewhere close by. I'm seeing the manager tomorrow.'

'Ah,' said Mrs Proctor, looking more settled on hearing this.

'They're desperate for workers so they won't be turning you down.'

Phyllis heaved a big sigh. 'That's a relief.' In a way, it was. She'd be away from a bad situation, though would miss the tobacco factory. Packing soap didn't faze her, but she would miss her friends.

Mrs Proctor tilted her head to one side in a quizzical manner. 'Just one question. How did you hear about me 'aving a room?'

'A friend who used to live round here,' said Bridget, instinctively knowing it wouldn't be a good idea to mention Maisie and her family as the last residents of this very house. 'I think she heard it from somebody who's since joined up.'

Ursula Proctor had the greatest regard for anyone who had joined up so her reservations vanished. 'So when would you like to move in?'

Phyllis exchanged a quick look with Bridget. 'Any time once I know I've got the job?'

A church clock struck close by.

'Good grief. Is that the time? Sorry, my birds, but it's time you departed. My boy Sam's due 'ome tonight – depending on the trains, that is. They're taking three times as long to cover a journey than before this war started. I'll await to 'ear from you,' she said as they began to descend the stairs, Bridget and Phyllis going first.

A draught of air flooded into the passageway and the cat ran forward and curled around a pair of masculine legs.

'Victoria! Me old queen!' On realising they had visitors, Sam Proctor smiled. 'Hello there.'

'Which old queen are you on about,' cried a joyful Mrs Proctor, laughter lacing her voice.

After lodging his kitbag on the floor, Sam Proctor took off his beret and smoothed back his hair. 'Give me a hug, then me old queen!'

Mother and son embraced.

'This young lady's taking the spare room,' she said, nodding at Phyllis.

'Ladies,' he said. His smile lingered on Phyllis a split second longer than on Bridget.

'As you've guessed, this is my son, Sam,' explained Mrs Proctor, pride shining in her eyes. 'Miss Mason hopes to get a job at the soap factory.'

'Good for her. First name?' asked Sam with the brusqueness of a sergeant major and enough charm to bring the birds from the trees.

'Phyllis. And this is Bridget.'

He shook both their hands, glancing at each of them in turn before his deep blue eyes again settled on Phyllis. And Phyllis looked right back and liked what she was seeing.

He had a shock of blonde hair that sat now like a thick cap on the top of his head despite all the efforts of the army barber to tame it. His face was as firm as his voice and there was a boyish lift to one side of his mouth, a trait he'd no doubt inherited from his mother.

He grinned at Phyllis. 'You'll have no trouble getting a job at the soap factory and it's only round the corner. Dead convenient. They're desperate. It ain't so much about soap but about glycerine. The army can't do without it. Trouble is, what with the call-up and more money to be earned in munitions, they're running short of workers. Mind you,' he said, wrinkling his nose. 'It is next to the bone yard. Has to be.' He saw the unsettled look that came to Phyllis's face. 'Sorry. Didn't mean to put you off. You'll be fine, princess. Don't listen to me. I've been away with only blokes to talk to for too long. I could go on for hours if you let me.'

His outspoken friendliness brought smiles to both their faces. He was a good-looking young man. Not only that but in a matter of minutes they both felt they'd known him for years.

'You'd better be letting them go, Sam. You're taking up their time and there's faggots and peas on the stove just waiting to be eaten.'

'Sorry, ladies.' He grinned impishly. 'Tell you what, Ma, how about I escort the ladies past the rough lot at The Duke of York while you get me grub on the table?'

'There's no need...' Bridget began.

Phyllis interrupted. 'That would be very nice.'

The truth was she'd seen the way he'd looked at her, and the prospect of him talking nineteen to the dozen made her feel happier than she had in a long time.

Bridget saw it too, the rapport between them. In the past, she might have condemned Phyllis and told her not to be so forward, but James had happened, so she had no right.

17

FRANK MILES

Frank Miles, his beard thick and bushy, was dead pleased with all he'd achieved. Cliff Venables, the manager at the slaughterhouse, trusted him implicitly and had no idea that his seemingly upright employee was lifting a bit of meat when he could. Some of it he gave to Vera, the rest he sold. Stealing from his employer didn't count as thieving in Frank's eyes.

Keen not to attract questions, he drank his tea alone, ate alone and, for the most part, went out on his rounds all by himself. One reason was that he didn't want anyone seeing him helping himself to an increasingly larger amount of meat. The other reason was he feared news might leak out of where he was to Eddie Bridgeman.

In the meantime, he was doing all right. Food, he realised, was the key to him making more than a wage. Nobody was getting enough from rationing and the situation was likely to get worse thanks to enemy submarine attacks on Atlantic convoys.

Having finished work for the day, he was off home for his evening meal, though he always made sure he timed getting home after the other three lodgers had finished their meals and gone to the pub or to bed, or even on night shift or air-raid duties. He'd no intention of offering to do air-raid duties. He didn't believe in doing anything that didn't bring in an extra pound note.

At seven thirty, he ambled into the kitchen, where a big black range sat like an iron spider in the heart of the old fireplace.

'Hello, love,' trilled his pink-faced landlady. 'I boiled up those pork bones with some onions,' said Vera.

He felt her eyes on him and knew she wanted to suggest he washed before sitting down to eat. She'd tried that before and had been taken aback when he'd snapped, 'I puts this food on the table, and got the right to choose whether I wash or not.' She hadn't dared suggest such a thing again and wouldn't do, he decided, not if she wanted to benefit from the bit of meat he brought in and the rent he paid. Both were enough to placate her and keep her from disrupting his happy – though hopefully – temporary residence under her roof.

He ate his meal without saying a word, not even complimenting her on the fact that the meat was so tender it had fallen off the bones and swam in a rich gravy with boiled potatoes, carrots and onions, topped off with a couple of suet dumplings.

Once he was finished, she took his dish, added it to the pile sitting on the draining board and poured his tea. She was flitting around, being attentive, yet he knew just by the way her fingers were wringing the tea towel that she wanted to know if he was off out tonight. What she really wanted was for him to keep her company – as if he would want that!

It seemed a while ago since he'd moved in and giving her a few bits of meat as well as rent had been enough to persuade her to take him to her bed. Getting to share her bed guaranteed she wouldn't be chucking him out any time soon.

For Vera's part, he was hardly the first of her lodgers she'd favoured and she had thought him worthy. Now she wasn't so sure. The only thing that held her back from dissolving the relationship was having less food on the table and a cold bed. She liked him there, lying beside her, the warmth of his body, the fact that he sometimes patted her and called her his prime bit of rump steak. She appreciated anything that sounded remotely affectionate.

'I'm off,' he said, the legs of his chair making a screeching sound as they scraped the red tiles.

Vera gritted her teeth and said nothing. She'd quickly learned that Frank didn't like any kind of criticism.

Standing tall now, he stretched his arms so his fingertips almost touched the ceiling and then he rubbed his stomach. 'That should keep me going until I get back. I shouldn't be too late. It all depends.'

She didn't ask him what he meant or where he was going but did say that she would keep an eye on the van.

'Don't need to,' he said. 'The van's going with me.'

'My word, they'll be working you to death at this rate,' she exclaimed. 'That's the third night in a row.'

To her great relief, she saw that she'd said the right thing. A secretive smile came to his face and he tapped the side of his nose.

'This is a bit of working in me own time.'

* * *

He'd found the right spot to trade, right in the centre of Bristol not far from the hospital but in a narrow alley. The buildings were tightly packed together, ramshackle gables jutting out from the first floors and keeping the lower floors in darkness. The streets and alleys all round were cobblestoned, very dark and frequented by those who preferred to do their business in the shadows.

The moment Frank backed into the alley, he was assailed by people who had read the name on the side of the van before it was cloaked in darkness. His customers only got a cursory glimpse of it, enough to make them trust it was bona fide.

'Got any 'orsemeat?'

'Got a bit.'

'How much?'

'Dead cheap to you, darlin'.' His salacious wink was picked out in the light of his torch. The women liked a bit of sauce and he reckoned that given half a chance they'd do more than blush for an extra pound of liver. Once he'd had this pitch for a while, he might take advantage of that, find a better billet and a more attractive woman than Vera. For the present, she'd suit – just until he got his sideline up and running.

The women, desperate for meat, thrust their money forward and Frank Miles was pleased.

'It would 'elp if you brought your own newspaper in future,' he shouted. 'I don't buy that many newspapers. Not enough to wrap everything you want.'

Bits of lamb, beef and pork sold first, buyers remarking that it had been a while since they'd seen even offcuts, and complaining that the four ounces per person allowed by rationing wasn't enough to keep body and soul together.

A woman with a clutch of kids hanging onto her skirt asked if he'd be in this same place every week.

He leaned forward, gave her a wink and said, 'Only if you promise me you'll be here too. If you stand me up, I'll cry...' He brushed laughingly at his eyes. 'Just don't tell the old man, eh?'

Even in the dense blackout, he saw a bashful blush suffuse her tired face. 'Bugger 'im. Left me with four kids to feed.'

As she shoved her purchases into her bag, he spotted what she was wearing. Not being in the least bit interested in what women wore, he'd firstly thought it a dress but now saw it was an overall identical to the one Maisie wore at the tobacco factory.

'See you again,' he shouted after her before he resumed selling other bits of meat, scraps in bags, bones that still had some meat on and even some chunks of liver, the bits that had been left behind after he'd cut the best pieces into slivers.

Horsemeat cut into thin steaks also sold well, the women who bought it stating in no uncertain terms that they'd pass it off as steak. Not that they were of a class to have had much steak – even frying steak.

There was soon little left but what there was he gave away to those who'd held back and counted the pennies before stepping forward.

'Give me whatever you can afford,' he said.

Once there was nothing remaining, he drove away, though pulled in at the side of a horse trough, took out a bucket and sluiced water around the most bloodied spots in the van. He winced as he did so. He'd made sure to wash all his wares, swilling away the smell that would have given away that the scraps of meat and bones were far from fresh. He'd had a whole load destined for the rendering yard. As usual, some of the bones still had scraps of meat hanging on them. He'd got hold of a sharp knife himself, sawed the best bits from the bones and wrapped these up in newspaper. Bones that still had meat on he'd placed in a bucket.

'Good for a stew,' he'd shouted out to the press of customers, all eager to buy at knock down prices. At sixpence each they were cheap, but he had plenty. The sixpences added up.

That was the great thing about delivering meat to the butchers. In return, you were loaded up with stuff the butcher had been saving up all week. Some of it ponged a bit, but not so bad that a swill in a bucket of water couldn't disguise. He reasoned that the meat would be devoured long before it became totally inedible. Besides, everyone was hungry and wanted something for nothing.

18

PHYLLIS

It was cowardly waiting until her mother-in-law was at one of her meetings before telling Tom Harvey that she was moving out, but he took it well.

His look was one of concern for her and worry about giving the news to his wife. She'd be furious.

'Are you sure about this?'

She'd told him that she was. 'I'm sorry I'm leaving you to tell Hilda, but you know how it is.'

He'd nodded and said, yes, he did know how it was. 'No forwarding address?' he asked, somewhat hopefully.

She shook her head. 'I don't think that would be a good idea.'

He nodded somewhat sadly. 'No. I don't suppose it would be.'

When Phyllis had been told that she'd be wrapping up tablets of soap and packing them in boxes, she'd had the idea that the soap would be sweetly scented, the sort rationed at one tablet a month and suitable for washing your face. It turned out they were big colourless blocks smelling vaguely of carbolic. What was more, the smell clung more stubbornly to her clothes than tobacco ever had.

Half a dozen women worked with her wrapping and packing, a close-knit bunch all living within the same area. They accepted her and were friendly enough, though nothing, to her mind, could replace her mates in the stripping room of W. D. &. H. O. Wills.

The evenings were still light when she left work and made her way to York Street. Having not been in work for some time, she found herself yawning on the way home, barely aware of passers-by or the odd bit of transport on Midland Road.

She was thinking of Sam when she suddenly became aware of a car pulling up beside her, a door opening and somebody grabbing her arm. A meaty hand was clamped over her mouth before she could scream as she was bundled into the back of a car.

The man who slid in beside her was the size of a wardrobe. There was another man in the front, one she surely did not know. He turned half round in his seat. His eyes were dark and intimidating. His clothes were well tailored and he smelt of cologne.

'Right,' he said. 'Now who might you be?'

She found herself fixating on the gold tooth which flashed at the side of his mouth. The hand that covered her mouth eased slightly then dropped away.

'Phyllis,' she said weakly.

'Right, Phyllis.' He began to use what looked like a small penknife to pick at his teeth. 'I seen you go into number five York Street. That's fine by me. What I wants to know is what you know about the Miles family that used to live there. Frank in particular.'

Phyllis shook her head so hard her hair whipped round her face. She was terrified. 'I never knew 'im.'

He arched his eyebrows. 'But you know who I mean?'

She nodded. 'I think I do, though I never met 'im. Not really.'

He stopped picking at his teeth and fixed her with a look that almost riveted her to the back of the seat. 'What does not really mean?'

Realising her small comment had tripped her up, she gulped. 'I saw 'im once outside the tobacco factory. That's all.'

Eyes unblinking, the man nodded slowly. 'What about that girl of 'is. Maisie. Do you know where she is?'

Phyllis shook her head even more avidly than before, determined that she'd not make the same mistake and give the slightest clue away. 'No.' Her voice sounded small, pixie-like and far away.

Those fathomless eyes fixed on her for what seemed like an age before he nodded slowly. 'Right, sweet'eart. I believe you.' He leaned towards her over the back seat, his face, his breath and the cloying cologne only inches from her face. 'Now you listen 'ere, Phyllis. If you do see Maisie, tell 'er Eddie Bridgeman wants to see 'er. Got that?'

Too scared to say anything, she nodded so vigorously it felt her head was in danger of falling off.

'Right.' Eddie Bridgeman nodded at the man who resembled a wardrobe.

She was free to go.

There was no time to head for The Llandoger and warn Maisie about this man, but it was Friday night and tomorrow the three Ms were meeting up for coffee in Carwardines. That, she decided, was the best place to tell her.

19

MAISIE

Hearing that Eddie Bridgeman was after her was like being doused in a shower of ice-cold water. Maisie was scared.

'He's after the old man,' she said without a trace of fear. She saw that Phyllis was scared and it would only make matters worse if she showed that she was to. She patted Phyllis's hand reassuringly. 'Don't worry yerself about it, Phyl.'

It was obvious from Phyllis's appearance that beginning a new life was weaving its magic. Her hair shone and although her clothes weren't new, they were clean and pressed and once again she'd painted her lips bright red.

Maisie went out of her way to reassure her friend and also to assuage the questioning look on Bridget's face. 'He don't know where I am, and you didn't tell 'im, Phyl. So nothing to worry about. Now, are you going to eat them biscuits or do I' ave to do it for you?'

* * *

The truth was that Maisie's cocky attitude hid a quaking fear. Eddie blamed her father for his short spell in prison and wanted to find him. God help him when he did! As for herself, Eddie would also be looking for her in the hope that she knew where Frank was hiding.

The place where she felt safest of all was in work at the tobacco factory, though even there was touched by dishonesty.

'Bloody 'ell. Somebody's pinched me liver!'

Somebody was stealing shopping left in the cloakroom.

'Well, that's your bloody fault for not bringing it in 'ere!' Aggie Hill stood with her fists resting on her ample hips, her voice booming round the stripping room.

Clara Bennet, a round-faced girl of twenty, was beside herself. 'That was fer me old dad's tea. 'E was looking forward to that. There was a turnip in there too.'

Maisie wrinkled her nose at Aggie. 'Can't blame 'er for not wantin' a pound of liver between 'er feet whilst she's working. You ends up smelling of it.'

Aggie's disapproving look swept over all those who worked under her watchful gaze for a guilty expression. 'I'll find out who it is, you mark my words.'

Bridget shook her head over a fresh pile of tobacco leaves. 'I can't believe somebody could be so mean.'

'Not mean. Desperate,' pronounced Maisie.

Still standing and a fierce look on her strong features, Aggie took command of the situation. 'We're goin' to do something about this. I reckon we should 'ang our bags in front of an open window. And we'll take it in turns to keep an eye on it. Raise yur 'ands all them that agree.'

Everyone knew better than to disagree with Aggie, hence a sea of hands shot up.

* * *

Maisie kept her spirits up all day, but by the evening back at the Llandoger, she fell a bit quieter than Aggie was used to.

Aggie gave her a nudge in the ribs. 'Care to tell me what's wrong?'

Maisie dipped the beer glasses into the warm water in the sink, kept her own problems to herself and referred to the thieving in the stripping room. 'We could set a trap.'

'And how do we do that?' Her face brightened; Aggie was like a mother to Maisie.

Heads together, she outlined the basic plan. 'We bring all our shopping in as planned, except one. That one we leave out in the cloakroom, but mark it with indelible ink.'

'You got any of this ink?' asked Aggie.

Maisie shook her head. 'We'll ask Bridget tomorrow.'

* * *

'I do,' said Bridget. 'Our Sean had some. Mum was going to throw it out whilst he was down in Devon. Makes a right mess, it does, and it won't come off. Ruined more than one of his pullovers.'

'Tomorrow then. That's when we're doing it. Strike whilst the iron's hot,' declared Aggie, her fist coming down hard on the table and setting the crockery rattling.

The following morning, Bridget arrived with a small jar of ink and a fine paint brush. At lunchtime, Aggie sent the girls out to purchase something irresistible to bait the trap.

'Something to make the thief's mouth water,' instructed Aggie. Her expression darkened. 'I don't like this thieving, not when we're all in the same bloody boat.' It was rare that Aggie swore but it had made her blood boil.

'Something meaty?' suggested Bridget.

Maisie looked thoughtful. 'Something sugary. It's sugar that we're missing the most, ain't it?'

'Raywards,' proclaimed Aggie with hardly a moment's thought. 'Pop in there and get a big bag of broken biscuits. If you can get some lardy cakes as well, all the better. Here. Take this carrier bag to put it in.'

'Or all the butter,' joked Maisie and despite the seriousness of their quest, they laughed.

The moment she pushed open the door of the biscuit shop, Maisie took a big breath and sighed.

'Sugar and biscuits 'ave a smell all of their own.'

'I know what you mean,' returned Bridget. 'You can taste it even before you take a single bite.'

They sniffed again and again as they went round lifting the glass lids on the big square tins ranged in rows from low-slung racks on the customer side of the counter.

Eventually they had a big bagful, mostly unbroken because Maisie had said they looked more tempting.

'Good job they're not on ration,' Bridget remarked.

From there, they rushed to get a place in the queue outside the bakery, where they bought a mix of lardy cakes and teacakes.

'I do feel a bit mean,' said Bridget once they were back at the factory, the ink bottle in one hand and a wavering paintbrush in the other. 'I mean, some of us are worse off than others.'

Maisie took the ink bottle, unscrewed the top, then gestured that Bridget should give her the paintbrush. 'Give it 'ere!'

'Not too much,' Bridget said, the tip of her tongue tickling the side of her mouth as Maisie painted on the ink.

'There,' she finally said. 'That should do it.'

She gave the bottle and brush back to Bridget who was as careful as she was not to get any of it onto her hands. 'It's a devil to get off if you do,' she said as she wrapped both items up in newspaper and put it into her bag.

Aggie was waiting for them when they got back into the stripping room.

'All done, is it?' she asked in a quieter voice, one that hardly seemed to belong to her.

They assured her that it was and that the carrier bag was left on a window ledge rather than hanging from any individually named coat hook.

It was just before tea break when Aggie, being in charge, waltzed off. On seeing her depart, Bridget and Maisie exchanged knowing looks. Would the carrier bag be gone?

At tea break, Aggie was already sitting at a table, her cup of tea and an ashtray sitting in front of her, along with a couple of Huntley and Palmer biscuits.

'They ain't any of the ones you bought, me chicks! The carrier bag is gone.'

'So what next?' Bridget looked at Aggie for leadership. She'd gone along with the plan but couldn't help being uncomfortable. It seemed so underhanded, so dishonest.

Maisie had no such reservations. 'Find out who's got inky fingers. That bag is now under the table inside somebody's shopping bag.'

Bridget pointed out that they couldn't look into personal belongings. 'Only security can do that.'

She saw Maisie's wicked wink. 'You're the one who brought in the ink. It's hands we're going to look at.'

'Not you girls though,' said Aggie. 'You've done enough. I think that's my job.'

There was something about her expression that was more thoughtful than usual. It suddenly came to Bridget that she already had a suspicion of who had taken it.

At the end of the working day, Aggie advised Maisie to go on home.

'I'll tag along later, after I've taken care of things.'

Maisie and Bridget left work together, though both harboured curiosity and felt just a little left out of this, the final conclusion of today's goings-on.

Oblivious to all this, male and female workers surged out of the entrance, all off home, though some would be doing war effort tasks for a few hours before they finally turned in.

Bridget was as keen to hear from Aggie as Maisie was.

'Doing anything tonight?' she asked.

Maisie grinned. 'I'll be serving for a couple of hours behind the bar – if you're up for it.'

Bridget pushed open the door of the Llandoger Trow with a feeling of apprehension. She wasn't used to entering a pub alone, especially one that was full of men. Heads turned and male eyes followed her progress across the uneven stone floor. A few raised their glasses in salute or touched the brim of their trilby or cap. Some made comment.

'Evenin', Miss. Looking for someone?'

'Me,' cried Maisie as she pushed her way through from behind the bar, slapping anyone who got in the way.

The group of men parted.

'Watch out! This one's got a kick like a goat and a tongue sharp as a razor.'

Their laughter quelled once Aggie came through. Even the roughest seaman respected Aggie Hill.

'Come through to the small room,' said Aggie. 'Curley and Gladys can manage to serve in the bar.

The two young women, both looking whip-smart in their best dresses, followed Aggie through to one of the many small rooms running along the front of the pub.

Aggie stood like a stone bulwark between them and the door they'd just come through. 'Edith Jones. Don't surprise me, though. Four kids, a 'usband that deserted 'er and a mother who drinks the money and rations that's meant for food. She tried to deny it until I grabbed 'er wrist and 'eld up 'er inky fingers.'

'Poor woman,' said Bridget.

Maisie was more circumspect. 'Now what?'

Aggie's lips twitched before speaking. 'She's 'ad a warning.' She hesitated before continuing. 'I told 'er to keep the biscuits and buns, but 'ad 'er promise not to do it again.'

Maisie frowned. 'You let 'er keep it?'

Bridget shrugged. 'I don't mind about that. I can't help feeling sorry for her.'

'That's what I thought you'd say.' Aggie turned to Maisie and her persistent frown. 'You all right with that, Maisie?'

Maisie was not quite all right with it. She could still smell that biscuit shop, but...

'If it's all right with you two, I suppose it's all right with me.'

'Right. That's settled then,' said Aggie, clapping her big hands together. 'It's a nice evening, so how about you two going off for a walk? Make the most of it before we've got winter darkness and the blackout to contend with.'

* * *

Aggie's cheerful expression waivered then disappeared once they were some distance off.

Sighing, she turned her back on the two young women and

looked to the other end of King Street where the sun still penetrated between the gabled rooftops onto the shiny cobbles.

Even before she heard the car engine, then saw it sliding to a stop in front of her, she knew who it was and her stomach cramped with apprehension.

His driver opened the rear door and a black and white shoe appeared, flash and snazzy. The other appeared and there was a man in a pinstriped suit, a little less fleshy than when she'd seen him last, but she knew beyond doubt that this was Eddie Bridgeman.

He shrugged himself into the padded shoulders of his double-breasted suit and eyed her challengingly.

A young woman got out behind him, who instantly brought a sour taste to Aggie's mouth and a hard look to her eyes.

'How's things goin', Aggie?'

There was not a vestige of a smile on Aggie's face. Her lips puckered. Eddie always brought a sour taste to her mouth, though not as much as the young woman he had with him.

'What do you want?'

There was a cruel twist to his lips, a black stare from his eyes. 'I'm back in town and back in charge. You owe me, Mrs Hill. You've 'ad a bit of a 'oliday since I bin inside. I'm in need of cash, Aggie.'

'I got none for you.' Aggie forced herself to sound firm and collected, though inside she was trembling with anger and fear. Tough she might be, but helpless when faced with this man.

Eddie Bridgeman shrugged his shoulders again and pulled in his chin as though she'd offended him and curled his arm round the pretty young woman at his side. 'Come on, Aggie. You can't begrudge me. After all I got your darling daughter 'ere to look after. She don't come cheap,' he said, shaking his head and smiling.

Aggie's anger multiplied when Angela smiled. Her own daughter had fallen through the cracks in the pavement and ended up with the likes of a small-time gangster. She'd be feeling sick to her stomach if she wasn't so angry.

'She can fend fer 'erself.' Never in her life would she ever have believed that she'd feel such ire towards her only daughter. As a child she'd doted on her. Perhaps, she thought, that was where she'd gone wrong.

Eddie slapped a kid glove over the palm of the other hand and shook his head. 'Aggie, that's a bit hard on yer own daughter. But there, if that's the way you feel.' His eyes hardened and he pushed the willowy blonde, so much like Aggie had been when she was young, away from him. He came close, his jutting chin only inches from her face. 'If you want my protection it 'as to be paid for. Ain't yer old man told you that? P'raps I'd better ask 'im. Right?'

Aggie held back a few choice expletives that came to mind. Arguing was futile and when she'd heard about him going to prison, she'd thought it was the last of Eddie Bridgeman. Whilst he was in prison, they'd sent one of his men packing when he'd tried to collect protection money. The thing was that since Eddie had gone inside his little empire had crumbled a bit and some of his gang had disappeared or at least been less reluctant to show their faces round the centre of the city where the police were always on the lookout for deserters or draft dodgers. Criminals were as likely to get called up as anyone else – and most of them were only a few feet ahead of the recruiting sergeants. Somehow, she couldn't think how it had happened he was out and inclined to make their lives a misery once again.

Aggie knew she couldn't win. 'Cyril's playing dominoes in the small room down on the left.' Her tone of voice was as grim as her expression, not just because his visit had surprised her, but fear for Maisie's safety. She knew the story of Maisie's father betraying Eddie to the law and Eddie always bore a grudge. If he didn't already know where Frank Miles was, it was pretty certain he had every intention of finding out. Whatever happened, he mustn't find out that Maisie was living here.

Mouth clamped tightly shut, she said nothing when he brushed roughly past her, up the steps and turned left.

Angela glanced at her mother, a smug smile on her lips. Her clothes were of good quality but far too tight and hardly ladylike, clinging like a second skin to her body.

A bitter hardness came to Aggie's face, but inside she was crying. She fixed her gaze across to the buildings on the other side of the road, wondering where the little girl she'd loved from the moment she was born had gone.

Everything about her daughter stabbed at her heart. Her hair had been softly brown when she was young. It was now peroxide blonde, almost white in fact. Even from a distance, she smelt of perfume – and not just any old perfume, but something expensive and doubtless stolen. Eddie Bridgeman was free to take advantage of the blackout and the black market.

Aggie was about to go inside, take off her slippers and put on a pair of shoes – dash off to find Maisie and hope against hope that Eddie wouldn't question where she was going, when she suddenly saw a flash of fiery red hair and a figure she recognised, a bouncy walk a confident air. It had to be Phyllis!

Phyllis waved and Aggie took off down the steps and lumbered along the cobbles, slipping and sliding thanks to the fact that she was wearing her slippers.

Phyllis was about to shriek with joy, which changed quickly to surprise at Aggie's headlong rush and the sense that something was wrong.

'What's the matter?'

Phyllis paled when a breathless Aggie explained what the problem was and what she wanted her to do. 'I didn't know you knew 'im,' she said in a surprised tone.

Aggie nodded. 'Maisie's gone for a walk up Brandon Hill with Bridget. Can you go after her and tell her not to come back just yet?' She jerked her head to the black and white timbered pub. 'Eddie mustn't know that Maisie's living 'ere. Best she keeps away until he's gone.'

Phyllis had been about to tell Aggie all about how her life had changed and that she was finally out of her in-laws' place, how invigorated she felt, no longer a mouse but an independent woman. Mention of Eddie Bridgeman pulled her up short.

'You'll likely find them up by Cabot Tower. Please don't bring 'er back 'ere, Phyllis me love. Not yet.'

Phyllis knew the story about Frank Miles shopping Eddie Bridgeman to the police and didn't need Aggie to tell her that he'd be pretty rough with anyone likely to know where Frank was living. She shivered at the memory of being bundled into Eddie's car.

'But Maisie doesn't know where he is. Nobody does.'

Aggie shook her head. 'Trouble is, he'll take some convincing.'

By the end of that evening, Maisie had made up her mind that she, just like Phyllis, had to move on. The question was where and could she keep a low profile before finding somewhere.

Bridget offered a temporary reprieve, one of the kid's beds.

Maisie countered that it wouldn't be wise. 'I don't want to bring trouble to me mates' doors.' Her eyes darkened with fear, then brightened again. She would not be daunted. She would not be beaten. 'Something will turn up,' she said at last. 'Just leave it with me and it'll be all sorted.'

'I'm afraid I must insist,' said Bridget. 'Just until you find something safer.'

Maisie looked sad until a cheeky grin lit up her face. 'At least there's no fear of Hilda Harvey hammering on the door.'

20

Towards the end of the month Sam Proctor came home again.

Phyllis was coming out of the soap works gate when she heard his cheerful whistle and him shouting her name.

Bubbling inside fit to burst, she slowed her footsteps just enough to allow him to catch up. She pretended to look surprised when his long stride brought her to his side within minutes.

She ran her fingers through her hair, looking at him dewy-eyed from beneath a playful fringe that refused to be tamed.

'Your mother will be pleased to see you.'

And she isn't the only one, she thought to herself. For days she too had been looking forward to his arrival. They'd clicked on that first meeting, had gone out to the pub and the pictures during that first leave, chatting and laughing as though they'd known each other for years rather than a few days.

'What's the old lady got for dinner tonight?'

'Fish pie with cheese – and a lot of vegetables.'

'It's always a lot of vegetables! Do you know how many tons of spuds the army gets through?'

She laughed. 'I couldn't say. You'll have to tell me.'

'Tons. That's all I know. Bloody tons!'

'Which means you don't know very much at all,' she responded coquettishly.

Throwing back his head, he let out a big throaty laugh. 'So how was your day?' Sam asked.

'Smelly.'

He laughed. 'Never mind. One day you'll meet the man of your dreams and he'll 'ave you out of there and down the aisle in no time.'

Phyllis laughed, a light hollow sound that just about hid the guilt his comment had aroused in her. The finger where she'd worn her wedding ring began to itch like a guilty secret that should be shared. The question was should she tell him she was married or widowed? As yet, she wasn't quite sure which.

'Phyllis, I've only got a week's leave, so I won't waste any time. Do you fancy coming out for a drink tonight?'

'Got nobody else lined up to go out with you?'

'I did phone Mae West, but couldn't get through.'

'So I'm second best to Mae West.'

'No. You were my first choice.' He took hold of her arm and off they walked back to York Street, talking all the way.

What with Victoria the cat waiting on the step and Mrs Proctor throwing her apron up over her face and bursting into happy tears, Sam Proctor stated that he really felt he was home.

'Me old queen, I smell something cooking.' His nostrils narrowed as he inhaled the smell of his favourite meal – faggots and peas – the meal she always made for him on the day she knew he was coming home on leave.

He looked disapprovingly at Phyllis. 'You told me it was fish.'

She grinned. 'I lied.'

After much talking and laughing, the meal was eaten and Mrs Proctor was told that they were going out.

'That's nice,' she said, yet Phyllis saw a flash of concern and a nervous tic flicker beneath her right eye. Before she'd moved in, Mrs Proctor would have had her son to herself, she thought. Well, Sam was a fully grown man and she a fully grown woman. His mother had to accept that.

They joined the queue at His Majesty's picture house and managed to get in the one and six's, though would have preferred the circle. All the same, they enjoyed themselves.

Sam held her hand all the way through the film and she felt protected.

'Did you enjoy the film?' he asked as they exited out of the stuffy interior and into the night air, their arms entwined.

'Loved it.'

The truth was she hadn't been able to concentrate. It had been an age since a man had sat so close to her, even longer since someone had held her hand. The flickering of the film had been hypnotic. She hadn't been watching people but a series of black and white flashes interspersed with her past and those who'd peopled it. Robert was one of them, of course, admirable at first until she'd realised that he was taking her over body and soul. Alan also figured, his easy-going manner and low-key irresistible sexuality.

It struck her that Sam was totally different to either of them. She didn't have to be anybody else but herself when she was with Sam. He didn't dominate as Robert had done. Even Alan, she now realised, had recognised her vulnerability and taken advantage.

Suddenly Sam's laughter burst into her thoughts. 'It was a bloody awful film. It might have been dark in there, but I saw you yawn. Thought you'd drop off at any minute.

'It was terrible,' she cried, her laugh matching his.

'Too right it was. My mind was elsewhere too. I reckon that

big shiny beam from the projector more interesting than the film!'

Laughing and with linked arms, they took a longer route home to York Street than the one they'd taken earlier. Sam was talking about the war and his part in it.

'I fancy serving abroad,' he was saying.

'Abroad!' Phyllis felt instant panic. 'Surely you don't have to go.'

'No. I don't have to. I think I want to. How about you? I reckon you'd look good in a uniform.'

Hilda Harvey came to mind and Phyllis burst out laughing.

Sam laughed because she laughed. 'Something funny?'

'Have you seen those middle-aged miseries protesting that women shouldn't serve alongside men?'

He shook his head. 'Can't say that I have. Who are they?'

Phyllis pursed her lips to stop herself from mentioning any names and certainly not admitting the woman who led them was her mother-in-law. This was not the time to tell him that. 'A women's church group.'

'It would be,' he said with a knowing grin. 'Do you know any of them personally?'

She opened her mouth to deny the fact, when a van pulled out from a side alley.

'Blimey, that stinks,' said Sam, wrinkling his nose.

Phyllis glanced at the driver. Although it was dark, a random handheld torchlight picked up features that looked surprisingly familiar. She held her breath. Though she'd only seen him once, on the occasion when he'd attacked Maisie outside the tobacco factory, she recognised Frank Miles. If it really was him, did he know that Eddie Bridgeman was looking for him?

'Do you know him?' Sam asked, noticing her gaze.

She barely stopped herself from blurting out that she did

know him but held back. To do so would mean her past unravelling in record time, so instead she shook her head. 'No. I don't think so. Let's get home. Terrible smell though.'

'Bone yard,' said Sam. 'I'd recognise that smell anywhere.'

As they crossed the opening to the alley, a number of people came out, some clutching bundles wrapped in newspaper, one or two carrying a brown paper carrier bag. Phyllis recognised a face; Edith Jones who worked in the stripping room at Wills's at the same time as she had.

One swift glance and Edith hurried on with her head down. Like everyone else, she was carrying a folded-up shopping bag beneath her arm.

Not wanting to be seen, Phyllis quickened her step. 'Come on. It's beginning to rain.'

Hurrying her steps, Edith Jones held tightly to her shopping bag. The smell of raw meat permeated the newspaper it was wrapped in. The family would eat well enough this week, what with bones for a stew, plus liver, lights tightly, the name applied to the pale meat of a cow's lungs, and a bit of caul. Mixed with onions and breadcrumbs, she'd bought enough to make at least six faggots.

Buying from the black market was a necessity but usually the prices were beyond the contents of her purse, so she counted herself lucky to have happened on this bloke. Her purchases had been incredibly cheap and carried out late at night so she knew it wasn't legal, but what did she care as long as it put a meal on the table?

Scurrying out from the alley, she'd kept her head down, only glancing up that one time, seeing the soldier and his girl cross her path. The young woman had looked vaguely familiar, all the better to get out of there and home as quickly as possible.

It wasn't until she was placing her purchases into the green tin meat safe that it came to her. Phyllis Mason – as had been – not exactly a workmate, but they'd known each other by sight. Phyllis had left and got married, though rumour had it that her husband had been killed. Now here she was out with another man! Well, she didn't let the grass grow under her feet, did she!

A bit of a smell wafted out from the gap between the meat safe and its door before she slammed it shut. The meat wasn't that fresh. Still, she thought, once cooked it would be fine. There was a war on. Eat it or starve.

21

THE THREE MS

October had been as glorious as September, but was replaced by the dark grey skies of November. Not a chink of sunshine split the heavy cloud and if it wasn't foggy or frosty it was raining. To Bridget's mind it seemed the dark days were only getting darker and her feeling of foreboding was difficult to shift.

It was a Saturday afternoon, there was no Sam Proctor and Phyllis had Saturday off work. Luckily so did Maisie, who had moved in with Bridget occupying the boys' old bedroom until such time as they came home from the countryside. As arranged, they met up for a spot of window shopping.

Their footsteps took them the length of Castle Street and nearby Mary le Port Street, a narrow medieval thoroughfare where an overhead footbridge imitating an Italian design, connected one side of the street with the other. After they'd drooled a while over the things in shop windows that they couldn't afford to buy on all of their wages combined – even if they had enough ration coupons – they headed for coffee at Carwardines.

Each of them was dressed in their best in honour of meeting up and the pleasure of being at the heart of the city.

Phyllis was back to her old self again, bright red lipstick and an application of face powder and eye make-up. The black snood she'd knitted at Hilda Harvey's behest had been discarded on the banks of the Malago, hooking on a stone in the narrow waters of the brook.

Despite the war, the shops were bustling, mainly with people who could afford to pay high prices without the need of handing over their precious ration books. The three musketeers were content to window shop, Bridget taking special notice of the cut of expensive clothes and the shape of hats. She couldn't afford them but she could memorise the details and pass them on to her mother, a dab hand with a pair of scissors and a needle and thread.

After ordering coffee and teacakes, they leaned closer across the table, all speaking at once, keen to hear news and pass it on.

Maisie and Bridget wanted to know how Phyllis was coping with her new life.

Phyllis, her face blooming with health and happiness, heaved a happy sigh. 'Now where do I start?'

Maisie's eyes bored into her, read all the signs and blurted, 'Start with Sam. What's 'e like?'

Bridget gulped. If there was one thing you could count on, it was Maisie getting straight to the point.

To her credit, Phyllis didn't hold back. Her eyes sparkled and her complexion was more peaches and cream than the deathly pallor it had been.

They sat back when the coffee and tea cakes arrived, the latter only lightly smeared with butter.

'I like butter on my tea cakes,' Maisie said to the waitress.

'There's a war on,' sniffed the waitress and left them to it.

Maisie pulled a disgruntled face. 'If I hear that once more, I'll strangle somebody. It's bleedin' obvious there's a war on! I don't need anyone to tell me that. It's just their excuse for being mean with the butter.' She lifted the teacake to her nose. 'If it is butter! I bet it's marge!'

Phyllis flashed Bridget a long-suffering look, which, to her surprise, Bridget did not return. Something was going on here that she was not party to, but she so wanted to impart her own news before she exploded. 'I'm in love,' she said suddenly. 'I'm in love with Sam Proctor.'

'That's nice, Phyl. And 'ow does 'e feel about that?' Maisie eyed her.

Phyllis sighed like a girl in love for the very first time. 'It's early days, but...' A faraway look came to her eyes. 'I've never felt like this before. When we're together, it feels as though we've known each other for ever.'

It occurred to Bridget that her life was quite simple in comparison to that of Phyllis.

'He looked a nice man when we first met him,' Bridget said brightly. She recalled the amiable expression, the honesty in his eyes and the way he'd addressed his mother and Victoria the cat. She badly wanted to give her sound advice, as well as set out a few home truths, but thought this might be tactless.

As it turned out, she needn't have concerned herself. Maisie jumped in with both feet and asked the question Bridget had left unasked. 'Does he know you're married?'

The smile vanished from Phyllis's face and her cheeks burned pink. 'No. I haven't told him. Anyway, I don't know for sure whether I'm still married or a widow. So I thought I'd say nothing, at least until I know for sure. But there is something else I want to tell you.' Her voice dropped to a whisper, her long hair in danger of dipping into her tea as she leaned closer across the tabletop. 'Guess who I saw a few weeks ago?'

'Surprise us,' said Maisie before shoving the last of her teacake into her mouth. Her manner was nonchalant.

'I saw your old man.' She directed her statement at Maisie. 'He was driving a van.'

For a moment Maisie's facial features froze. She took a deep breath. 'What kind of van?'

Phyllis shrugged. 'Some kind of butchers' van. No,' she said, on reconsidering and remembering what Sam had said. 'It was something to do with a slaughterhouse out at Ashton.' Her frown deepened. Ashton was sandwiched between city and countryside, where there were more cows and sheep than people, yet she'd seen him in the heart of the city. The van was a long way from where it should be. Phyllis frowned. 'I've seen 'im going into the rendering yard too, though driving a lorry not a van,' she exclaimed.

'Crikey,' said Maisie. 'Don't tell me he's got a job?' She'd never known Frank Miles to have a job. 'That'll be a turn-up for the books.' She fell to silence and took a sip of lukewarm, weak tea, a worried look on her face. She felt Bridget's eyes on her.

'Sean and Michael's bed is yours for as long as you want it.'

'Until they come 'ome,' ventured Maisie. 'But I'm a bit scared about Eddie Bridgeman finding me. I 'ave to make plans.'

'What are you going to do?' Bridget asked.

'Just a thought,' said Phyllis, 'but couldn't you tell Eddie Bridgeman where your old man's working? Then he could take it from there and wouldn't be after you.'

Maisie shook her head. 'I don't want to get tangled up with Eddie Bridgeman. Once he's got his claws into you, he don't let go. I'd only shop the old man if I've got to, unless the old sod's done somethin' really rotten.'

Phyllis frowned. In her mind, she saw again that dark alley, Frank Miles and the writing on the side of the van. She pushed her cup and saucer to the middle of the table and looked at each of her friends. They had looked out for each other from the start and they still did – would forever, she hoped. 'A lot of people came out of that alley where the van came out of. According to Sam, it's a well-known haunt for people flogging stuff on the black market.' Her eyes flashed at Maisie. 'Meat being one of them.'

For once Maisie said nothing, too busy thinking of what might happen if Eddie Bridgeman ever did catch up with her.

'I saw somebody else too,' Phyllis went on. 'I saw Edith Jones. Is she still working in the stripping room?'

'Yes, she is. That poor woman,' said Bridget, shaking her head. 'I don't blame her buying on the black market, not with four hungry mouths to feed and no husband.'

Although she was putting on a brave front, Bridget could tell by the dark lines beneath her eyes that Maisie was worried.

Maisie puffed out her chest. 'I plan to rent somewhere, but it means clopping around like a ruddy cart'orse until I do. I've got a copy of the classifieds from the Evenin' World. One of them's bound to suit. I'm gonna give it my all next Sunday.'

Bridget arched her eyebrows. 'I'll go with you.'

'We'll both come with you,' said Phyllis with an air of finality.

'That's a good idea,' said Bridget, nodding enthusiastically.

'Next Sunday,' said Bridget, raising her empty cup.

'Sunday here we come,' added the other two.

22

THE THREE MS

Sunday came. Accompanied by her best mates, Maisie was off to find somewhere to live.

The day was cold thanks to a sharp easterly wind broadcasting in no uncertain terms that winter was coming. Unusually for them, Maisie, Phyllis and Bridget, walked in silence, each contemplating their individual problems.

There was little traffic on the roads and even fewer people out and about. Piles of fallen leaves rustled beneath their feet and all three were wearing winter coats that they'd had the good fortune to buy before the outbreak of war.

During the week, there existed a sense of urgency in the city, crowds of people, men and women, some in uniform. In contrast, the weekend was sombre, the sky, the buildings and the river varying shades of grey.

Maisie had circled a couple of rooms to let in the newspaper's classifieds. None of them were close to the tobacco factory or at a rent Maisie could afford, except for one in a grimy five-storey house in Stokes Croft.

Maisie peered above the knitted scarf entwined round her

neck at the grim looking building. 'Blimey. It's worse than York Street.'

'A lot worse,' stated Phyllis. Although living in York Street was a bit of a comedown, she felt obliged to go on the defensive. Sam lived there, which somehow made it a lot better than it actually was.

So,' said Bridget, her hands thrust deep into her pockets. 'Do we chance going inside?'

'Might as well,' grumbled Maisie.

Phyllis merely grunted something about preferring to stay outside.

Bridget grabbed her arm and tugged her inside. 'We said we're sticking together and we are.'

The landlady's eyes were buried in wrinkles. Her eyebrows were as bushy as old-fashioned sideburns and the chenille blouse that strained over her breasts was breaking at the seams.

The outside of the house had been bad enough, but one look at the peeling plaster, the smell of damp, grime and cats' pee confirmed the reliability of their first impression.

The landlady kept six cats in her ground-floor flat and proudly stated that they were never allowed out but wandered the building from top to bottom.

'They'd get runned over, dear,' she'd said, wiping a trickle of brown snuff from her nostrils with a handkerchief the colour of mud. 'Come on up and I'll show you the room.'

There was a stove and kitchen cupboard behind a faded curtain, a threadbare carpet on the floor, peeling wallpaper and a bed covered with a dirty eiderdown.

Maisie considered what else might be in that bed, more so when she spotted a cockroach crawling up the wall.

Before she'd even opened her mouth, the landlady held out her open palm. 'Ten shillings a week.'

It was cheap, but nothing could persuade Maisie to share her living quarters with bugs and cockroaches.

'I'll get back to you,' she said, gagging against the rising bile as she headed for the fresh air, Bridget and Phyllis right behind her.

'Better hurry up about it, dear. At that price, it won't be around for long. There's a lot of foreigners around and they ain't as fussy as you!'

The last comment was accompanied by a slamming of the door.

'I can still smell that place,' said Phyllis as they strode off towards St John's Arch, an old city gate that straddled a narrow street. She wrinkled her nose. 'What a pong.'

Bridget shook her head disconsolately. 'How could anybody live in a place like that?'

Maisie suddenly burst out laughing. 'Plenty of company though. Cockroaches and cats. What more could you want?'

They were still laughing when Phyllis suggested they walk through St Nicholas Market.

It was only a little before six forty-five and it was far darker in the narrow alleys of the ancient market than in the streets around it. Before war had been declared, wall-mounted gas lights threw pools of light over the uneven flagstones. Even late in the afternoon, it was like entering a dark cave. Now the darkness was total, the gnarled stone slabs beneath their feet dependent on the muted light of a torch.

Bridget came to an abrupt standstill. She held up her finger and bade them listen.

They stopped, glanced to either side of them, as if that might help them hear anything any better than they could see anything.

Bridget reached out her hand. On her left, she touched Maisie's arm, on the right Phyllis.

The sound was enough to set their teeth on edge. Starting

from a low whine, the sound of the air-raid siren soared to an ear-screeching wail.

'Oh my God. Please say it's a false alarm.' Phyllis's voice began as a tremble but ended up a whine.

'I've got a feeling it's not,' said Bridget. 'In which case we must get to the nearest shelter...' Her need to do something positive outweighed her fear and her mind worked quickly. She recalled seeing a map of air-raid shelters. 'The nearest is between Fairfax Street and Castle Street in the old castle wall. Come on, follow me.'

Hampered by the impenetrable darkness, they stumbled and slid over the old flagstones. They didn't see the man they bumped into, but they did see his uniform in the light of his torch, his shouted warning that they should take shelter.

Bridget informed him where they were going.

'No time for that.' His torch arced through the air as he swung it back and forth, urging them to follow.

The few people who were out and about all seemed to converge in the alley, sweeping them back in the direction they'd come.

'Down in the cellars,' somebody shouted.

'Where do we go?' shrieked Phyllis, who had never really believed this could happen – not in the middle of Bristol. Up at the aircraft factories or in the docks, but not here.

Bridget grabbed hold of her arm. She'd half expected this reaction from Phyllis. 'Come on, Phyl. Do as the man says.'

Pushed from behind by other people caught in the raid, they descended a set of rough stone steps. What with the press of the crowd and the darkness, they were unable to see their feet, feeling their way slowly and surely. Fresh air was replaced by a mustier, more enclosed smell that told them they had left the outside behind and were now possibly below ground.

'Crikey,' said Maisie, who was right behind them. 'I can smell sherry.'

Some grumbling, some stunned by fear to silence, the small crowd spilled into an old and dimly lit wine cellar, where huge wooden casks loomed dark against distempered walls. Cobwebs hung in the corners, but there were benches to sit on and bare light bulbs threw a welcome but gloomy light. This was one of many such stores built in the eighteenth century where the wine fermented in cool temperatures accorded by being below ground.

'Bristol Cream,' said Phyllis after taking a big sniff. Maisie was right. Even though the barrels might be empty, the sweet smell of sherry, a beverage Bristol was famous for, still prevailed.

'It would be,' said Bridget, her interest aroused. 'Port wine especially. It became popular during the war against Napoleon when no French wines could be imported. Fortified wine, what we call port, travelled better.'

Maisie rolled her eyes. 'Bridget Milligan, I used to think you'd have made a good teacher. Isn't it vicars that give sermons from the pulpit?'

'Take no notice,' said Phyllis on seeing the sudden hurt look on Bridget's face.

'I didn't mean it,' said Maisie.

The current of fresh air from outside was cut as the door in the arched entrance slammed shut.

Once the benches were filled, people sat on the floor, or the luckier ones on upturned casks bearing names like Jerez, Amontillado and Ruby Port and still smelling of what they had once contained.

Talk became whispers and even whispers became muted. Frightened eyes turned towards the door as the sound of anti-aircraft guns intensified. Bridget put an arm around Phyllis. who was, like many others, staring wide-eyed at nothing in particular, but waiting for whatever it was that might happen next.

Maisie was looking around her with great interest. Something about this place, possibly because of its age, reminded her of the Llandoger. The ceiling was low and barrel shaped. The smell was alluring and oddly exciting, as were the shadows.

As the guns got louder, Phyllis began to shake. 'Are those bombs?' Her voice was brittle and as tremulous as her body.

'No,' answered Maisie. 'I've already told you. Just anti-aircraft guns.'

'Better times ahead, Phyl,' Bridget said quietly. 'They give the guns names,' she added brightly, in an effort to take Phyllis's mind off things. 'The biggest is named Purdown Percy.'

The Information aroused no response. Phyllis's eyes were round as marbles. She was scared.

'Makes you wonder, all these barrels,' Maisie piped up. She jerked her pert little chin at the biggest barrels sat on wooden trestles lining the walls. 'They looks as though they've been 'ere for years.'

Bridget had merely glanced at the barrels, but now she too looked at them in more detail. Telling a bit of a story might help. 'Wine's been coming into Bristol since the Middle Ages, if not before. Five hundred years at least. It wasn't so busy when wine was coming in from France, but got busier once England lost Gascony and a lot of wine began coming up from Portugal and Spain. For some reason, it made the port of Bristol more convenient...'

'Because of the winds,' Maisie pronounced. 'Some of the sailors in the pub told me that. If you're coming from the Atlantic, it's easier to go with the wind up the westerly approaches – less trouble than sailing into the Bay of Biscay.'

Before Bridget had chance to make comment further, there

was a huge explosion. A shower of loose plaster and fine dust fell from the arched ceiling. A toddler clasped to its mother's breast began to wail. Women screamed and men, some haunted by the events of a previous war, threw themselves to the ground and covered their heads.

The three friends crouched but, gradually, once they were sure it was only dust that was falling on them, they straightened, though still held on to each other.

The sound of another explosion came and again everyone covered their heads.

'That was close,' said the ARP warden. His bloodshot eyes looked up at the ceiling, perhaps fearing it might collapse, or even that he could see through it.

'I was quite fancying doing a bit more window shopping before we headed home,' Bridget said as brightly as she could. 'Not that my clothes coupons are likely to buy much round here, but still, a girl can dream.'

More explosions and the crashing of buildings sounded close by. People covered their ears and closed their eyes. Some prayed. Others were more defiant, determined to rise above what was happening outside and keep doing the ordinary things, to speak loudly and not huddle with fear.

'Well, I was 'oping to get enough stuff to make a Christmas pudding. I likes to make mine early.'

The woman who spoke had a round face, her hair tucked into a black beret with a small feather on one side.

'My cook makes the pudding very early too,' said another woman in a more refined voice, suggesting she had strayed from Clifton or another of the upmarket suburbs north of the River Avon. 'She's been collecting ingredients since August and we did save some plums from those we picked in the garden. No doubt we'll manage, but it isn't going to be easy.'

Listening to the conversation about Christmas made Bridget think of her brothers and sisters. It would be the first time ever that the family had not been together at Christmas. She wondered at the chance of travelling down to Devon. It wouldn't be easy but worth it to see their smiling faces – and there was James of course.

It seemed in that moment that the bombs were no more than the hammering on a base drum like the ones the Salvation Army used in their marches. Concentrating on James and that warm day in a barn smelling of hay took her mind away from where she was now. She told herself that she really was attracted to him and that it had nothing to do with the last letter she'd received from Lyndon telling her about his family arranging a marriage for him. He'd hurt her and she'd reacted. Should she feel regret or triumph? She wasn't sure.

'I sometimes wonder what the baby would have been like,' Phyllis suddenly whispered into her ear. 'But being born into this... and no father?' She flinched at the sound of another explosion. 'I'm starting afresh and reckon that Sam's the one. In fact, I'm sure he is.'

Although she sounded breathlessly determined, Bridget had seen her infatuated before. Sam seemed nice, but he was away in the army and she wondered whether being apart might dent Phyllis's feelings. Still, she thought, at least she's away from the Harveys. She couldn't blame her for not regretting that.

An old man curled half asleep in the corner began playing the hymn 'Nearer My God to Thee' on a mouth organ. When somebody suggested he played something more cheerful, he began playing 'Pack Up Your Troubles'.

Somebody who lived in one of the apartments above the cellars defied what was going on and brought down a bucketful of tea.

'No sugar and go easy with the milk.'

It was a familiar statement and nobody complained. In the meantime, the building trembled with each blast.

'I wonder how long it will go on,' said Maisie, clutching an enamel mug of hot tea with both hands.

Nobody chanced an answer.

The old man who'd played the mouth organ, took a pocket watch on a bright silver chain from his waistcoat, sighed, shook his head and put it away again.

It was hours later when a tinny chime from the old man's pocket watch announced it was midnight. Just seconds after its chime faded, the all-clear sounded.

The steps up from the wine cellars were dark. The air was full of smoke and the sound of fires raging out of control thundered in air that seemed devoid of moisture. The fiery glow lit up where the alley met Corn Street so no torch was needed to see their way.

'Looks like a long walk home,' said Maisie as they eyed the devastation, the three of them still as statues.

Men shouted at them to stand back.

'But I need to get home,' cried Phyllis. 'I need to get back to York Street.'

'It's past Old Market,' explained Maisie.

The man's face was black with soot. 'No chance. Castle Street, Mary le Port Street and everything around 'as gone up in flames. If you can't get 'ome, a relief centre's been set up in a tent in Queen Square. And stay away from Park Street. It's an inferno.'

'We can make it home,' Bridget declared. 'I'm sure we can.'

Sombre and feeling a deadness inside, they looked one more time behind them at a city in flames. Vast fires had taken hold of so many ancient buildings, some of which had been in existence even before Queen Elizabeth the First had declared St Mary Redcliffe the finest parish church in all England. It was now difficult to identify the once charming facades of black and white, the later buildings of the Georgian and succeeding ages were now like giant bonfires, monstrous flames lighting up the sky.

The orange glow lit their way for a considerable distance. Everywhere heaved with people, some armed with nothing more than buckets and stirrup pumps, faces black, tin hats perched lopsided on their tired heads.

They sprang between road and pavement. Above them, people hung out of first-floor windows, staring to where the great fire consumed the heart of the city.

Phyllis began to sob. 'Poor Bristol.'

Her two friends hung their heads, sorrowfully silent.

They made their way along East Street, the bells of fire engines and ambulances jangled as they raced past them and towards the city centre.

Suddenly Bridget stopped in her tracks. 'We should have asked whether there were many casualties.'

Maisie shrugged. 'Why? What could we have done?'

Her mind went back to the day she and Bridget had gone in disguise to visit Phyllis. She'd liked wearing that uniform but didn't think she could ever be a nurse and get used to the sight of blood. She sighed as she faced what seemed an incontrovertible fact that somehow saddened her; she was just a tobacco girl and always would be.

It was a hard slog home from a city centre smelling of smoke, the air full of cinders, being diverted away from the chaos, the red sky like a halo above burning buildings.

It was gone three in the morning before they made it to the Milligan house in Marksbury Road.

Bridget wasn't surprised to find her father waiting up for her and Maisie, no more than a shadow in the doorway.

'Where the bloody hell, do you think you've been? It's gone three.'

Bridget opened her mouth to say something, but it was as though her tongue had cleaved to the roof of her mouth. Phyllis and Maisie stood behind her.

Suddenly there was the thudding of feet coming downstairs and there was her mother, an off-white shawl thrown round her shoulders.

'Oh thank God!' Mary Milligan brushed Bridget's dirty hair back from her face. 'We heard the bombs and your father...'

Once they were inside the house and the light was lit, she saw copious tears streaming down her father's face. He didn't bother to brush them away but hugged his wife and daughter for dear life, then threw back his head and closed his eyes. On opening them again, he declared that her mother had prayed that night. 'And so did I,' he added. 'Though the bombing was in the heart of the city, not out here.'

Mary Milligan smiled through her tears. 'The first time in years,' she said as she wiped the wetness from her face. 'Now look at me going on like this. You and Maisie are safe and so's Phyllis. It's lovely to see all three of you together again. Make the most of it, girls. There's some tonight who'll never be seeing the one they love again,' she said sadly.

'I can't get home,' said Phyllis, her glossy hair now smelling of smoke and clinging damply to her face.

'Of course you can't. Don't we have plenty of beds here,' stated Patrick Milligan, now swiping at his eyes with a man-size handkerchief. 'Thank God the kids are in Devon.'

'Thank God,' his wife added.

23

They slept like logs and in the morning were awakened by the smell of something frying and the low murmur of the wireless. Bridget stretched her arms as she tried to dissemble what was real and the dreams she'd had. The smell of smoke was fainter now thanks to the wash she'd had before going to bed, but the fire was still vivid in her mind.

Pushing both images and bedclothes aside, she switched on the small table lamp beside her bed and got dressed more quickly than she usually did. She enjoyed her job, but today its place in her life was going to be even more welcome. It was her firm belief that the routine of stripping the tobacco leaves and the company of her workmates at the factory would help her forget the sight of a city in flames.

When she got downstairs, her mother was frying bread in the kitchen, the sound and smell of beef dripping both appetising and, in a strange way, almost sickening. There were bound to be some this morning that would not wake up to a tasty breakfast, some indeed who would not wake up at all.

Her father stopped fiddling with the knob on the Bakelite wireless and looked up.

At first there was moistness in his eyes before his whole face shone with affection.

'You're up bright and early. I thought you might not go in.'

'I have to.' She fiddled with her hands. On tying back her hair, she noted that a little at the side of her head was singed, though she couldn't recall noticing it before. 'I'd better give Mum a hand.'

'No need,' he said with boyish merriment. 'Your friend's already out there.'

She heard Maisie call from the kitchen. 'Be ready soon. Pull up a chair.'

Bridget laughed sheepishly. 'Sounds as though she's taken over.'

Her father said nothing but frowned at the dance music playing on the wireless. He wore a troubled frown. Not for a minute did Bridget believe he was listening to the music.

'What did it say on the news?' she asked cautiously, hoping against hope that thousands hadn't been killed by the bombs or burned alive.

He clenched his hands and kept his eyes fixed on the wireless. 'Two hundred killed and over a thousand injured. It would have been more if it hadn't been a Sunday and all the shops closed.' He shook his head. 'The buildings in the old city are all gone. St Peter's Hospice, the Dutch House. A lot,' he said sadly. 'Course, they were old, half-timbered and burned easily, but still... part of this city's history.'

She glanced out to where Maisie was chatting to her mother nineteen to the dozen between taking bites out of her fried bread. Despite a harrowing night, Maisie had retained her appetite.

A creepy, scary feeling churned in Bridget's stomach as

though she was looking down from a great height and afraid of falling; she'd never liked heights, but that wasn't what this feeling was about. 'What about the Llandoger Trow? It's in the heart of the city.'

Her father shook his head. 'Not mentioned, but...' he shrugged. 'Who knows what's been destroyed until the heat's died down and they sift through what remains.'

Hopefully no more bodies, thought Bridget. She thought of those like her father who had seen the destruction of war first-hand. To those left behind, it had seemed a world away, but in this war, it had come home to roost.

'Glad I'm living here with you,' Maisie sad with a shudder. 'I bet a few bombs fell 'round York Street what with it bein' close to the marshalling yards.' A wistful grin appeared. 'Shame Frank Miles ain't inside it if it's gone up in flames.'

She was tactful enough not to mention her hope for the destruction of York Street once Phyllis was tottering down stairs looking like hell. After all, Mrs Proctor and her son lived there now.

Phyllis refused breakfast. 'I don't think I can.' She looked at her hands. Her brightly coloured nails were broken and dirty.

'What will you do today?' Bridget asked her as she stirred her tea and took a bite of the fried bread.

Phyllis kept her gaze fixed on her hands. 'Sam was coming home today, but whether he'll get here or not...' An angry expression came to her face. 'It's just not fair! This bloody air raid will hold up his train.'

Bridget caught a look flash between her parents, who no doubt thought Phyllis selfish to talk of trains being late when their beloved city was in flames.

Maisie noticed too. 'Never mind about the train being late, what about them that's died or were injured.'

'I didn't mean it like that.' Phyllis looked offended. 'I just wish things could be normal again.'

Bridget swallowed the shock she felt. Phyllis had lost no time in declaring herself in love with Sam and totally rejected any well-meaning advice that she should be a little less impetuous. After all, they hardly knew each other. But then, thought Bridget, look what happened to you. One week in the August sun and face to face with a man who resembled Lyndon, and you threw caution to the wind. And the funeral, she reminded herself. The funeral moved you. Thankfully her period had arrived on time so she wasn't going to end up like Phyllis and marrying because she had to instead of because she wanted to.

Even though they'd had little sleep, Maisie and Bridget made their way into work. Phyllis went with them, intending to get a bus or tram to Old Market. As it turned out, there were very few. The tramlines had been blown up, along with the Bedminster tramway station. Phyllis had no alternative but to walk.

Most of the women and girls working in the stripping room had made it in, though some stools were unoccupied and there were gaps at tables.

Subdued and somewhat sullen, Aggie muscled her way in smelling of smoke. 'We lost the last two gables. We've got five now instead of seven. Still, thank God for small mercies. We'll be open as usual.' She shook her head dolefully before shouting for the wireless to be turned on.

The newscaster's plumy accent cut like a knife through an odd silence in a room that was usually full of conversation and comment. *'Last night, enemy aircraft bombed a city in the south-west of England. Although great damage was sustained, fatalities were light and a number of enemy aircraft were shot down...'*

Aggie's voice boomed out like a foghorn. 'A city in the south west...! It do 'ave a name, you know!'

Despite the fact that the announcer couldn't hear her, she glared at the wireless as though she could see through it to the man who dared treat the city with such anonymity.

Maisie gave Bridget a nudge. 'If that bloke were 'ere now, 'e'd be quaking in 'is boots.'

One, two, three... Bridget counted and placed names to the empty stools.

'None of our girls were bombed out,' said Aggie on seeing her anxious face. 'They're just 'aving a bit of trouble gettin' in this morning. I did meself...'

Aggie was proved right when two of the missing came rushing in. Only one person did not. Edith Jones.

'Anyone know where she is?' shouted Aggie over the bent heads of women and girls keen to pass the piecework threshold and gain a bit of extra money.

Heads were shaken. Nobody seemed to know until Ted Green, one of the managers, walked through and whispered something into Aggie's ear that made her face turn pale.

Gathering herself, she clapped her hands. 'A bit of quiet if you please. Edith Jones and her kids were carted off in an ambulance last night. They're all in hospital. They ain't been bombed out, but I reckon we should 'ave a whip-round. Give whatever you can.'

There were gasps and questions racing from one person to another, all trying to guess why Edith and her family had been carted to hospital and generously plonking coins into the canvas bag Aggie used for all her collecting.

'What about 'er old lady?' somebody shouted.

Ted responded that he didn't know. 'Might still be in the Barley Mow buried under a beer barrel,' he added in a sarcastic manner.

As assumptions sprang up like mushrooms, Maisie sat with

her brow knitted in a deep frown. What with the bombing, it wasn't easy to find out what was going on in the city and the fact that the Battle of Britain was being fought on their doorstep. Telephone boxes had been blown off their perches and many lines were down. Like the tramlines, they would take some time to repair – if it ever happened.

Aggie admitted to having been listening to the wireless from early that morning. 'Lot of clearing up to do, so I 'ad a fag and listened to the wireless. Lord Haw Haw's been on the wireless on about Bristol wanting to replace the trams with buses, and their bombers 'ad done the job. Bloody cheek.'

'But what about Edith,' said Maisie. 'Anyone been around to her 'ouse?'

'We could ask a neighbour, I suppose,' ventured Bridget.

'Or phone the hospital. You're good at that, Bridget.'

The two of them exchanged looks of understanding. The last time they'd phoned the hospital it had been about Phyllis.

They'd heard from one of their workmates that lived in that direction that there was no damage around Midland Road even though it was a prime target.

From necessity, a great need to lift the gloom, the conversation turned to more pleasant matters.

Maisie had received letters from Sid, the closest thing she'd ever had to a real boyfriend. At first, she'd been a bit lazy replying, but of late she wrote to him a bit more often, mostly because his letters had become more interesting. He was somewhere in the Middle East but couldn't tell her where. '*There are a lot of camels here, the sun's hot and the sea is the deepest blue you could ever imagine.*'

She'd even let Bridget read them, who'd immediately surmised that he was in Egypt.

'You got any letters from abroad?' Maisie asked her as she

tucked her letter into her overall pocket. The inference was obvious and caused a deep blush to come to Bridget's face.

'No. I don't know anyone in the armed forces,' she snapped, loath to even mention Lyndon by name, let alone admit that he was likely engaged to somebody else.

'I was meaning your RAF bloke down in Devon. Thought 'e might 'ave gone abroad.'

Both Maisie and Bridget knew she didn't mean any such thing. Bridget's reluctance to talk about Lyndon was noticeable and the only reason she had mentioned James was because his story was intertwined with that of her evacuated brothers and sisters. She'd admitted nothing else, certainly not of any intimacy shared.

* * *

One of the girls in work who lived close to the city centre remarked on the damage she'd seen, of rubble and glass strewn over the roads and gaping holes – like missing teeth – amongst those buildings still standing.

As they made their way to one telephone box that was still standing, Maisie and Bridget had spotted a staircase hanging against the remaining wall, a collapsed roof and a bed sitting on top a pile of rubble.

Sleet beat against their faces as they waited for the queue to use the telephone box to diminish. Once it was their turn, they both huddled inside, Bridget taking off her woollen mittens before dialling. As before, Maisie got out a handful of pennies.

Having learned from their earlier experience, Bridget proclaimed herself Edith's sister.

'I need to know whether I have to make room in my place for the children,' she explained.

'Ah yes,' said the voice on the other end. 'Two children of a family of four died in the early hours of this morning. The mother and surviving two children are critically ill.'

As the news sank in, Bridget replaced the phone.

'Poor Edith.' Her voice was little above a whisper. Edith's children were as much a casualty of this war as the widow and children attending the funeral of a father killed at Dunkirk.

'What killed them? Was it gas?'

Bridget shook her head and relayed what had been told to her, eyes moist with unshed tears. 'They died of food poisoning – eating bad meat.'

Maisie froze. She couldn't speak. She could barely blink. Everything that Phyllis had reported came back to her. Up until now she had resolved not to shop Frank Miles, unless he did something that she couldn't possibly ignore. This was that something, but how best to shop him without betraying her whereabouts to Eddie Bridgeman and bringing his vengeance down on her head?

Weary from work, Maisie fell into bed but couldn't sleep. Tossing and turning, she stared into the darkness, her thoughts diving round all over the place. She *would* shop him. She *had* to, but not directly. She had to get somebody else to do it, somebody who hated him as much as she did; somebody who would savour the sweet taste of revenge.

An hour or two after midnight, she came to a viable conclusion. There was one person who hated Frank Miles more than she did, one who might be able to distract any semblance of blame falling on her.

Grace Wells, her natural grandmother, blamed Frank Miles

for killing her son after finding out about his relationship and the child he'd had with Maisie's mother – resulting in her birth. There was, it seemed, no other option than to visit Totterdown and ask for her grandmother's help.

24

PHYLLIS

When Phyllis had first escaped from Hilda Harvey, she'd almost skipped to her job at the soap factory, but familiarity now festered with contempt. She hated the smell of the place. It wouldn't be so bad if she worked in the office rather than in the steamy, smelly area where the liquid was boiled then left to cool and solidify.

It did have a small office, but she didn't see much of an opening for a secretary or even a humble filing clerk. However, she did mention it to Mr Grove, the manager, who'd leered at her, groped her bottom and said that he would see if there was an opening for her – if she played her cards right.

She understood his meaning and from then on had done her best to keep out of his way.

Although she hated the job, and the house in York Street was far from being a spacious hotel, Mrs Proctor had made it far cosier than when Maisie used to live there. Not that its cosiness was Phyllis's chief reason for not moving on to better things. Other jobs beckoned and so did other lodgings, but Sam Proctor was the most wonderful man she'd ever met. He was also a superb lover, something she'd found out one night when Mrs

Proctor had gone to the Odeon picture house with an old friend. The front room sofa had a few loose springs that squealed in time with their lovemaking, so much so that Sam had made a joke about it.

'If they springs get much louder, the whole street will know what we're up to.'

Driven by their passion, their laughter was short-lived.

'Are you sure?' In the dim glow of the standard lamp standing like a spindly lighthouse in the corner, she saw both passion as well as reluctance in his eyes. As an act of reassurance, but also a signal of her impatience, she pushed his hand up her skirt as far as her stocking tops.

For a moment he held his breath before he gave in and his hand travelled further. His body was hard, his touch gentle and it wasn't long before they were rushing to take their clothes off.

Phyllis's knickers, recently made from an old silk chemise she'd bought at a Salvation Army thrift counter, slid like water down her silk stockings – bought at enormous expense from a spiv with a suitcase who hung round down behind the engine sheds at the edge of the marshalling yards.

This evening, Sam was due home again on leave and hopefully they'd get the chance for a repeat performance. It all depended on his mother having somewhere else to go.

On entering the house, the smell of something cooking wafted out along the narrow passageway. Its smell was welcome after that of the soap works, as was the glow of the cosy interior, and she blocked her mind to what other people were enduring following the air raid.

As she went upstairs to get changed, music drifted out from the wireless in the living room – 'Moonlight and Roses' – and then she heard his voice, deeper above the delicate tune that she so loved.

Phyllis's heels clattered down the stairs. She was wearing her best shoes and her best dress, hair loose and cascading down her back, make-up newly retouched.

The moment he saw her, he put down his teacup and got up from the chair.

'Phyllis!' Even though his mother was still present, he gave her a massive hug. 'I bin thinking about you all day!'

'What with the air raid, I thought you'd be late,' she cried excitedly, aware that Mrs Proctor was frowning at such a public display of affection.

Sam's beaming expression changed and suddenly he was holding her at arms' length.

'Me and the regiment are being posted overseas. Can't say where of course, but...'

Phyllis froze. It was as if the floor had opened beneath her. 'No.' It was all she could say and in a very tiny voice. 'Do you know for how long?'

'I've already asked 'im that,' declared Mrs Proctor, her expression tighter than usual.

It was hard for Phyllis to read the look on Mrs Proctor's face. There was concern of course that her son was being sent overseas, but also something that bordered on relief, which was more difficult to understand.

Phyllis's legs felt weak and she was scared at whatever it was she was about to hear.

'As long as it takes to win this bloody war, I suppose,' he responded with a 'chin up' sort of smile. 'But we'll do it,' he said with a sudden burst of joviality. 'And then there's no more going off to foreign parts for me. Blighty for me forever!'

Though tears pricked her eyes, she smiled back at him. One question remained to be asked, but Mrs Proctor answered it before she had the chance.

'Off on the train to Southampton tomorrow.'

Sam elaborated. 'Nine o'clock tomorrow morning. Temple Meads.'

'I'll come with you,' she blurted.

He shook his head. 'No. I don't want any waving hankies and crying buckets at the station. I'll say goodbye to you both 'ere.'

Tears flowed from his mother's eyes. 'Sam! My darling Sam!'

'Don't you worry, Mum. I want my best girls to take good care of each other whilst I'm away.'

'It's so unfair,' said Phyllis in a tremulous voice, her bottom lip quivering.

He laughed. 'Hardly. I was thinking we could pop along to the Duke of York for a quick one. You up for that? Mum's coming too.'

For a moment her heart soared. Phyllis would get to have a little time with him before he left. As it was, his mother would be there. She'd never been hostile towards her, yet tonight it seemed that something had changed. The only thing she could put it down to was that his mother was jealous of her relationship with her son, which reminded her of Hilda Harvey.

* * *

The morning came too soon for Phyllis's liking. Cloaked in a thick fog, York Street took on a ghostly look, even though it was only seven thirty in the morning.

Sam's arms were warm around her, but still she sobbed.

'Now come on. I said no tears. No fretting about me getting there in time neither. I've been taught 'ow to quick march, ain't I,' said Sam. In order to prove his point, he marched a short distance up and down the pavement, turned and marched six more.

Phyllis laughed whilst brushing threatening tears from her

eyes. His mother called him a silly sod and told him to stop messing about.

Sam put his arm round his mother and kissed her on the forehead. 'Now don't you worry about nothing, Ma. I can fight as well as march, even run if I need to!'

Even in the dim light, Phyllis could see his attempt at a cheery expression, though it did nothing much to diminish her concern.

On letting his mother go, he put one strong arm round her, pulled her close and kissed her. After that he whispered into her ear, 'Wait fer me, Phyl. I'll do right by you when I get back and that's a promise.'

After heaving his kitbag over his shoulder, he disappeared swiftly into the fog without looking back.

An ominous silence accompanied the two women as they went back inside the house, each careful not to let the light from the passageway fall out into the street before the door was closed.

Mrs Proctor stood in front of Phyllis with her lips pursed and hands tightly clasped in front of her. 'I want a word.' Her tone was unusually harsh.

The warmth of the living room and the smell of recently eaten breakfast still lingered in the air. Coals damped down for the night were already glowing and the kettle normally singing on the gas stove was now sitting on the hob at one side of the fireplace.

Mrs Proctor turned to face her, arms folded and a hard look on her face. In fact, thought Phyllis, her eyes looked harder than nubs of coal.

She swallowed her apprehension. It couldn't possibly be anything serious, could it?

'Is something wrong?' she asked.

Mrs Proctor's jaw stiffened. 'Yes. You're a wrong 'un and I want you out of here.'

Phyllis opened and closed her mouth like a breathless gold-fish. 'You can't do that! Sam expects me to be here when he gets back. Me and him – well – we might be getting married.'

Mrs Proctor shook her head and glowered. 'I don't think so.' She began to tap her fingers on the elbows of her folded arms. 'What about the husband you already got? What you going to do about him?'

The whole room seemed to spin round at an alarming rate.

'I'm... a... widow,' she managed to stutter.

There was no let-up in Mrs Proctor's angry glare. 'Not according to your mother-in-law. She's 'ad word that your old man is still alive.'

'What?'

It was as if all the blood had drained from Phyllis's body. Robert was alive?

'I could accept you getting involved with my boy and being a widow, but you didn't say that. You said you were single. I let it be last night, seeing as Sam was due 'ome, but he won't be back for a while. Whilst he's gone, I think the best thing you can do is pack your things and get out of here.'

'I receive a widow's pension!'

Mrs Proctor shook her head. 'That ain't what you told me when you first come 'ere. Anyways, I don't believe you. I want you out.'

'But where will I go?' said Phyllis, more to herself than to Mrs Proctor. She was devastated, angry but also confused and afraid.

'That's your problem, but I want you out of this house and away from my boy. He don't deserve to be lied to!'

25

MAISIE

Rehearsing in her head what she would say, Maisie knocked on the door in Totterdown that she had only visited once before. A voice sounded from the other side.

'Who's there?'

'It's me. Maisie. Your granddaughter,' she added more loudly.

The sound of a bolt being slid grated from behind the closed door and there was Grace Wells.

'Well, you ain't bin 'ere for a while. And now you show up,' came the grumbling from within.

For a moment Maisie suspected the door might be slammed in her face. Her grandmother narrowed her eyes and peered searchingly into her face and she fumbled round her neck, her fingers eventually closing over a pair of spectacles hanging on a black bootlace. Her eyes were amplified by the thick lenses.

'I need your 'elp.'

Grace drew in her chin and shook her head. 'Don't count on me if yer in the club. I don't do that any more.'

'That's not the kind of 'elp I want. It's about Frank Miles. I want to shop 'im to the law, but can't. I thought you might be able to 'elp.'

It was as though she'd batted at Grace Wells's face with a carpet beater. Her expression changed. She stood back level with a now wide-open door. 'I'd strangle 'im with me bare 'ands if I could.'

Maisie stepped inside, the thick rugs doing nothing to mute the creaking floorboards beneath their feet.

As she entered the rear room where frightened women had once come to terminate pregnancies they did not want, it struck Maisie that what she was about to ask might go some way to levelling out what her grandmother did for – or rather – to these women.

Grace sat herself heavily in an old armchair that squealed in protest. She'd put on a considerable amount of weight since Maisie had last seen her.

The smell of food was as before, but there was also that of drink. It seemed it wasn't only Edith's mother who was hitting the bottle.

For a moment Grace said nothing, though Maisie noticed a flicker of interest from behind her thick glasses.

'Is it a 'anging offence? I 'ope it bloody well is. My boy won't rest in peace and my mind won't be at ease until Frank Miles 'as breathed 'is last breath!' Her voice was more gravelly than Maisie recalled, as though she was trying to swallow something that couldn't be swallowed.

She outlined what had happened and her plan for putting him away for good. 'Two kids are dead 'cause of 'im, two more ill and the mother, Edith Jones, is still sick thanks to 'im selling rotten meat.' She stopped as something occurred to her. According to what Phyllis had told her, there had been a whole crowd of people buying that meat. How many more had fallen ill? she wondered.

'Edith Jones you say. Is she Betty Morland's daughter?'

Maisie had hoped the family would be known to her grandmother and it seemed from this remark that they were. 'Is that 'er name? Drinks a lot of gin.'

'Grace nodded. 'Drowns 'erself in anything she can get 'er 'ands on.'

Maisie chose her words carefully. 'I know it's a lot to ask, but I thought that in some way you could shop 'im, point them in the right direction, as it were.'

Grace sucked in her lips, making it appear as though she had none at all. 'I'm not sure any evidence I'd give would carry much weight. Besides that, I wouldn't want to come up before the beak and say that I'd been buying rotten meat so that's 'ow I knew.'

Maisie sighed. This was the same problem anyone would have if they admitted seeing him flogging tarnished meat. 'I thought you might be able to think of some way round it.'

'So why ain't you gone to the police?' Grace's eyes fixed on this granddaughter that she hardly knew but instantly loved because she was her son's offspring. Not that she was one for showing her feelings, but that didn't mean she had none. She'd had a hard life, seen grim things that could hurt bad if she let them. So she kept her feelings to herself.

Maisie swallowed. 'I don't want nothing to do with 'im or Eddie Bridgeman.'

Grace's eyebrows rose. 'What's 'e got to do with it?'

Maisie blinked, swallowed her nerves and took a deep breath. 'Eddie will be after me if 'e finds out I knew where Frank was working and I didn't tell 'im.' She shivered. 'And I didn't like the way 'e used to look at me – as though 'e was stripping me clothes off.'

The light of understanding shone in her grandmother's eyes. She knew enough of what men were capable of when taken with devilish desires, uncaring of the consequences. The consequences had been her stock in trade until her eyes began to fail. Luckily she had foreseen old age and infirmity robbing her of that particular line of business. Young women still came knocking at her door desperate to get themselves out of a difficult situation. The sad young women were sent elsewhere. There was always somebody to help as long as they could pay for the service.

Grace Wells was a money lender as well as an abortionist. She'd made the decision early on to reinvest what she earned from one line of business to finance lending money at a high interest rate. The more she lent, the more she made, and once her boy John was gone, making money became her saviour. What had started small-scale had bloomed, so much so it had enabled her to buy this house from a landlord who'd fallen on hard times. She even knew Eddie Bridgeman but wouldn't tell Maisie that.

Things had changed the day Maisie had showed up following the death of her mother. She hadn't foreseen it happening. The girl wasn't to know how much she resembled her father, Grace's son: the same dark brown hair and eyes; the pert chin that reminded her of her own when she was young. The slight build was inherited from her too and she didn't doubt that inside Maisie's pretty head was an astute brain.

Grace clenched her jaw. 'Is there anything else you can add to what you've already told me?'

Maisie dredged up every last little detail she knew. 'Edith bought rotten meat and her mother must 'ave known she did. They wouldn't throw 'er into prison seeing as she's lost most of 'er family – would they?'

Grace nodded thoughtfully.

For her part, Maisie felt that a great weight had been lifted from her chest. She sighed, then chirped, 'How about I put that kettle on and make you a cup of tea while you think about it?'

Without waiting for Grace to reply, she popped up from the chair, filled the kettle and lit the gas.

With Frank out of the way and Eddie unaware of her whereabouts, she could forge a new life and would leave Bridget's house as quickly as possible. It had been good of them to take her in, but it was a borrowed bed, short term until the kids came home. Anyway, she still didn't want them implicated in anything.

'Leave it with me,' Grace said at last.

Maisie thanked her, but even once she was outside, the pavements crisp beneath her feet as the first frost of December took hold, she couldn't resist looking nervously over her shoulder – just in case Eddie Bridgeman was closer than she thought.

* * *

After Maisie had gone, Grace sat hard-faced before the fireplace staring at the one remaining photograph she had of her son before checking her ledger for the name and address of Edith's mother. Betty Morland was no big borrower, but she hadn't been out of debt for years. Beside her address she'd written down the names of the pubs she frequented, most of them rough cider houses. That's where she would find her, and perhaps between them they could bring Frank Miles to justice. They were two old ladies with a great deal in common.

Bridget had related what she knew about Edith and her kids to her workmates. A sombre mood fell on the stripping room from then on.

Every so often, her gaze drifted to Edith's empty stool. Physically she was still alive, but how would she be having lost two of her children?

Tears pricked her eyes. She'd never met Edith's kids, but she ached for their terrible predicament and that of their mother.

Maisie so wanted to assure Bridget that the person who'd harmed the Jones family would be punished, but that would mean having to explain about her grandmother, who she was and what she was. She was sure Bridget would disapprove.

The sudden wailing of the air-raid siren brought an instant scraping of chairs as the women grabbed handbags, shopping and gas masks. It sounded like a thundering of hooves as hundreds of heels thudded along the corridors and down the steps into the cellar.

Aggie lit the gas under the tea urn. Bridget helped her set out mugs and teacups.

Mr Parker, one of the factory's air-raid wardens, stood guard over the milk and sugar, a pair of tongs in one hand.

'One lump of sugar per person,' he called out.

Aggie attempted to take them off him, but he was having none of it.

'I'm not taking sugar meself,' said Aggie. She patted her ample hips. 'Got to take care of me figure.'

Mr Parker was unrelenting, but despite his grim-faced frugality, a unique cheerfulness prevailed.

Aggie poured tea and Bridget added milk. Mr Parker added sugar in a very particular manner.

'What the 'ell's up with 'im?' remarked Aggie.

Bridget smiled. 'I think he must have read *Oliver Twist* and is waiting for somebody to say, "Please sir. Can I have some more."'

Aggie chuckled. 'I've read that book.'

'I know you did. I leant it to you.'

Aggie looked surprised. 'Did you?' she chuckled again. 'Yeah, I s'pose you did, you being the great reader that you are. Must admit, I likes reading better than I ever did. Especially now in this war. I can pretend I'm somewhere else when I'm reading.'

The siren had ceased its monotonous wail. Their ears strained for the sound of aircraft, though it was difficult to hear much down where they were.

Bridget placed a record on the gramophone, wound up the shiny handle and once it was up to speed, placed the needle onto the edge of the record.

There was laughter and then a glorious sing-along to 'The Sun Had Got His Hat On'; and the Jack Hylton Orchestra.

Maisie's slender feet tapped in time to the music and then she was on her feet, tap dancing, swinging her arms, laughing as she danced. Everyone was mesmerised. Nobody had seen her dance before. Her slight frame spun on slender legs, her arms held gracefully to either side.

She made saucy jokes about Hitler that she'd heard in the pub before she'd moved in with Bridget. At first, Aggie Hill's face was a picture of astonishment, and then she was laughing along with everyone else, tears of mirth rolling down her cheeks.

Bridget laughed, though at the same time wondered what was happening in the world above them. Seeing the devastation of bombing had affected her. Besides the sad fact that people had died, there was also the realisation that there would be no more window shopping round Castle Street, which was now little more than piles of rubble.

Normally in December the Christmas lights would be brightening the streets, and the smell of horse chestnuts roasting from kerbside braziers would perfume the air and warm the hands. There had been no lights for two winters now. Shop windows had been decorated but unlit which gave them a dour greyness despite their attempt at festive jollity. Everyone had commented how much better they'd looked when the lights were on, but even the greyness would have been better than the present situation. The lights had gone off in those shops forever. There was nothing left except blackened ruins.

Bridget hid her heartfelt sigh behind a bright smile. Maisie was belting out another song along with the record on the gramophone and everyone was joining in, 'The Village of Christmas Pie.' One or two were marching round in time with the music. Aggie's voice was louder than everyone else.

'Heard from your chap?' asked Maisie, flopping beside her, breathless from all that dancing and singing.

For a moment Bridget was inclined to ask which one she was referring to, but held back. She plumped for James because he was the one she was most likely to see again though always her thoughts went back to Lyndon. She still felt let down and something of a fool.

'You mean James. I get the odd letter. He's on Ops but hoping to get home for Christmas, but there's no guarantee.'

'There's a war on,' exclaimed Maisie. Her brown eyes shone with interest as a new record – a Fred Astaire and Ginger Rogers' number – danced its way round the turntable.

Just as she got to her feet, ready to twirl round the cellar, the all-clear sounded.

'Come on, you lot. Back to work,' shouted one of the foremen.

'And there was me just getting into me stride,' trilled Maisie, flushed with exertion and tendrils of glossy brown hair framing her face.

'Now Carwardines is gone, we need to decide where to meet up on a Saturday afternoon and for that we need Phyllis.'

Aggie confirmed Phyllis had not been to the Llandoger asking for them. 'I only seem to be gettin' unwelcome guests these days,' grumbled Aggie.

Recognising that Aggie preferred to mind her own business, Maisie had not pried into why Eddie Bridgeman had visited her. In time, Aggie would tell her, but if she didn't, there was nothing she could do about it.

* * *

It was Saturday afternoon when they made their way to York Street meaning to find Phyllis at home and drag her out to somewhere they could talk in peace.

The street itself was unchanged since Maisie had lived there, scruffy urchins swinging from a rope hanging from a lamp post, women gossiping on their doorsteps. Hostile eyes glanced at them until they recognised her.

'All right, Maisie me luvver? Ain't seen you for a while.'

Maisie gave them a weak smile and pulled her hat low over her eyes, her collar up so it hid her face. She hadn't wanted to come back here, fearing who she might see.

The house looked cleaner and less neglected than it used to be, the windowpanes and net curtain as white as any others in the street, perhaps even whiter.

Having not seen Bridget since she had accompanied Phyllis to her door, Mrs Proctor looked askance. 'Can I help you?'

Bridget explained. 'We're Phyllis's friends and usually we meet up at Carwardines on a Saturday afternoon, but it's all gone now, so we were going to catch up and sort out where we'll be going in future.'

Mrs Proctor retained her sour expression which Bridget found a trifle worrying.

'She is all right, isn't she?'

Mrs Proctor's face soured. 'She ain't 'ere and I don't want 'er 'ere.'

Maisie dared to ask why.

Mrs Proctor's glowering look switched from Bridget to Maisie. 'Because she's a dirty little liar. Messing about with my Sam when she's already married.'

'Widowed,' said Maisie. 'She's widowed.'

'Missing in action, presumed dead,' added Bridget, sensing something was very wrong and that such a piece of information might make Mrs Proctor look less angry.

'Well, that ain't what her mother-in-law said! Now I'll thank you to clear off and let me get in out of the cold.'

Bridget gaped. Mrs Harvey had been there! Well, that explained it!

Maisie butted in. 'Mrs Harvey ain't all there. Reckons the War Office is lying to 'er and don't know what they're doing.'

'I don't care what she thinks. All that I know is that Phyllis told me and my Sam that she was single. No 'usband was ever mentioned, widow or otherwise. Now, if you don't mind...'

Seeing that the door was about to close on them, Maisie jammed her foot into the gap. 'Can you tell us where she's gone?'

'I don't know and I don't care.'

Her foot was shifted and the door slammed shut.

'I wonder whether she still works at the soap factory,' said Bridget.

Maisie strode across the street and asked one of the women who had worked at the soap factory all her life.

She shook her head. 'No. Left when that stuck-up bitch living in your old 'ouse chucked 'er out. It was dark, but I 'appened to be up in the bedroom, 'eard the racket and took a look.'

The two friends fell silent as they left the street until Bridget shook her head.

'I can't believe she didn't come to us for help. Where can she be?'

Maisie understood what it was like to want to hide away from people who frightened you. In Phyllis's case, she was trying to leave her old life, just as she had done, but in the process she was relying on her heart and wasn't using her head.

'P'raps she's got another chap,' she said.

Bridget proclaimed she didn't believe that was the case, but a doubt set in. Phyllis had always adored being the centre of attention and there was no doubt she was very attractive and adored flattery. Phyllis getting involved with Sam had shocked her. She had to concede that to some extent Maisie might be right, but she didn't want to believe it. In that direction was trouble.

27

Bright moonlight shining from a clear sky made the frosty ground glisten like icing on a cake.

Frank Miles's wide grin exposed a number of missing teeth. He knew he looked ugly. He also knew that they could be replaced, though of course that cost money. Perhaps by the end of this war, if not sooner, he might be able to afford a gold tooth like those Eddie Bridgeman sported. The rate his bit of shady business was going, it wasn't totally impossible.

Tonight even the moon was shining in his favour, giving him enough light to drive without even turning on the blinkered headlights. What with the white-painted kerbs, he could see his way well enough. Turning on the headlights meant others seeing him – especially the authorities – and he could well do without that.

Thanks to the cold weather, the meat of late had kept well and wasn't stinking so bad that he had to wash away the green bits before selling it to his regular customers. A few of them had asked if he was the bloke flogging the bad meat reported in the newspapers. He'd asked them if they'd been ill, to which they'd replied that they hadn't.

'Then it can't be me then, can it!' he'd exclaimed. 'I'm still 'ere and so are you!'

From what he knew, it was only one family affected and two kids had died, though he refused to believe it was down to him. Kids were susceptible to illnesses: measles, chickenpox and stuff. He'd had some himself as a boy, though couldn't swear as to what diseases they had been.

In the meantime, he was doing pretty well, thanks of course to the day job. What a stroke of luck that had been, and in more ways than one. Few people could get hold of petrol, but seeing as the van was commercial and used in the transport of food products and likewise the lorry which ferried essential commodities such as bones for rendering down, he didn't have too much of a problem. It didn't take much extra to enable him to continue in his sideline of flogging off condemned meat. All he had to do was slot in his activities between visits by agents of the Ministry of Food and Agriculture, and so far in that aspect too, he'd been lucky. They were busy people.

The alley where he usually set up shop was untouched by moonlight, black as the Ace of Spades in fact. That too he decided was lucky, all the better to cloak his black-market and highly illegal shenanigans. He liked that word, *shenanigans*; it sounded a clever word and made him feel a bit clever.

The blackness was total, so for a moment at least he was obliged to turn on the headlights, the top halves of which were painted black to prevent them being seen by enemy aircraft.

Small pools of light picked out patches of ice and frost on the cobbles, plus stout shoes and up legs as far as the knees.

As he slowed, it occurred to him that the crowd were surging around and behind him. Faces, and to some extent, upper bodies were difficult to distinguish, such was the blanket blackness of the alley. Here and there he thought he detected the gleam of a brass button.

'What the...'

Suddenly he was blinded by the glare of a flashlight.

'Sod it!' He used a few other choice words under his breath. He was rumbled. Caught in a trap. Somebody was out to get him.

The gears crunched as he attempted to slam the gearstick into reverse. The crunching noise increased to grinding. The van shuddered. Thrusting the gearstick forward coincided with the door being tugged open. A burly set of hands reached in, grabbed him by the shoulders and hauled him out. Half in and half out, he tried to brace his hands against the door frame, kicked out and tried to hook his feet under the steering wheel.

'Come on, Frank. Best for you if you comes quietly.'

The first burly hands were joined by another pair and he was passed like a parcel from one policeman to another until he was standing more or less upright.

'I ain't done nothing,' he shouted.

The flashlight lit up the iron-hard features of an older man. 'That ain't what we heard,' he said. The insignia of a sergeant was caught by the carefully focused light.

'You can't do anything and it ain't my van,' he shouted.

'We are arresting you on suspicion of selling contaminated meat – might be manslaughter, even murder, so anything you do say will be written down and given in evidence...'

Frank burst into almost maniacal laughter. 'You ain't got no evidence for that. I works for the bloke who owns this van. It's legit.'

He thought the accusation of murder or even manslaughter was a bit much and from past experience knew he could be off the hook on the other charge of selling rotten meat unless a witness could be found. He very much doubted anyone would step forward and admit to buying food on the black market. They had families to support and were unlikely to want to get involved.

'We've got a witness,' the sergeant declared and sounded mighty pleased about it. 'You're for the 'igh jump this time, Frank. You'll be inside for the duration and for a long time after that.'

No matter what they said, Frank continued to protest his innocence all the way to Bristol's Bridewell Station. Constrained with handcuffs, he was still protesting when they manhandled him through the big double doors of the police station. Though he dragged his legs, the toes of his boots scraping over the floor, their strong arms held him upright.

Being surrounded by coppers was the stuff of nightmares, but he hadn't been prepared for what happened next. Shouting obscenities normally the domain of dockers or other rough men, a woman burst through the cordon surrounding him. In one swift move, she swung a leather shopping bag, clouting him on the side of the head. Whatever it contained it weighed heavy. His head spun and his eyes seemed to rattle like marbles inside it. His legs splayed in all directions when he stumbled over two or three large King Edward potatoes that rolled across the floor. That explained the weight of the shopping bag!

Somebody he did not recognise dived under the arms of the coppers holding him.

'You killed my grandchildren and I'd like to 'ang you meself,' she screeched, her long fingernails clawing at his face.

'Now, now, Mrs Morland...'

Arms whirling like a windmill in a brisk breeze, even the uniformed constables found her a challenge.

As his vision cleared, Frank caught sight of the woman screeching at him; small and wiry, her hat sitting like a fat black crow on a nest of wiry grey hair.

Self-preservation in life was second only to making money. He drew back, wary of those sharp nails drawing more blood. 'Get 'er off me!'

The stink of booze came with the sharp finger she pointed his way. 'My daughter bought yer rotten meat!'

He looked helplessly at the coppers. 'I don't know this old cow. She's mad. Get 'er away.'

Taking pleasure from Frank's discomfort – a bloke they'd had occasion to run in before but never for anything as serious as this – the smug-faced bobbies smiled.

Encourage by their attitude, Edith's mother lunged in anew.

'I knows who you are and so did my Edith. She seen you before when you was attacking yer daughter outside Wills's. A bit of asking around and I knew who you were, Frank Miles.'

The colour drained from Frank's face. For the first time since being arrested, he was scared. 'Did Maisie tell you where to find me?' he said in a spit-curdling snarl.

She looked at him askance. 'Who's Maisie?'

'My daughter...' His words fell away.

The old crone looked puzzled. 'I ain't never met yer daughter. Told you, my Edith knew 'er.' Her expression turned sorrowful as she addressed the station sergeant behind the desk. 'My poor Edith. You ought to see 'er in that bed, all white and pale, barely able to talk she was, but she knew you. That she bloody well did.'

Their hour of entertainment over, the police began to push Frank towards the door that he knew from experience led down into the white-tiled cells of the clink.

'Off to the cells for you, Frank me lad. Get used to it. You ain't likely to be out for a long while.'

* * *

Grim of countenance, Edith's mother left the Bridewell feeling satisfied, though still angry. Frank Miles wasn't to know that in one way he'd turned her life around. After what had happened to her family, she'd sworn that if the police brought him in, she'd give up the drink. She'd had her last brown ale earlier that evening.

Other customers in the pub had treated her promise to give up the booze with disbelief but, out of consideration for her terrible loss, kept their mouths shut.

Only one other woman had been there, the one who had primed her with the details of the man who had killed members of her family. She'd known Grace Wells for years; in fact, they'd been at school together. She'd also borrowed money from her, and it had come as something of a surprise when Grace said she would wipe the slate clean as long as she put the finger on Frank Miles. Even if Grace hadn't promised she'd be debt-free, it would have been a great pleasure to do it anyway.

28

PHYLLIS

It had been some weeks since Phyllis had left York Street and moved into her new address. Numbed by her sudden eviction, she had walked as if in a dream to where she guessed she could move in right away.

The room in Stokes Croft with its dingy interior, hard-bitten landlady and a houseful of cats that she'd viewed with Maisie had still been available.

'Five shillings a week,' said the landlady.

Phyllis carefully counted out the money from what remained of her last wages, the beige suitcase that had once been her father's sitting solidly against her leg. If only she still had her army pay book – or widow's pension – whichever was appropriate – but that was locked in Hilda Harvey's bureau. She was within her rights to go round there and demand she give it to her, but truth was, she shuddered at the thought. Better to work her socks off than find herself a virtual prisoner there.

It plagued her to wonder whether Robert was still alive or not. For his sake, she hoped he was, but either way she would never go back to him. For the first time in her life, she was free. She would not give it up easily.

Her rented room was some way from the soap factory and she would have stayed there if Hilda hadn't also gone round there and made good her story. 'She's been carrying on with another man, and her husband away fighting.'

Her employers had let her go. That too was something of a relief.

Though Christmas hadn't yet come, let alone New Year, Phyllis made resolutions that for now at least she intended keeping. The first one was that she would write to Sam at his last known army address before he was posted overseas. He was her first priority and she had to make the effort to explain why she hadn't told him the truth. Hopefully the letter would follow him to his new posting. She only prayed that his reply wouldn't be redirected to York Street, where Mrs Proctor would probably throw it onto the fire.

The news that Robert might very well be alive had come as a shock. Was Hilda Harvey telling the truth, or still clinging on to her dearest wish?

The other thing she didn't yet want to face was telling Maisie and Bridget what had happened and her present dire circumstances. They'd gone out of their way to help her. She felt guilty but reassured herself that she hadn't really let them down.

For a time, she wandered the city streets thinking through her options. She also wrote to Sam hoping against hope that he would get her letter.

As she assessed her options, she worked casually behind the bar of a pub, did a little waitressing in a coffee shop. One such coffee shop was directly opposite the devastation that had once been the series of streets where she and her friends had window shopped. All that remained was rubble, twisted metal and solitary second-floor doors hanging from crumbling walls, swinging windows from what remained of a frame.

She stared for a while, numb but determined to climb out of this hole she was in. Everything had changed or was changing and so was she.

Christmas was only a week away and people had done their best to decorate windows already plastered with gummed paper to prevent injury from flying glass.

Her spirits low, Phyllis plodded on, winding her way through crowds of uniforms and shoulders displaying the insignia of many nations.

It was surprising how jolly everyone sounded. She didn't feel jolly, that was for sure.

Consumed by deeply depressing thoughts, she ignored friendly smiles and words and at first didn't hear her mother's voice calling out to her.

'Phyllis. Phyllis.'

It wasn't until a set of painted fingernails closed over her arm that she came to a halt.

For a moment she was tongue-tied. Her mother was wearing a leopard-skin hat that was most probably home-made, but elegant all the same. Her coat was black checked with big patch pockets and a fox fur, glassy eyes shining, was draped across her shoulders.

Beside her was a man. He had a kindly face and dark bristly black eyebrows, a thin moustache above his top lip and a few silvery streaks ran through his blue-black hair. He wasn't tall but gave the impression of being strong, having wide shoulders and firmly placed legs.

Her mother smiled like a shy young girl, her eyes fluttering up at her beau. 'This is Matthew Horsley. Matt, my fiancée,' she said with a lisping sound, her cheeks turning candy floss pink. 'Matt, this is my daughter, Phyllis.'

'Pleased to meet you, Phyllis.' A strong hand clasped hers, bright white teeth flashed when he smiled. There followed a slightly more serious frown. 'I'm sorry to hear about your husband. Have you heard anything?'

Unwilling to disclose her mother-in-law's visit to York Street and losing her job, she shook her head. 'The news stays the same. Missing in action, presumed dead.'

'It must be hard for you.' Matt Horsley had kind eyes and sounded genuinely caring. She suddenly understood why her mother had fallen for him.

'Yes. It's the not knowing. I don't know what to do until I know for sure.'

'Mrs Harvey came round and said she had news of Sam. Insisted that you had to be told and where could she find you.' Her mother frowned. 'I directed her to York Street. Did I do wrong?"

'It was the worst thing you could have done. She came round and made a right racket and caused me to be evicted. I won't go into the details. I had to get out of there dead quick. I managed to find a room and a temporary job, until something better comes along.'

'Oh, Phyl. I'm so sorry. Surely there's something we can do.' There was a flicker of guilt on her mother's beautifully made-up face before she addressed her handsome Canadian officer. 'Do you have any suggestions, Matt?'

Phyllis inwardly groaned. She knew her mother was only trying to be helpful, but she considered her behaviour too sugary, like a young girl.

Matt Horsley took his arm from round her mother's waist and adjusted his tie. 'Well, seeing as you've got no kids, you could join up.'

It didn't seem like much of an option to Phyllis. She'd seen some women who'd joined up clomping around in heavy shoes and thick lisle stockings. And all that marching about on a parade ground which although she had once considered the idea had put her off. 'But I don't know anything.' It seemed a reasonable enough excuse.

'You might know more than you think. You can write, can't you? Clerical workers are always needed, and you might even be able to get some extra training – like typing for instance. The army, navy and air force always need typists and not just to type letters.'

Suddenly all the exasperation she'd harboured for quite some time exploded like a sky rocket. Perhaps, after all, something good had come out of her nights bashing away on a typewriter and falling for a man who said she was good at it. It was a far-fetched hope, but she might even end up posted close to Sam – wherever that might be.

'Thank you,' she said, her spirits climbing up to new and dizzying heights. 'I've always wanted to work in an office. Do you have any idea who I might approach?'

Matt nodded in the direction of a large sign saying:

Recruiting Office – Women's Auxiliary Airforce

There was a queue outside. Some women were clutching handbags nervously to their chest. Some looked very young. Others were replenishing their make-up, glittering compacts held aloft before their face, powder-puffs patting their cheeks, fresh lipstick applied.

Phyllis suddenly felt as though a door that she thought firmly shut had sprung open.

Both her mother and Matt looked surprised when she planted a kiss on his cheek before planting one on that of her mother and sprinting off to join the crocodile of girls and women waiting to join the war effort.

She suddenly felt desperate to let her hair fall free and put on a bit of make-up.

'Excuse me,' she said to a girl that was applying powder and lipstick. 'I've left mine at home. Do you think...?' She nodded at the make-up.

The young woman smiled. 'Course you can.'

As she retouched her make-up, it occurred to Phyllis that serving with girls like these would be similar to working with the tobacco girls who never failed to help each other out if they could.

'Quite exciting, isn't it,' said the pretty blonde who had let her borrow her make-up.

'Quite,' said Phyllis. Suddenly there were butterflies in her stomach. This really could be a new and exciting episode of her life.

Questions were asked by an officious woman wearing the smart uniform of the WAAF as the queue ambled forward. Mostly it was about where you lived and what you were hoping to do. Some were joining in the hope of being closer to their boyfriends. Others wanted to travel.

'Any particular skills we might make use of?'

'I can type,' replied Phyllis.

'Home or abroad? Not that abroad is an option – unless you're an officer.'

'I wonder whether I can be posted close to my fiancé?'

It was stretching the truth a little, but she decided it was worth it.

Names were called out. The queue shuffled forward.

A row of desks were lined up inside the recruitment office. Behind each one was a man in uniform.

Each woman was given a card with a number on and told to wait until their number was called. Finally it was Phyllis's turn.

The bespectacled man sitting behind the desk who vaguely resembled Clement Attlee, the Labour Party Leader, asked for her name and address.

'Mrs Phyllis Imogen Harvey. Number 10a, Stokes Croft.

He wrote it all down, along with her age.

Without moving his head, his eyes looked up from the form he was filling in. 'So you're a married woman. Husband in the forces already, is he?'

She clenched her hands over her handbag. 'He's dead. I'm a widow, but do have a fiancée, though I'm not sure where he is. I wondered if it would be possible to be posted close to him – you know – seeing as we're...'

'Possible, but difficult.' Expression stiffly unchanged, he scribbled something on the form before looking up again in the same distanced manner as before. Phyllis wondered if his neck ached being cricked into that position all day.

'Do you have any particular skills that might be of use to the air force?'

'I can type,' she said and felt instantly proud of the fact. He suddenly looked more interested in her than he had been.

'Do you have a qualification?'

She shook her head, her raised spirits slightly dented.

'I was taking a course, but the war came along so I didn't get chance to gain my diploma. But my teacher said that I was very good at it and shouldn't have any problems at all.'

He nodded as though this was all quite understandable, the

war getting in the way. It was the excuse for everything. 'How fast can you type?'

She thought quickly and embroidered the truth. 'About seventy words a minute.'

He grunted as though it was average, but Phyllis detected that he was somewhat impressed. His next comment confirmed it. 'That's very good, and I'm sure you'll get even faster and more accurate. Practice makes perfect, and we need people who are familiar with a keyboard.'

She beamed. 'Thank you. Thank you very much.'

'You'll receive confirmation of your posting within the next three days.'

'Have you any idea where I might have to go?'

He became very still, his eyes narrowing slightly as he made up his mind whether to disclose any further information.

'Don't hold me to account, but with your skills I'm recommending you go to West Drayton.'

Uncaring that he'd told her she would only be paid two thirds of the comparative rank wage, she sailed out of that office, her feet not seeming to touch the ground. She'd signed on. She'd joined the RAF! The women's division of course. Nobody could stop her now.

She wondered what she might find at West Drayton. Probably a lot of girls all training to be secretaries and clerks to the service's high standards. Still, the qualifications she received would stand her in good stead after the war.

She wanted to tell the whole world, but the world was a big place. There were two people above all others, though, that she was bursting to tell. With that in mind, she headed for the entrance to the tobacco factory in East Street. By the time she got there, it would be dark, but she had her torch and refused to allow the darkness to suppress her excitement.

29

THE THREE MS

Pools of light directed from a mass of handheld torches fell onto the pavements, followed by the footfall of the employees leaving the tobacco factory. Along with them came the sweet smell of tobacco but not a sliver of light.

Phyllis chanced searching the sea of faces, resulting in a few harsh comments about the enemy being able to see it from miles up.

There was nothing for it but to shout. 'Is Bridget Milligan and Maisie Miles there?'

'Phyllis?'

Two figures, one smaller than the other, burst through the crowd.

'Phyllis. What are you doing here?'

'And where you bin?' Maisie added.

'Fancy a coffee? I'll tell you then.'

Over coffee at Cardwardines, the East Street branch, of course, seeing as Castle Street was no more, their eyes bright with excitement, Phyllis related all that had happened, including being evicted from York street and ending up in Stokes Croft.

As she talked, Bridget took in her carefully applied make-up, the luscious red lips and tumbling auburn hair. A while back, she'd looked washed out. Meeting Sam had bucked her up and so had this new venture. However, she couldn't help having reservations, though she masked these by looking interested and happy for her.

'So where's Sam stationed. Do you know yet?'

The exuberance lessened a little. Phyllis fiddled nervously with her cup. 'I haven't heard yet, but I have written to him. Not that I'll get sent overseas just yet. I have to do standard training first and I hear only officers are sent overseas. Still,' she said suddenly, a new brightness in her eyes. 'That should only be for about six weeks. After that, they'll send me to wherever he is.'

'Phyllis, I'm really thrilled for you. It all sounds very exciting,' said Bridget and really meant it.

Phyllis sighed happily. 'I think I'll enjoy it. So how about you two?'

'I'm still taking up a bed,' explained Maisie, 'though it's only temporary.' She shook her head. 'Poor old Aggie. I do worry about her. Not that she says much. Keeps it close to 'er chest that one. But she's right to fear Eddie Bridgeman. Scares the life out of me,' she said with a shiver.

'Me too,' said Phyllis recalling the time she was dragged into his car. 'Is he still looking for Frank?' Phyllis asked. Like Bridget, she knew that although Frank had brought her up – though dragged might be a more fitting word – he was not Maisie's father.

A bright smile perked Maisie's lips and made her eyes shine. 'We all know where Frank is.'

She went on to explain about him being responsible for flogging rotten meat and killing people. Her look soured. 'I think 'e should 'ave been 'ung. Poor old Edith…'

Phyllis pulled a face. 'I hope it's decent food in the WAAF.'

'An army marches on its stomach,' declared Bridget. 'Napoleon said that.'

'Good. Hope the RAF and WAAF know that too. And no Hilda Harvey to worry about'

For a moment there was laughter until Bridget turned thoughtful. 'Just suppose that Robert is still alive, what then?'

Phyllis looked vaguely startled, but recovered quickly. 'I'd get a divorce,' Phyllis snapped. This was not a question she wished to face because it made her feel guilty.

Maisie frowned. 'No letter from the War Office?'

Phyllis shook her head. 'Not to me, but maybe that old bat...'

'You going round there to find out?'

'Not bloody likely.'

Fearing the situation might get out of hand, Bridget poured just enough oil on troubled water. 'Let's face it the world is turned upside down and a lot could change before this war is over.'

'You sound like my mother,' Phyllis said petulantly.

All three of them lingered before leaving the warm atmosphere. Newspaper headlines from somebody close to the door screamed out at them.

'FOOD CONVOY LOSSES.'

Maisie grimaced and grumbled as she turned on her torch, Phyllis holding back the blackout curtain so they could slide more easily behind it and get out..

'The way things are going we could all starve to death,' mumbled Maisie once they'd arrived at the bus stop where Phyllis intended getting a bus to Stokes Croft.

They didn't wait too long. The dark shape of the bus lumbered towards them, barely distinguishable from the buildings round it.

'I'll let you know the minute I'm off,' cried Phyllis.

Her lithe figure was swallowed by the blackout.

Bridget and Maisie walked home in shared silence.

Maisie was thinking of moving on, after all living with the Milligans had only ever been meant to be a short-term solution.

For her part, Bridget was concerned about Phyllis. The Phyllis she'd known and loved had bounced back from her disastrous marriage, yet she felt troubled. One husband, one lover, a few casual dates and now Sam; somehow she didn't think it would stop there. Phyllis needed romance in her life. She was of an affectionate disposition and her heart most definitely ruled her head. The trouble was, such a combination could easily lead her into hot water.

Bridget's parents were over the moon when the Cottrells wrote to say they were willing to put them up over Christmas. On this occasion, there were a number of parents travelling down to call on many other billets in the area. With this in mind, a coach would be awaiting them at the station local to South Molton. Maisie had arranged to stay with her grandmother over Christmas, though Bridget's father had generously offered to see if he could wangle it for her to go with them.

Maisie had declined quickly, a slightly furtive look in her eyes. 'I need some time with me gran. I need to 'ave a good 'eart-to-'eart with 'er.'

Busily folding and packing, Mary Milligan chattered and laughed at the prospect of spending Christmas with her children. 'Do you think Sean will like this yellow pullover? I'm not sure about the colour, but, well, I did my best.'

When Bridget didn't reply, her mother noted her wan expression and the slowness of her packing.

'You look as though you don't want to go.' She hugged the

yellow pullover to her as she regarded her daughter's face. 'You do want to, don't you?'

'Of course,' said Bridget, adopting as bright an expression as she could muster. 'I'm looking forward to it.'

It was a lie. She wasn't looking forward to it. James would be there. His mother had said so.

Over the last few months, she'd forced herself not to dwell on that one night in the hay. When she heard from him it was by way of one of the little cards members of the military were issued with therefore, unless they were written in very small letters, it was difficult to say very much. At least she heard from him, unlike Lyndon marooned on the other side of the Atlantic. At this moment in time her love life seemed extremely hopeless.

Sometimes when she lay in bed at night she got the two of them confused. They looked alike. In her mind she was finding it difficult to divide one from the other.

When she thought about that roll in the hay it was Lyndon she thought of, him who aroused her desire and not James.

Going back down to Devon was going to be embarrassing, though she could hardly tell her mother that. As far as her parents were concerned, this Christmas would be as no other.

At first she'd thought her mother had left the room, but Bridget became aware that she was still there, a deep frown furrowing her brow and something else in her eyes. She actually looked guilty.

Bridget stopped rolling up a pair of stockings and looked at her.

'What is it?'

Her mother looked as though she was making a painful decision. Finally she sighed. 'I might as well give it you. It might cheer you up.' Her mother blushed a bit deeper and the look of embarrassment was superseded by guilt. 'The fact is... well... your American did write, but as you were no longer leaping out of the front door at the postman, I thought you'd got over him. I thought it for the best...'

Her mother's hand tightened on the socks she was now rolling into a ball.

'I don't understand,' Bridget whispered, a small frown denting her brow.

Her mother left the room, went downstairs, then came back holding a letter.

'This came for you this morning. You haven't been checking the post of late, so I didn't think you were interested in what he had to say – that American boy. I wasn't going to bother you with it.'

Bridget stared speechlessly and her hand shook as she took it.

'Sorry, me darling, but I thought it for the best. He unsettled you, he did, so when you said that his parents were out for him marrying one of his own class... well... there seemed no point in him upsetting you any longer.'

'And now?' said Bridget, her face flushed with anger.

Her mother took a deep breath. 'It suddenly occurred to me that I was being unfair. 'Tis you must make your own decisions. Sorry, love. My fault.'

Her fingers as numb with shock as the rest of her, Bridget tore open the envelope.

My dear Bridget,

I've had no reply from you to my previous letters, including the one telling you that I'd avoided my parents' attempts to get me married off! I escaped! None of my letters have been returned, so I am presuming – and hoping – that you are fit and well.

I can only imagine how difficult things are; we're hearing a lot about food shortages thanks to Ed Morrow and his broadcasts from London, along with details of enemy air raids.

I fondly remember that day when you took me to see the historical sites of Bristol. It was all quite an eye-opener – as are you of course.

I feel it in my bones that I will return there at some time in the future and perhaps we might even meet up again. However, I quite understand that you may by now be favoured by another admirer – which is not surprising at all. Your sparkling charm will stay with me until I'm in my rocking chair.

Please respond if only to confirm that you are safe and well, after that, if you no longer wish to hear from me then so be it.

Fond memories and best wishes,

Lyndon.

'How many letters,' she asked her mother, her words trembling on her tongue. 'He said 'them'. More than one?'

Her mother swallowed. 'I threw them on the fire.'

Bridget was still feeling numb when she boarded the train with her parents. Her mother looked sheepish, and her father confused, which meant except for the one letter that he had asked his wife to keep, he hadn't known about the letters which came later and what his wife had done with them.

Unlike their last trip down when it had only been them and they'd been picked up by car, on this occasion a whole load of parents was taking the opportunity to visit their offspring. As they took their seats on the coach, Bridget found that listening to the fussing and regional accents – mostly London – took her mind off what her mother had done. Bags and parcels wrapped in brown paper and tied with string were pushed onto overhead shelves or piled onto laps. Some voices were louder than others, bragging as to who had suffered the worst bombing, how far it got to their street, how much damage had been done to their house and of the thieves taking advantage of empty houses.

'If I gets the buggers who pinched my aspidistra, I'd swing for 'im I would!'

'Someone stole your aspidistra?' remarked Bridget, unable to understand why anyone would wish to steal a plant.

'It was in a mother-of-pearl pot,' declared the same woman. 'Me mother gave it me.'

'Oh I see,' said Bridget sympathetically. 'A family heirloom, was it?'

'Yeah. Me gran got it from a 'ouse she used to work in. The lady of the 'ouse owed 'er wages. Wouldn't pay 'er. Said she was lying when she said the woman's 'usband had been too free with 'is 'ands.'

There was laughter as well as congratulations that her grandmother had got something out of an unpleasant situation. Some level of jollity persisted for most of the journey, quietening as one lot of parents got off the coach to join the families their kids were billeted with.

Bridget knew for a fact that not all the houses who'd taken in evacuees were as big as Winter's Leap, so goodness knows how they would fit them all in.

One set of parents after another were dropped off until only Bridget and her parents remained, the farm being that much further out from the town.

Day had long gone by the time the tall chimneys of the old manor house came into sight, stark and solid against a blanket of blackness.

Bridget's mother almost sprang down the step of the coach,

impatient to see her children and breaking into a quick run towards the house.

'Where are they? Where are they?'

The strong odour of mud and manure reminded everyone that although this was a manor house, it was also a working farm.

With a care for the blackout, it wasn't that easy to see the door, just a sliver of light for a split second until the figure of Mrs Cottrell blanked it out and her voice rang across the yard.

'You must be dog-tired, me dears. Now come on in. James is here too but gone out to 'elp a neighbour with a difficult calving,' she said as she pressed back against the wall to let Bridget in. 'He'll be like a dog with two tails when he sees you, me dear. Everyone's in the best room, including Ruby and Katy. The vicar brought them out earlier. It's more convenient if they stay overnight.'

The warmth inside took the chill from their bones. Logs that were only a little less in size than tree trunks crackled and glowed in a huge inglenook fireplace. The eldest three children were red-faced, toasting forks held at arms' length. A large china butter dish was placed out of danger of melting behind the youngest girls.

There were shouts of joy and a scrambling to welcome their much-loved parents, toast retrieved so it wouldn't get burnt. For a moment their supper was forgotten until Sean offered his father the first slice.

Mrs Cottrell laughed. 'Good job I baked two more loaves today and churned extra butter.'

One of the things that impressed everyone from the city was the proliferation of food available in the country. Chickens scratched all day in the yard, pigs rooted in the ancient orchard where gnarled apple trees presided above the last of the fallen fruits of autumn. There were plenty of eggs, cheese, butter and meat. Even bread, despite the Ministry of Food taking the lion's share of cereal, was eaten warm from the oven.

Bridget's parents were more than satisfied that their children were being well looked after.

As the children chattered and their parents fawned over them, commenting how much they'd grown and were they looking forward to Christmas, a thick mutton stew was served with the toasted bread. As they ate, Mrs Cottrell outlined the sleeping arrangements.

Bridget's parents were given the same double room they'd had before with a blue eiderdown on the bed and pale wallpaper sprinkled with forget-me-nots.

To Bridget she said: 'Seeing as all the girls are staying, I've put them in the room you had last time, so I've made up a bed down in the small sitting room. Hope you'll be comfortable there.'

The small sitting room was set off the huge kitchen and was warmed by the range which kept going all night.

Bridget stared at the narrow bed. James would have known before he'd gone out that she would be sleeping here. Would he knock at her door when he got back? What would she do if he did?

At first, she slept lightly, hearing attuned to the sound of James's small car. She considered what to say to him. If she hadn't received the letter from Lyndon she wouldn't have been so confused. Everything would have been so very straightforward because Lyndon would not have figured at all because he'd been more or less engaged. Now it appeared that it just wasn't so.

Tired by the journey, the light sleep deepened and her apprehension vanished.

In the feeble light of a winter morning, she arose, got dressed and made her way to the dining room, where the smell of breakfast wafted in from the kitchen, not just fried bread like at home, but bacon, eggs and field-picked mushrooms.

Her mother's morning would be taken up helping with the Christmas feast and decorating the house with boughs of greenery brought in by Patrick and her boys. Her father had occupied himself in adjusting the fine grandfather clock that sat at the bottom of the stairs in the hallway.

An eerie silence existed between mother and daughter. Every so often, Bridget's eyes met hers, saw her lips form a soundless *sorry*.

After collecting the few eggs laid at this dour time of year, Bridget sat on a wall, retrieved the letter from her pocket and read it again. Reading the words made the day seem much warmer. It was a lovely letter and explained a lot. On the other hand, Lyndon was still on the other side of the Atlantic, though he seemed certain that they would see each other again.

'My mother said you didn't eat much breakfast. There's a war on. Make the most of it. You're in the country now.'

James!

The wind whipped at her hair as she turned to face him.

He was out of uniform, wearing typical farmhand gear of corduroy trousers, wellington boots and a scruffy brown jumper with leather patches on the elbows. His face was made ruddy by the wind and his hair was awry, not typical for an RAF flyboy.

Furtively and swiftly, she tucked the letter into her pocket.

He took her in his arms and looked surprised when she pushed him away. It angered her that he was simply picking up where he'd left off. There had been many months in between and the few little postcards saying nothing in particular irked her.

'You've got a nerve,' she said. 'Those cards must have been

dashed off in a minute flat. You could have said more, written a proper letter.'

He shook his head. 'Too busy. I've been up there,' he said, one finger pointing upwards at the glowering sky.

She looked him squarely in the face. 'One night doesn't mean to say that you own me.'

His smile cracked as he shoved his hands into his pocket. 'Same here, but the memory is still with me. Will be till the end of my days.'

She shook her head. 'It was a mistake. It shouldn't have happened.'

He gave an offhanded toss of his head. 'You were missing the other bloke. I was the understudy. Isn't that right?'

She felt her face grow hot. 'Of course not!'

There was accusation in the way he looked at her. 'I don't believe you.'

The morning air was cold and pinched at her cheeks. She hung her head and grabbed at the egg basket. In her haste, the basket turned over and the eggs fell out, some rolling whole on the stony ground, some smashing and spilling. 'Now look what you've made me do!'

Eggs were precious. All food was precious. She felt so guilty at wasting any of it. She scrabbled on the ground, picked up those that she could. James also picked some up.

As each picked up the warm eggs, their eyes met.

'I'm sorry,' he said. 'I should have been more thoughtful. It was a difficult time. I've lost a few mates.' He shook his head and there was sadness in his eyes. 'It's best not to care too much in these times. Live for the moment, that's what most of us are doing.' He shrugged. 'How do we know tomorrow will ever come – our tomorrow that is, our personal tomorrow?'

She had been going to carry on being harsh with him, her

way of coping with her own guilt. She understood better when she recalled that last visit and more especially the widow and children attending a graveside in a pretty country church. Her own life had not been touched up close by loss, but his had.

After making sure the eggs were safely gathered, her fingers brushed the letter in her pocket. James was right in that he had been a substitute for Lyndon and that in itself had been unfair. 'Let's just forget it ever happened,' she finally said.

He shook his head. 'I can't do that.'

She started when he stroked her chin with one finger, lifting it slightly so her eyes met his.

'I will try to make amends. You're the sort of girl a chap would like to marry and I promise I will stay in touch – if you don't mind that is.'

Of course she was flattered, but more cautious than she'd been on that heady evening in the hay, a perfect evening, a night full of stars. Despite the fact that Lyndon was on the other side of the Atlantic and James was here, sounding as though he wanted to begin anew, she found herself unable to trust him. She was on her guard and would stay friendly, but keep her distance.

31

Christmas had worked out better than Maisie had hoped. She'd stayed with her grandmother in Totterdown. It had been a pleasant day. Grace had shown her photos of her father from when he was young. His looks had surprised her, his complexion darker than her own, but with the same eyes and unruly thatch of dark hair.

She'd washed up after they'd eaten, placed a blanket over the old lady and took the empty sherry glass from her hand once she'd fallen asleep. It was good to have somebody to look after, also to feel that she belonged with the old woman, that she was part of her.

She'd explained about living with Bridget in an effort to keep out of Eddie's way, but that it couldn't be permanent. 'Bridget's brothers will want their room back, though I don't know when that might be.'

'You can move in if yer like.'

The offer came out of the blue. Her grandmother wasn't to know that she'd had it in mind to ask her if she could. The worry she'd been carrying on her shoulders dropped away.

'That would be lovely, Gran.'

A wide-lipped smile appeared amongst the heavy wrinkles. 'Might as well. We're all the family we got. And not too far to your work.'

'Best Christmas present I could 'ave, Gran.'

'So's this,' said Grace Wells, patting the blanket that Maisie had bought from a church hall jumble sale.

Following Christmas Day, she'd spent time with her half-brother. It had taken some courage to tell him what had happened to Frank Miles, after all he was Alf's natural father.

He shook his head when told about the rotten meat he'd been selling. 'Will the old bugger never learn?'

Maisie asked cautiously if he was going to visit him in prison, where he was awaiting trial and sentencing.

Alf looked pensive. Finally, he replied. 'No. 'E made 'is bed, 'e can lie on it.' He shook his head again. 'Killing two nippers! What the bloody 'ell was 'e thinkin about?'

'Money.'

Alf took in a lungful of cigarette smoke and funnelled it out through pursed lips.

Maisie adored her brother. He'd always been decent, always handsome. His time at sea had made him more rugged. No wonder he attracted admiring glances from good-looking women in the pub where they were having a drink. It wasn't in him to return their looks. She could count on one hand the number of times he'd gone on a date with a girl. None of them had lasted more than one or two nights. On occasion, she'd caught sight of the troubled look on his face and recalled his closeness to a sailor on a night out in the pub at the end of York Street. He'd shaken his head when she'd asked after he'd been on one date if he was going to see the girl again. 'Not for me,' he'd said. 'Not my type.'

He hadn't asked who'd shopped his father to the police, and

she didn't venture any information that might mar their relationship. She'd told him the reason she was no longer living at the Llandoger, that she was living with Bridget's family though only temporarily.

He winced at mention of Eddie Bridgeman.

He sounded bitter and looked concerned. 'Keep out of 'is way, sis. Promise me you'll do that.'

She nodded. 'He won't catch up with me. I've got plans.'

Maisie's plans for New Year had not included drawing incendiary duty from six to nine up on the roof of the tobacco factory. Keen to get away, she'd breezed through filling buckets with sand and had also borrowed a pair of binoculars, which she trained on a moonless sky.

'Nothing up there,' she finally said, sighing as she passed the binoculars back to their owner. In her mind, the minutes were ticking by.

Fred Black accepted the binoculars with great alacrity. 'And ain't we glad there's nothin' up there,' he exclaimed. 'You off now, are you?'

Maisie pushed her tin hat back and mopped at her brow with a crumpled handkerchief. 'If it's nine, then I am.'

'It's five minutes to.'

She pulled a face. 'Don't be mean. My brother's just gone back to his ship and me best mate is off to join the war tomorrow. Me and Bridget are going to the station to see 'er off.'

Taking off his tin hat, Fred scratched what remained of the hair on his head. 'Women in the army. Well, they did during the last lot and they proved their worth. Reckon this time it'll be tougher. Best of luck to the girl.'

* * *

Clouds of steam billowed up from the locomotive hovering like low lying cloud in the iron rafters of Temple Meads Station.

Phyllis was feeling pensive.

'Fancy another cup of tea,' asked Bridget.

Phyllis shook her head and pushed the teacup away. 'The more tea I drink, the more I want to use the lavatory. I could get caught in there and miss the train if I'm not careful.'

Maisie munched on the remains of the teacake Phyllis had declined on account of a sickly feeling in her stomach. 'Crikey, how many pennies 'ave you got through so far?' she asked once the last piece was swallowed.

'Enough,' returned Phyllis with a light laugh and meant it. She'd pushed half a dozen pennies into the slot of the brass door locks of the lavatory cubicles. Her nerves were playing havoc with her system.

A waitress came with the bill, which Bridget settled.

The air out on the platform was ripe with the smell of cinders and white with steam.

Maisie breathed it in. 'That smell reminds me of Wright's Coal Tar Soap.'

Bridget remarked that some of the women here must also be joining up judging by all of them carrying a single suitcase as per instructions.

'I hope so,' said Phyllis. Her nerves had not subsided one iota, but she upheld her confidence by imagining being closer to Sam. 'They try and put you close to someone you know,' she said with great confidence and much hope.

The fact that she was trying to reassure herself wasn't lost on either Bridget or Maisie, who exchanged slightly worried looks but said nothing. Phyllis needed buoying up before setting out on this great adventure.

The guardsman blew his whistle. A green flag was waved at the end of the platform.

'Time for you to climb aboard,' said Bridget.

Maisie gave her a peck on the cheek and asked if she had her sandwiches. Phyllis swallowed her nerves and nodded.

Carriage doors were hanging open in the section of train closest to them, though others at the back of the train were being slammed shut.

Suitcase in hand, Phyllis hugged her friends, who wished her luck and told her not to worry. That would have been it, but for the sudden furore spreading like a storm in their direction. Shouts of protests arose from the crowds waving off loved ones or waiting for the next train.

'Hey watch it, missus.'

'I demand you stop that woman right now!'

The unmistakable figure of Hilda Harvey hurtled through the crowd, shoving people aside, knocking over suitcases and small children alike.

Maisie gave Phyllis a push. 'Quick. Get on the train.'

One big step, and Phyllis was aboard.

Bridget slammed the carriage door, then stood side by side with Maisie forming a barrier between the departing train and Phyllis's mother-in-law.

Wearing a furious expression, eyes glinting and frothing at the corners of her mouth, Hilda Harvey ignored the pair of them and waved her clenched fist over their heads. 'Get off that train, you hussy. You're a married woman! You've got no right going away. You've got a husband in the army.'

Bridget adopted a calm manner and soft but firm voice. 'Mrs

Harvey, whether Phyllis is married or single, it doesn't matter. Women can join up if they want to.'

The threatening fist was lowered to wave at them.

Bridget backed off and found herself dangerously close to the gap between platform and railway carriage. Maisie grabbed her arm, pulled her back and then, like a terrier confronting a bull or a bear, stood defiantly between them.

'Now just you listen, you crazy cow! Phyllis don't belong to you and for that matter, your son don't belong to you either! What they do is between them, so get off 'ome and leave 'er alone.'

Maisie had always been the outspoken one, but on this occasion her tenacity had taken even Bridget by surprise.

For a moment, Phyllis's mother-in-law looked dumbstruck. Then suddenly she was lunging forward.

Maisie grabbed one of her arms and Bridget the other. Keeping a tight hold on her arm, Bridget did her best to dissuade her from continuing her wild onslaught.

'There's nothing you can do. It's a free country.'

Maisie kept her mouth shut and used all her strength to hold Mrs Harvey back.

The carriage doors slammed with an air of finality. The train was about to leave the station.

All around them, people who had watched the scene with open-mouthed curiosity now turned their attention to the departing train, waving at loved ones leaning out of windows.

Only once it had built up sufficient speed and the tail end of the train had passed the sloping end of the platform did they release Hilda Harvey's arms. If they thought that was the end of it, they were mistaken. Her poker face flushed with anger, Hilda rounded on them, pointing a sticklike, black-gloved finger to each in turn.

'You'll pay for this,' she hissed, spittle flying from the corners of her mouth. 'I'll be watching you two. Just you see if I don't.' She stormed off.

Bridget took a deep breath and suggested they wait a while before following her out.

Maisie grinned. 'Old witch. I bet she's got a broomstick outside. What a start to the New Year, eh?'

Bridget did not share her humour. 'She lives in Bedminster.'

'So she keeps her broomstick in Bedminster.'

'I live in Bedminster and Phyllis's mother lives in Bedminster, plus we both work in Bedminster.'

'You're worrying too much.'

'Perhaps I am,' mused Bridget as they headed for the concourse.

'Excuse me. Have you got platform tickets?'

The ticket inspector at the exit had a grim countenance and a stiff moustache.

'Course we 'ave,' said Maisie.

His steely gaze shifted to Bridget. 'Both of you?'

They both said yes in unison.

'Then show me.'

They both got out their penny platform tickets and the inspector eyed them disdainfully.

He nodded and looked slightly disappointed that they were entirely legal. 'Right. You can go now.'

Bridget was relieved, but Maisie, who'd always had a less than trusting attitude for anyone official, questioned why he'd stopped them.

'I don't know what you mean.'

Maisie was having none of it. 'Yes you do. An old witch with a poker face and a scratchy voice put you up to it. Ain't that right?'

He cleared his throat and attempted to punch the tickets of

people coming off the platform and heading for the concourse. 'I was told you'd sneaked in without buying one.'

'By a mad-looking woman in black?' asked Maisie, her jutting chin and straight mouth emphasising the challenge in her voice.

'Could be,' he said and turned away.

'Ain't as though we told Phyllis to join up,' said Maisie, her soft lips set in grim defiance. 'She wanted to be near Sam. That's the reason, ain't it?'

Bridget rolled her eyes. 'Let's hope Mrs Harvey doesn't find out about him!'

Maisie shook her head. 'The army's big and they're marching about all over the place. Phyllis won't 'alf be disappointed if she don't get posted close to 'im.'

Bridget frowned as she thought about it. 'At least she'll be typing in an office, or so she reckons. It was always what she wanted to do so perhaps in time Sam might not matter so much as all that. Anyway, she'll be way behind enemy lines so not likely to get shot.'

Maisie laughed. 'Thought the same meself. Great minds think alike.'

32

BRIDGET AND MAISIE

Twelfth night had come and gone and the girls in the stripping room were as morose as the weather.

Maisie had moved in with her grandmother in Totterdown. Grace Wells's eyesight was going, but her intellect was sharp and despite her suffering, she had a lighter air about her, which in Maisie's opinion was due to the fact that Frank Miles was awaiting sentence for his involvement in the deaths of two children by way of selling rotten meat.

'Don't care if 'e 'angs,' declared Maisie after she'd confided in Bridget at lunch. 'I'd pull the rope if I was asked.'

Being of a more lenient disposition, Bridget winced and manoeuvred the conversation in another direction. 'Heard anything from Sid?'

Maisie grinned. 'Funny you should ask. I got a letter from 'im. Fancy reading it?' She brought out a folded piece of lightweight paper from her overall pocket. 'Go on. I don't mind if you read it,' she said on noting Bridget's hesitation.

'All right.' Bridget opened the letter and read the few lines Sid had written to Maisie. The first line was about how hot it was.

The second was that he could see the sea from where he was and it was very blue. The third line suggested they regarded themselves as engaged. 'He wants you to get engaged,' she said with some surprise.

Maisie smirked. 'Silly bugger. I'm too young. I've already told 'im that. And what about you? Made your mind up yet?'

The blue eyes of Bridget Milligan stayed fixed on the job in hand – eating her lunch. 'About what?' she said, as though she'd not understood the question.

'Your bloke in Devon and the American. Who's your favourite?'

'You make them sound like a couple of racehorses,' Bridget replied indignantly.

'Well, they are in a race – of a kind – aren't they?'

'No they are not! Anyway, what's the hurry? I'll consider getting married once this war is over. Whenever that might be.'

Maisie frowned, then shrugged her shoulders casually. 'Bridget Milligan, you're going to be left on the shelf if you ain't careful.'

'Or I might become a nun,' returned Bridget.

'Really?' Maisie's eyebrows arched in surprise, and on seeing Bridget was only joking, the pair of them burst out laughing.

The canteen was warm and moist thanks to the steam given off by the cooked vegetables displayed on the server. They'd been lucky enough to bag a table for two in a tight little corner.

Maisie eyed Bridget over the top of her teacup. It had long occurred to her that Bridget was a bit standoffish with men; she didn't go on loads of dates like Phyllis, nor as many as she did for that matter. She liked Bridget, but sometimes she seemed so far away and had things buried so deep inside, they were never likely to see the light of day. 'The trouble with you is that you think too much.'

Her sudden comment caught Bridget unawares. 'What?'

'You've got something on yer mind. Come on. Spill the beans!' She was, thought Maisie, like a stone angel in a churchyard; beautiful but stiff and silent. Maisie put down her cup and leaned closer across the table. 'A problem shared is a problem halved – or is it the other way round?'

'Don't keep on.'

'I will too!' Maisie flashed that resolute, challenging look that told Bridget in no uncertain terms that she was going to keep asking, like a terrier with a bone.

With gruff deliberation, she sprang from her chair and headed for the exit and the corridor leading back to the stripping room.

A rather hurt and dumbfounded Maisie looked after her. 'Bridget!'

'Everything all right?' Aggie pulled out the chair Bridget had recently vacated.

Maisie shook her head. 'I always thought Bridget knows 'er own mind. No muddles in 'er brain. Now I'm not so sure.'

33

BRIDGET

The pong of the gasometer fouled the fresh evening air as Bridget made her way home across the cut. A cold wind chilled her bones and whistled between the gaps in the houses. Every so often, the light from her torch picked out small movements; dried leaves racing across the frozen ground, the more furtive scuttling of a rat, the beating of wings followed by a scream as a water vole was taken by an owl's sharp talons.

In peacetime, the glow from windows would lend a welcoming light to finding her way. So would that of street lamps, but in the dense blanket of blackout there was nothing except her torch.

The other girls she'd been with had fallen behind and she was all alone with her thoughts. She recalled Maisie's words about people in love. She hunkered down further into her coat and pulled up her collar against the cold wind. Maisie was young, brash and outspoken. That's what she told herself, yet deep down Bridget accepted she'd always possessed a wisdom beyond her years.

At long last, she had left the gasometer behind her, though

the impenetrable darkness persisted, the circles of light from her torch like stepping stones across the dark ground. In the past she had used her key to get in, but due to blackout regulations she now knocked at the door of her own home, giving her mother chance to turn out the hallway light and draw back the curtain before opening the door.

She heard her mother's voice, hushed and urgent. 'Bridget. We've a visitor.'

The door was closed and the curtain drawn behind her. The hallway light, a dull single-bulb affair in a tulip-shaped glass shade threw a dubious glow over the small hallway.

Curious as to who the visitor might be, she took off her coat, adding it to the bundled mass already hanging on the wall mounted coat hooks. On following her mother into the living room, she found her father sitting in his favourite chair closest to the window. Seated in the matching armchair on the other side of the fireplace was Mrs Cottrell. She held a handkerchief in one hand, her expression was strained and her eyes red from crying.

'I'm the bearer of bad news, me dear. It's James. He's been injured. In hospital at the infirmary.'

'In Bristol?'

'It was the nearest hospital with an orthopaedic surgeon experienced with broken bones.' Kate Cottrell explained.

Bridget's jaw dropped. 'Oh my God. Is he all right?'

His mother nodded and, though a fresh bout of tears threatened, Mrs Cottrell swallowed the impulse. 'They tell me he'll live, but he is badly injured. I've got to get back to the farm, but I wondered if you could call in on him. He said he'd love to see you. We did notice, 'is dad and I, that you seemed to get on. So if you could...' There was pleading in her voice and in her eyes. Bridget was touched.

Despite the shock she'd suffered, Mrs Cottrell was a pragmatic country woman. She went on to explain that she was staying that night but had to go back to Devon the next day.

'I've made up one of the beds in the other room,' Bridget's mother explained, though Bridget had already guessed that. 'You can stay longer if you wish,' her mother added, but Mrs Cottrell flung her shoulders back like a soldier and declared that she had duties that could not be shirked.

'It's the farm. Labour is short and there's the children to think of.'

As a matter of duty rather than affection, Bridget promised to go in and see James the following evening straight from work. 'If I'm allowed, seeing as I'm not a relative. They're very funny about visiting hours.'

'Not for members of the armed forces,' stated Mrs Cottrell. 'Extenuating circumstances, anyways I told them his girlfriend would likely be calling in. It's not a problem.'

But it is, thought Bridget, or it could be if I dwelt on last summer. By rights she should marry him, shouldn't she? Even though it was only a moment in time. That's what nice girls were supposed to do, weren't they?

* * *

Their footsteps echoed along the hospital corridor, the smell and sound of Bristol Royal Infirmary unchanged since her last visit here with Maisie.

That very morning, she'd told Maisie what had happened and that she was visiting the hospital straight from work.

'I'm coming with you,' declared Maisie in that no-nonsense tone she used when determined to have her own way.

The news had spread far and wide throughout the stripping room. Sympathetic looks and comments abounded, weighing

Bridget down, stifling the urge to explain that he was just somebody she knew and not her boyfriend or fiancée as some of them assumed him to be.

She peered through the porthole-type windows set at eye level in the double doors of the ward.

'Can you see him?' asked Maisie.

She shook her head. All she could see were a series of low lights in cone-shaped shades, nurses, doctors and ward sisters moving soundlessly between the beds.

Nerves on edge, Bridget took a deep breath. 'I don't know that I can do this,' she whispered.

'You can walk away right now if you like. It's your life.' Maisie gave her shoulder a reassuring squeeze. 'I'll wait out 'ere.'

The door swished closed behind her and there she was, coldly upright walking up the centre of the ward, rows of beds on either side of her. As she approached each one, she sought his familiar face and blonde silky hair. Finally, she found him lying white-faced, his eyes closed and a frame encompassing his legs.

Although she told herself that he meant nothing to her, the sight of him pained her eyes and her heart. His mother had been reluctant to explain the details of his injuries. She now thought she knew why. His legs! She remembered him striding across fields, climbing the ladder in the hay barn, the hardness of his thigh muscles against hers. He'd laughed then. Looking at him now lying here, she thought she might never hear him laugh again and that would be a great shame. She couldn't help feeling pity for him.

She approached him softly so as not to disturb him, trying to find the right words to say – as if there would ever be 'right words'.

Suddenly, without her saying anything, his eyes opened.

'Bridget?' His smile was wide and warm. 'Thanks for coming.'

She leaned over him, caressed his hair, then kissed his forehead.

His eyes closed and his smile vanished as though both had required too much effort.

Bringing a chair beside the bed, Bridget glanced at the frame holding the bedclothes away from his legs.

The ward sister came along to check his pulse. Her eyes met Bridget's.

After the nurse's clipped footsteps had strode off down to the far end of the ward, his voice suddenly broke into her thoughts. 'It was bad luck. Flak over Holland. Untouched all the way there but caught it on the way back.'

She leaned in closer, placed her hand on his shoulder, and although he hadn't said so, she knew beyond doubt that he would never fly again. 'Just get better,' she whispered, her eyes filling with sadness for a life ruined. 'Your parents need you down on the farm.'

His eyes looked tired when he trained them on her. 'What about you? Do you need me?' She noted the bitterness in his voice, the need for somebody to want him, now he was no longer a healthy and handsome specimen of a man, though even without legs he was still quite a catch.

Her heart felt as though it was climbing into her throat. What could she say? He looked so pitiable, so in need of good news to take away his pain. Much as she'd primed herself to stick to the truth of how she was feeling, she took the coward's way out. Between copious tears, she told him that she needed him too.

'Are you sure?' He sounded like a small boy needful to feel that somebody really cared for him.

The sobs racked her shoulders as she threw herself across him, felt his fingers running through her hair, the warmth of his cheek, the sinews standing proud of his neck.

Her eyes locked with his and in that moment they were back rolling in the hay. Everything had seemed so simple on that one warm night.

He looked dismally at the frame covering his legs. 'I was thinking we might get engaged, even get married. Seize the day, somebody said. In war, there's a hundred times more of a reason to do that. So how about we get married, though I won't be able to walk you down the aisle unaided. I might have crutches or... false legs.'

She wanted to remind him that it had only been a one-night stand, that they barely knew each other. His predicament stilled her tongue and kept the truth inside.

'It's both legs,' he said to her almost spitting the words. 'Both bloody legs!'

There was great anger, but who could blame him? The floor of his world had disintegrated and he'd gone crashing through it. Giving solace and a sense of hope was one thing that she could do, at least in the short term.

She asked him if he'd had any other visitors besides his mother.

'Only a friend based with me.'

His eyes flickered as though reliving the visit, but he didn't go into detail, his eyes once more fixed on the frame covering his legs. She sensed his seething anger building up inside.

After telling him she would visit again the following evening, she rejoined Maisie outside in the corridor. She felt her friend's searching look as they made their way to the lift and the outside world.

Maisie remarked that she was white as a sheet. 'How is he?'

'He's lost his legs.'

'Oh.' It was all Maisie could say. She was totally lost for words, sorry for both James, who she'd never met, and her dear friend

Bridget who she suspected would fall in with whatever James wanted, mainly because she felt sorry for him. Should she broach the subject? Criticism might not be welcome. For now at least she would mull it over before making comment.

Their mutual silence lasted all the way along the corridor until the hospital, its echoing silence and its antiseptic smell was behind them. Outside, as they pulled on their gloves and got out their torches, Maisie sniffed and said, 'I take it you're going to see him again.'

'Of course.'

'Should you? I mean, he might get the wrong idea.'

'I can't help that. He's been injured. I have to do something.'

It was exactly as Maisie had feared. 'You're too soft fer yer own good, Bridget. He's injured and you want to make 'im feel better.' She shook her head.

'I'm just being kind!' Bridget exclaimed.

'Or riddled with guilt?'

Bridget rounded on her. 'Guilt about what? I've nothing to be guilty about.'

It wasn't entirely true, but Bridget was befuddled. She didn't think it was love but they had had physical contact. It had to mean something, surely.

'He's very dejected,' Bridget finally proclaimed.

'I know what yer saying, Bridge, but what if 'e takes it the wrong way?'

Bridget licked the dryness off her lips and walked on. Although her feelings were muddled, she told herself she would sort them out. He just needed somebody to care for him, to even think that there might be some future for them as a pair. A man with no legs was bound to feel dejected. There had to be hope and if she conveyed that hope, she'd let it be. If it helped him, then all well and good – at least for now.

34

'You're not going to let this idea go, are you.'

The words were said through an eddy of thick cigar smoke and were a statement rather than a question. Lyndon O'Neill the second, had long come to the conclusion that his son, Lyndon O'Neill, the third, was a chip off the old block and capable of filling his shoes. Only he wanted him to do more than fill his shoes; he wanted him to fly in higher circles – become something in government. Hell, if that old bootlegger Joe Kennedy could rise to becoming ambassador to the Court of St James with ambitions for his sons, why couldn't his son move in similar circles?

Lyndon's response was terse, almost to the point of discourtesy. 'No. I'm not.'

He eyed his father through his own fug of cigar smoke, chin as stubbornly set as his sire and determined that he would go his own way, do his own thing. He'd lost patience with his country's attitude to the war in Europe and had voiced his opinion that at some point – debatable as to when – they would have to stand their ground.

'You'd be going into a war zone. OK, the US isn't directly

involved in this war, but that doesn't mean to say that the day won't come when we are involved. We got sucked in back in nineteen seventeen. And it don't matter that we're neutral. Hitler has categorically stated that neutral shipping is not exempt from attack. You'll be in danger from the minute you head across. Don't that worry you, son?'

His father's eyes narrowed as he awaited his son's response.

'Dad. A few years back everyone was saying that Hitler wouldn't be so bad once he had the responsibility of power. Well, he got that power and sorely abused it. We can't ignore it indefinitely. I'd like to go over there. I'd like to see what's going on.'

His father grunted and lowered his eyes to his desk and the letter lying there. Lyndon's answer was not unexpected. He was prepared for this.

On raising his eyes to meet Lyndon's, he said, 'You're my son and as stubborn as I am. A real chip off the old block. So I've pulled a few strings in Washington. You're not going on any holiday. It'll be a working visit. Will Oakby is a pal of mine; works for Cordell Hull.'

'The Secretary of State?' Lyndon pulled a surprised face. It never ceased to amaze him how many famous and influential people his father knew.

'The very same,' said his father in a tone of voice that made it sound no big deal. 'I've arranged for you to accompany a delegation attached to the embassy. Their job will be to get a "hands-on" feel for what's going on over there. The likes of Ed Morrow are all very well, but the president wants feedback from others besides broadcasters and journalists. He wants to know what's happening on the ground and wants bona fide reports from people he can trust. The British are doing something similar. They've set up a unit entitled Mass Observation Department. To feedback groundswell opinion that helps form government policy. That's what we want to, but from our own sources otherwise we'd be accused of being swayed by British propaganda.'

Blood rushing with excitement, Lyndon leaned forward in the chair, elbows on knees, cigar dripping ash onto the dark green carpet. 'When do I leave?'

His father smiled through the fug of the cigar that he was smoking. He wouldn't say it, but he was proud of his son and the fact that he was off to do something useful. His wife would be furious when he eventually told her. But there, she'd have to live with it.

'The delegation departs in three weeks on one of our own planes. You'll land in Croydon, just south of London. After that, your job is to observe how things really are.' A sudden twinkle came to his father's eyes. 'And not just in London. Fact is, I want you to call in at our biggest buyers. Report back to me how W. D. & H. O. Wills are faring.'

Lyndon's head jerked up. 'In Bristol?'

His father smiled. 'Sure. Might be able to look up that little friend of yours whilst you're there.'

'Bridget. You mean Bridget,' said Lyndon, his eyes shining.

'If you say so.'

'I do say so. Thanks Dad.'

He sprang to his feet, shook his father's hand, then left the walnut panelled room, his feet seeming to be at least six inches above the floor. He was going back to England after all this time. He would see Bridget. He only hoped she'd be pleased to see him.

35

BRIDGET

The first snowdrops were in full flower, greeting the first months of 1941 with their pristine whiteness, and Phyllis had written from West Drayton, where she was training to be even faster at typing than she currently was.

I'm also getting to use other more specialised equipment. They've even given me a promotion already which they tell me will broaden my options. I'm not sure what they mean by that. One of the girls said they might be earmarking me to go abroad. I've never been any further than Weymouth, so it does excite me. I might also meet up with Sam. He did say he was being posted abroad, though didn't quite know where and was wary of telling me.

The stockings are scratchy and the shoes pinch my toes. As for the underwear!!! I'm sure I can make two pairs from each pair of bloomers. They're huge.

Missing you both so much. Please write as soon as you can.

Love, Phyllis.

The letter had arrived at Bridget's. Both she and Maisie had taken it in turns to read it.

'I'm almost envious,' declared Maisie. 'I wonder if she *will* get posted overseas. Bet she'll 'ave a fine old time if she does.'

Bridget sighed, smiled weakly and refolded the letter. 'I just pray she stays safe.'

'I just pray we don't get the push,' said Maisie. 'We ain't receiving nowhere near as much baccy as before the war. And we ain't producing so many fags either.' She glanced at the floor. 'I've never seen this floor so clean. Every little speck's bin swept up and chucked back in the bin. Reckon this rate some'll be smoking dust and splinters of wood. Aggie said that there's a rumour they're bulking fags out with horsehair. Imagine that! Glad I don't smoke.'

The sudden interruption of the air-raid siren was wound up to full crescendo, enough of a noise to put nerves on edge.

Almost as one, those working on the factory floor and those from the offices and other facilities began to make their way en masse to the cellar, feet clumping thunderously down the steps and into it.

Maisie had been trying to get a decent conversation out of Bridget all morning, but hadn't quite succeeded.

'Are we still friends?' she asked.

'Of course we are. Why shouldn't we be,' Bridget responded, her voice somewhat brittle and an uncompromising look in her eyes.

To Maisie's mind, she didn't look at all herself and was behaving out of character. It was as though there were two Bridget's inside her at odds with each other.

'Seeing James again tonight, are you?'

Bridget said that she was. Mrs Cottrell had gone back to the demands of the farm and the evacuees she'd taken under her wing. 'There's no one else, except somebody from the base.'

'One of his mates?'

'That's right.'

She felt Maisie's searching look, dark eyes as sharp as steel.

The air raid seemed to be going on a bit – if there was one going on that is. It was impossible to hear explosions down deep below ground and Vera Lynn singing her heart out helped, plus anyone who had a voice was singing along in the hope it would steady their nerves.

Although she was younger than Bridget, Masie felt very protective towards her. She mulled over, thought and mulled over again. Finally she couldn't hold it in any longer.

'Just you be careful, Bridget Milligan, that your feeling sorry for 'im don't go too far. I'm tellin' you now, I ain't gonna let you make the same mistake as Phyllis.'

Bridget retaliated. 'For goodness' sake…!'

'Phyllis married that bloody awful Robert 'Arvey because she got persuaded into it – oh, and it turned out a bit 'andy when she found she was up the spout. I ain't saying you're gonna get yerself in the family way, but you might end up doin' it because you feel sorry for the bloke.' She shook her head dolefully. 'That ain't right, Bridget.'

It wasn't in Bridget's nature to get flustered or angry but she did now, raising her voice in a way that she rarely did. 'You wouldn't know. You've never had a sweetheart, and before you say it, Sid doesn't count, even though he's asked you to get engaged.'

Maisie sniffed. She knew very well that she and Sid had a very casual relationship, but it wasn't so bad for all that. 'We understand each other,' she said loftily. 'When he gets back – if he gets back – we'll just take up where we left off and see where it goes.'

Maisie was hurt. Bridget confused and frightened. In consequence, both fell to silence.

The all-clear sounded and the crowded cellar emptied, everyone heading back to their work, chattering as they went, some still singing the latest Vera Lynn offering.

Bridget and Maisie lingered before bringing up the rear, climbing the wide steps back up to the ground-floor corridor where management and those who worked in the offices came up from the far end cellars and threaded off back to their cosy domains.

Bridget contemplated her options. She and James hadn't made any commitment, yet for all that she felt obliged to give him comfort. Just as a friend, she told herself. There was nothing else and no one else in her life at the moment – nobody close to hand that is.

And then everything changed. It was as though a sunburst had broken through the low hanging clouds of despair.

'Bridget! Hey! Bridget, honey!'

'Blimey,' said Maisie, her jaw dropping on spotting who it was. 'He's here!' She sounded as though God had suddenly landed on earth.

Bridget gasped.

Lyndon O'Neill was back. Nearly two years on, he was just as well dressed, his complexion more tanned, his hair a more sun-kissed blonde than before.

Seeing her friend's shocked face, Maisie made herself scarce. 'See you later, darlin'.'

Bridget was dumbstruck. Was she dreaming? No. She could smell him, his clothes, the oil on his hair. 'Lyndon. I didn't know...'

'It seems I got here before my letter. I did write. I'm here courtesy of Uncle Sam.'

'Uncle Sam?'

'The United States of America. It's a government directive that I couldn't refuse.'

When he came close, she felt she was drowning in the smell of him, the close proximity and warmth of his body.

Her mouth felt dry, but at last she came to and said, 'I have to get back to work.' She didn't want to. She wanted to stay here, to talk to hug, to kiss until she was too dizzy to kiss any more.

He shook his head. 'No you don't. I've cleared it with management.' He took hold of her arm and led her upstairs into an area she hadn't ventured for some time. The Medical Unit was to her left, but Lyndon took her onwards and upwards to more hallowed areas where the carpet was thick and the walls panelled in a reddish coloured wood.

'We've got the boardroom to ourselves.'

'The boardroom?'

Going upstairs into the management area was something ordinary workers never did and certainly nowhere near the boardroom.

'It's a matter of national importance,' he said to her as he pushed open one of the pair of solid mahogany doors.

More mahogany lined the walls. The eyes of past chairmen looked down at them from frostily posed portraits. Here and there were portraits of a number of employees who had served a lifetime with the firm, even the workers from the factory floor.

Lyndon held out a chair and motioned for her to sit. His hand brushed her shoulder, then caressed her face.

'Please,' she said, jerking forward so he would know not to do that. 'Don't do anything until I know this isn't a dream.'

He looked slightly hurt. 'I'm sorry. I've no right. I was just hoping...'

She said nothing, just sat there staring down at the highly

polished table that seemed to run almost the whole length of the room. He was here. She'd dreamed of seeing him again. She should be throwing herself into his arms, but found it difficult to do that, almost as though he'd become a stranger all over again.

'It's like this,' he began. 'The idea is to gather first-hand experiences from the British people, though not just the politicians and high-ranking military. I've been asked to measure morale, to get some idea of what ordinary people are feeling. Thing is, I need to know where to find these ordinary British people and who best to observe. That's where you come in. I want you to take me to see ordinary people like you.'

For a moment, she was tongue-tied. This was like a dream that she'd dreamed many times, dreams that had featured Lyndon, though certainly not the US government!

'Will you do that,' he asked when no answer was forthcoming.

She thought quickly of how best to explain what her country was going through, not the military side of it, but the home front and not just about food, fuel and clothing. The emotional side mattered too. When she at last opened her mouth, this was exactly what she said to him and he agreed with her.

'As usual, you understand what's needed.' His smile lit up her world. 'That's exactly what we want. How the war is affecting lives, women and relationships. It all counts. I recall you telling me about your dad, how he came back injured from the Great War. If we could touch on something like that...'

'We can,' she said, nodding her head vigorously. 'We can.'

She had to mention James. There was no getting away from it.

'I've a friend who's in hospital. He was shot down.' She licked the dryness from her lips. 'He's lost his legs.'

She hung her head, afraid of meeting his eyes, but she felt his disappointment.

'Does he mean something to you,' he said slowly, all the joy of being reunited gone from his voice.

She shook her head. 'I don't know – not really. We had a bit of a fling. Nothing much. No more than a night really.'

There. She'd said it. She waited for his response, the rejection that surely must come.

'Just a fling.'

She nodded.

'And now you're thinking you're Florence Nightingale.'

'What?' Her head jerked up. 'Don't make fun of me! James needs me to be there for him even though...'

'Even though you don't love him. You love me.'

It happened so quickly, him putting his arms round her and her burying her face against his shoulder, breathing in the smell of him, feeling the warmth. Her hands clutched him so tightly. His hands were warm against her back. What was that he'd said? That she loved him?

'You're right. I do love you, Lyndon, but I thought I'd lost you. Then your letter came, then I found out about the other letter – or letters. I'm not sure which.'

For a moment he held her at arms' length and eyed her questioningly. There was no alternative but to tell him what her mother had done.

'She kept telling me that we were of different classes so could never have a future together.'

He shook his head and without hesitation pressed his lips to hers. If their bodies had been close before, they were even closer now, not even a hair's breadth between them.

'Our future together is as positive as that kiss.'

She smiled through her tears. She hadn't meant them to come to her eyes, but she just couldn't help it.

'We're going to have a fine future together, Bridget. It can work. We'll make it work.'

Everything was so right, she thought. Everything could be so complete. There was just this niggling concern about poor James who had made her come alive on that warm summer night.

'You're right,' she said. 'I really do love you. Honest I do, but I don't know how it happened, well I do and I know why. The only thing is...'

'You've got to visit this guy and get it off your chest.'

Their embrace lessened as she nodded.

'So when are you aiming to see him again?'

'Tonight. I promised.'

Lyndon heaved a sigh. 'Well, like my old grandpappy used to say, you should never break a promise.'

She almost laughed. 'He must have been a very wise man.'

He kissed her again. Her feeling of responsibility towards James seemed much more foolish now, though she would still visit him. 'He's been through so much and his family have been so good to the kids. All but two are billeted with his parents on the farm. They're good people. They work hard to grow the food we need, plus taking in members of my family, and now this with James though at least he won't be flying any longer.

A thoughtful look came to Lyndon's face. 'They sound a typical British family; putting in the extra effort in order to obtain final victory, plus a serving pilot. How about I bring my notebook and take down a few details for this project I'm working on?'

She couldn't see James objecting to that and so agreed

'Tonight then,' he said, his index finger running down her forehead and nose until it rested on her lips.

'Yes. I'd better go now. I've got work to do.'

'We both have,' he said. 'For the rest of our lives.'.

Together they entered the hospital. Every so often, Lyndon eyed her enquiringly.

'You OK?'

She nodded. 'Fine.'

The truth was there was a knot of sheer nerves twisting and turning in her stomach. How would James be? Would he fall apart once she'd made it clear that there was nothing between them, that there never had been?

There'd never been any spoken commitment and those trite little postcards couldn't compare to a romantic letter of the sort Lyndon wrote to her. It wasn't in her nature to harden her heart. She couldn't help but feel sorry that his mother was his only visitor. Besides, she told herself, getting involved in Lyndon's project might lift his spirit and give him something interesting to talk about and so he would know that somebody cared for him, that there was still a life beyond flying.

She shoved aside that it might not be a good idea to bring them together, these two men who looked so alike and had touched her heard. Bringing them together did worry her. How would they react to each other? She couldn't be sure but it still seemed good to do something.

As they approached, James's head jerked in their direction. His smile was hesitant as he eyed the big man with the looks of a film star.

As she introduced the two young men, Bridget saw them do a double take.

'You could be my twin, except you've got legs,' James said grimly.

'In which case we were separated at birth. I'll ask my mom,' returned Lyndon. 'Pleased to meet you.'

He took James's hand and shook it vigorously whilst carefully avoiding letting his eyes rest on the frame positioned over his legs. The guy was understandably sensitive about his injuries; Bridget was in tune with that, caring soul as she was.

He gritted his teeth when Bridget gave James a friendly peck on the cheek. The sharp-eyed pilot noticed Lyndon wince. He clenched his jaw, devilment in his eyes.

'Bridget and I have been talking about getting engaged.'

Bridget blushed. 'That's not true, James.'

It struck her then how much James liked to be in charge, to control the proceedings, whatever those proceedings might be. Her thoughts went back to how the children had adored him. Now she saw how much he'd enjoyed their admiration and positively encouraged it. But it wasn't only that now. Telling a lie and casting aspersions was his way of coping with how he was. If he wasn't going to be happy, he didn't want anyone else to be happy either.

Lyndon's response was stilted, not quite believing but unwilling to give offence. 'Oh. Congratulations. I didn't know that.'

Bridget's response was instantaneous. 'James is elaborating.'

Lyndon's expression was very controlled. He was here for a purpose and would give James no reason not to help him with his research into British morale. He was here to support Bridget, but also to carry out a task for his government.

'I see. Well, let's get to the reason I'm here – and it's not to steal Bridget away – though I have to say I'd like to.'

There was a grim set to James's jaw as Lyndon explained why he was there and what he was doing.

James made comment. 'So, you Yanks are weighing things up before you enter the war.'

'I can't confirm one way or another whether that will happen,' Lyndon replied courteously. 'This is basically to report on the lives of real people. I understand your parents run a farm. That in itself is of interest. Keeping people fed.'

At mention of the farm and his parents, James nodded. 'I see.'

Bridget could see his prickliness had lessened but was in no doubt that he sensed Lyndon was more than a friend. The rest of the conversation circled around how James had felt on coming home, what his family thought, how both he and they would manage when the war was finally over. This last question – how he would manage – obviously hit a raw nerve.

'As best I can,' James said grimly and his eyes locked with hers.

Every inch the professional, acting on behalf of his country, Lyndon gave no indication that he knew about the fleeting relationship between Bridget and James.

The visit and the notetaking eventually came to a close. A brief goodnight and they headed for the door.

Bridget tried not to feel prickly at James's behaviour, but it did annoy her that he'd made it seem as though they were engaged when it wasn't true at all. Her first impulse was to go back in there and sort it out, but what good would that do? James was feeling sorry for himself and lashing out, muddying the waters, acting like a spoilt child. Because his life had been spoilt he wanted to spoil it for everyone else'. Laying her frustration aside, she adopted a business like air. 'I trust that was useful to you?'

Lyndon said that it was.

For some time, their footsteps echoed along the bare corridors. The working day was over by the time they left the hospital. The night was dark, but Lyndon had his own car hired by his country's government so that he might more easily facilitate the work asked of him.

Not a word was said until they were parked outside her home in Marksbury Road.

When he turned the lights off, it left them in total darkness. It felt to her as though they were submerged in ink.

The flame from his lighter fell onto his features. He lit a cigar and wound down the window. The night air drifted in as the smoke drifted out. 'It's great to see you again.'

'You too.'

'You do mean it, don't you?'

She knew what he was referring to and threw herself into his arms.

'Yes. Yes, I do love you.'

'Bridget. You're fixed in my mind.'

She nodded. 'And you in mine.'

'I can understand how it happened – you and James. My own stupid fault, telling you about my folks plans to get me married.'

He threw the unfinished cigar out of the window and hugged her closer, kissed her hair, her ear, her nose and then her mouth.

Over his shoulder she fancied movement by the front door. Her father was out making sure she was all right.

'I've got to go.'

'Your old man's waiting by the front door. Am I right?'

'How did you know that?'

'Because if I had a daughter as beautiful as you, I'd be doing the goddam same.'

She laughed then pushed open the door and got out.

She couldn't be unkind to James, but the path to her future was clearing. Lyndon was back and although she did feel slightly obliged to James she had to commit herself one way or another.

A postcard arrived from Phyllis:

> *Darling, having a whale of a time and answerable to nobody. I've been declared top of my class and given another promotion. It's been confirmed they're sending me abroad. I'm excited. Take this advice from me. Be true to yourself.*
>
> *Best of love to you.*
>
> *PS. This card is for you and Maisie. I need to save on stamps.*

'Sounds as though she's enjoying herself,' said Maisie, flipping the card this way and that as if by doing so they could tell what she was up to.

Four words above all others burned into Bridget's mind.

Be true to yourself.

The rest of that day might have passed in a blur if some special things hadn't happened. The first was a message from Miss Cayford, inviting her along to her office.

It was well known that Miss Cayford had quite a few house plants growing in pots on top of her filing cabinets. Bridget recognised the plants growing there now as winter greens and carrots – in pots! Things were certainly changing fast.

'Do sit down,' said Miss Cayford, flicking open a file in front of her.

Bridget did so, wondering all the time what was happening here.

'You haven't joined any of the women's military services, have you?'

She shook her head. 'No. I've got younger brothers and sisters though they have been evacuated. My help is sometimes needed at home. And my father was invalided out of the merchant navy in the last war.'

Miss Cayford nodded. 'I see. Well, I must say we appreciate you still being here, which is why I called you in.' She leaned back in her chair, fingers intertwined and a very satisfied look on her face. 'I'm offering you promotion to the packing department. It's a little more money of course. Can you show me your hands?'

Bridget did as requested, already knowing that anyone with dirty fingernails would not be allowed to become a cigarette packer. Luckily for her she had just been to the ladies' cloakroom so her fingernails were pristine despite having been stripping leaves all morning.

Miss Cayford turned her hands over and inspected her palms. 'Very satisfactory,' she said at last. 'The job is yours.'

'Do I have a choice?'

Miss Cayford frowned. She'd never had a girl turn down a promotion. 'Yes. Of course you do, but be warned, if you do turn it down, there might not be a second chance.'

A second chance, she thought as she came away.

Maisie almost knocked her over, face alive with curiosity. 'What did she want you for? Promotion? It's got to be. Have you accepted?'

Bridget took in Maisie's avid enthusiasm. 'How could I

possibly leave you in the stripping room all by yourself! You'll get into trouble in no time.'

Maisie looked quite taken aback. 'Go on! I don't believe you.'

Bridget smiled. 'Yes. I've got a promotion.'

'What about the men in your life? What's 'appening?'

'I'm seeing both of them tonight.'

'Greedy girl!'

'First one and then the other. You're a cheeky mare, Maisie Miles!'

Maisie offered to go with her to the hospital, but Bridget declined. There was much thinking to do on the way there and just as much – if not more – on the way back.

Although it was still daylight, the sky was leaden and the weather truly awful. The buses were crowded, condensation running down the windows and rising in a steamy fug from wet coats and hats. Water ran in rivulets over the gnarled pavements and beat on ruined buildings and piles of debris.

The wet and wintry gale tugged at the hem of her skirt, her stockings clung damply to her legs and her shoes were soaked.

Just before she reached the doors to the ward where James was lying, she chanced on the ward sister coming out.

'I know I'm early, but is it possible that I can go in and see him?'

The ward sister, a woman of mature years with tightly permed grey hair, eyed her sidelong. 'I'm sorry but he already has a visitor. We're only allowing one at a time until he's more recovered.'

She spoke hesitantly and there was pity in her eyes.

'Perhaps I could wait?'

The woman looked thoughtful, came to a decision and nodded. 'Just as long as you keep out of the way.'

Time ticked away. There were no chairs, but she didn't mind. *At least I've got my legs*, she thought. She looked through one of the round windows. A screen pulled halfway across the ward prevented her from seeing James or his visitor. He'd said that one of his friends from the base was coming in regularly. She vaguely recalled him saying the friend was on leave.

Judging by the wall clock, its thick black hands jerking round over the seconds and minutes, it was getting close to her normal time of arrival.

Just as the big hand locked into place, she became aware of footsteps coming towards her on the other side of the doors. Readying herself to enter, she stepped forward. The doors swung open.

The young woman who came out wore the uniform of the Women's Auxiliary Air Force of the same dark blue as the men. She was pretty, blonde and had a trim figure.

For a moment their eyes met and they exchanged a fleeting smile. Then she was gone.

Suddenly Bridget felt as though she'd awoken from a deep sleep. In her mind, she ploughed through a whole raft of questions as she entered the ward. It was only a short space to James's bed, but enough time for things to solidify.

Sensing her approach, his eyes flashed open. There was no smile and neither was he moved to explain that he'd already had a visitor – another female visitor.

'Not got your American with you.' He sounded contemptuous, yet at no time had Lyndon been that way towards him and it riled her.

'He's only trying to help.'

'If he wants to help me, tell him to bring a pair of legs with him next time,' he grumbled. His attitude was incredibly hurtful and she fancied it had a purpose.

'You're more of a coward than I thought,' she said, both hands clasping her handbag.

A nerve flickered beneath one eye and puckered his jawline. His look was piercing.

'If you think that, what are you doing here?'

Pity evaporated and she now felt a great sense of release. 'I saw your friend. She's very pretty. How much pity do you want? How many girlfriends do you have visiting you? How many women fawning over you will it take to make you feel better?'

There wasn't a flicker of response. His jaw remained rigid and those bright blue eyes were as frozen as a lake in winter.

When they'd first met his handsome features had reminded her of Lyndon. She could now see differences, a selfish brooding look on his face. She sensed his manner would become manipulative over time, his character more self centred.

'I still need you, Bridget. We have something special.'

She shook her head. 'James, all we ever had was one solitary night when I lost self-control because it came home to me that in war there's not necessarily going to be a tomorrow for any of us.'

'Never mind,' he said petulantly. 'I've still got Deirdre. That's the name of that pretty little blonde you've just seen leave. She won't let me down. Not like you.' There was spite in the way he said it and told her all she needed to know.

Bridget smiled and readied her handbag and her umbrella. 'Then good luck to you and Deirdre. Goodbye, James. Good luck.'

Once outside the hospital, the heavy rain that had stayed in all day was gone and the afternoon sun was shining.

Some way ahead of her a rainbow formed a bridge between The Horsefair and Stokes Croft where Lyndon awaited her. She'd read that a rainbow prophesied a new beginning. It was enough for her, at least for now.

MORE FROM LIZZIE LANE

We hope you enjoyed reading *Dark Days for the Tobacco Girls*. If you did, please leave a review.

If you'd like to gift a copy, this book is also available as an ebook, digital audio download and audiobook CD.

Sign up to Lizzie Lane's mailing list for news, competitions and updates on future books:

http://bit.ly/LizzieLaneNewsletter

Why not explore the first in the series, *The Tobacco Girls*.

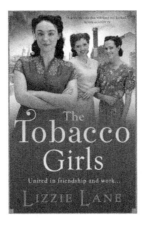

ABOUT THE AUTHOR

Lizzie Lane is the author of over 50 books, a number of which have been bestsellers. She was born and bred in Bristol where many of her family worked in the cigarette and cigar factories. This has inspired her new saga series for Boldwood *The Tobacco Girls*.

Follow Lizzie on social media:

 facebook.com/jean.goodhind

twitter.com/baywriterallatı

 instagram.com/baywriterallatsea

bookbub.com/authors/lizzie-lane

ABOUT BOLDWOOD BOOKS

Boldwood Books is a fiction publishing company seeking out the best stories from around the world.

Find out more at www.boldwoodbooks.com

Sign up to the Book and Tonic newsletter for news, offers and competitions from Boldwood Books!

http://www.bit.ly/bookandtonic

We'd love to hear from you, follow us on social media:

facebook.com/BookandTonic

twitter.com/BoldwoodBooks

instagram.com/BookandTonic